I0565635

A MOVEABLE FEAST OF MURDER

A MOVEABLE FEAST
OF
MURDER

———◆———

Agata Stanford

A JENEVACRIS PRESS PUBLICATION

A MOVEABLE FEAST OF MURDER
A Dorothy Parker Mystery / June 2012

Published by
Jenevacris Press
New York

This is a work of fiction. Names, characters, places, and incidents either are the product of the author's imagination or are used fictitiously. Any resemblance to actual persons, living or dead, events, or locales is entirely coincidental.

All rights reserved
Copyright © 2012 by Agata Stanford
Edited by Shelley Flannery
Typesetting & Cover Design by Eric Conover

ISBN 978-0-9827542-9-0

Printed in the United States of America

www.dorothyparkermysteries.com

For Brenda Bright, who loves a good mystery.

Also by Agata Stanford

The Dorothy Parker Mysteries Series:

The Broadway Murders
Chasing the Devil
Mystic Mah Jong
Death Rides the Midnight Owl

Acknowledgments

I am fortunate to have the expert technical and artistic skills of Shelley Flannery and Eric Conover, who work as a team with me to bring my stories to my readers. Thank you, Shelley, for suggesting the title of this book. Thank you, Jeannette Sinibaldi, for "pardoning my French," correcting my French spelling and applying the appropriate accents where required, answering my questions, and helping me to map out a parade route through the streets of Paris. Thanks also go to Gina Grant for additional assistance on the Paris section of this book. I send heartfelt thanks to architect and artist Benedetto Puccio for photographing the Paris landmarks featured in this book, and to author Anatole Konstantin (*A Red Boyhood: Growing Up Under Stalin*) for sharing his insights and knowledge of the Soviet Union and communist activity in Europe in the 1920s. Thank you, Michael Alan Mayer, author of *Time Trippers: The Nights of the Round Table*, for passing on to me so many details about France in the 1920s. Thanks go to Les Dean of the National Railroad Historical Society for details of 1920s European rail travel.

I appreciate Facebook's Virtual Ocean Liner page, and its anonymous patron, who has answered all my questions about steamship crossings. Thank you, Frank Pelkey at Crandall Public Library in Glens Falls, New York, for assisting me in my research. Finally, I must express my gratitude to the members of The Robert Benchley Society, who are continually educating me about all things Benchley.

Contents

Who's Who in the Cast of
Dorothy Parker Mysteries

The Algonquin Round Table was the famous assemblage of writers, artists, actors, musicians, newspaper and magazine reporters, columnists, and critics who met for luncheon at one P.M. most days, for a period of about ten years, starting in 1919, in the Rose Room of the Algonquin Hotel on West 44th Street in Manhattan. The unwritten test for membership was wit, brilliance, and likeability. It was an informal gathering ranging from ten to fifteen regulars, although many peripheral characters who arrived for lunch only once might later claim they were part of the "Vicious Circle," broadening the number to thirty, forty, and more. Once taken into the fold, one was expected to indulge in witty repartee and humorous observations during the meal, and then follow along to the Theatre, or a speakeasy, or Harlem for a night of jazz. Gertrude Stein dubbed the Round Tablers "The Lost Generation." The joyous, if sardonic, reply that rose with a laugh from Dorothy Parker was, *"Wheeee! We're lost!"*

Dorothy Parker set the style and attitude for modern women of America to emulate during the 1920s and 1930s. Through her pointed poetry, cutting theatrical reviews, brilliant commentary, bittersweet short stories, and much-quoted rejoinders, Mrs. Parker was the embodiment of the soulful pathos of the "Ain't We Got Fun" generation of the Roaring Twenties.

Robert Benchley: Writer, humorist, boulevardier, and bon vivant, editor of *Vanity Fair* and *Life Magazine,* and drama critic of *The New Yorker,* he may accidentally have been the very first standup comedian. His original and skewed sense of humor made him a star on Broadway, and later, in the movies. What man didn't want to *be* Bob Benchley?

Alexander Woollcott was the most famous man in America—or so he said. As drama critic for the *New York Times,* he was the star-maker, discovering and promoting the careers of Helen Hayes, Katherine Cornell, Alfred Lunt and Lynn Fontanne, and the Marx Brothers, to name but a few. Larger than life and possessing a rapier wit, he was a force to be reckoned with. When someone asked a friend of his to describe Woollcott, the answer was, "Improbable."

Frank Pierce Adams (FPA) was a self-proclaimed modern-day Samuel Pepys, whose newspaper column, "The Conning Tower," was a widely read daily diary of how, where, and with whom he spent his days while gallivanting about New York City. Thanks to him, every witty retort, clever comment, and one-liner uttered by the Round Tablers at luncheon was in print the next day for millions of readers to chuckle over at the breakfast table.

Harold Ross wrote for *Stars and Stripes* during the War, where he first met fellow newspapermen Woollcott and Adams. The rumpled, "clipped woodchuck" (as described by Edna Ferber) was one of the most brilliant editors of his time. His magazine, *The New Yorker,* which he started in 1925, has enriched the lives of everyone who has ever had a subscription. His hypochondria was legendary, and his the-world-is-out-to-get-me outlook was often comical.

Jane Grant married Harold Ross but kept her maiden name, cut her hair shorter than her husband's, and viewed domesticity with disdain. A society columnist for the *New York Times*, Jane was the very chic model of modernity during the 1920s. Having worked hard for women's suffrage, Jane continued in her cause while serving meals and emptying ashtrays during all-night sessions of the Thanatopsis Literary and Inside Straight Club.

Heywood Broun began his career at numerous newspapers throughout the country before landing a spot on the *World*. Sportswriter and Harlem Renaissance jazz fiend, he was to become the social conscience of America during the 1920s and beyond through his column, "It Seems to Me . . . ." His insight and commentary made him a champion of the labor movement, as did his fight for justice during and after the seven years of the Sacco and Vanzetti trials and execution.

Edmund "Bunny" Wilson: Writer, editor, and critic of American literature, he first came to work at *Vanity Fair* after Mrs. Parker pulled his short story out from under the slush-pile and found it interesting.

Robert E. Sherwood came to work on the editorial staff at *Vanity Fair* alongside Parker and Benchley. The six-foot-six Sherwood was often tormented by the dwarfs performing—whatever it was they did—at the Hippodrome on his way to and from work at the magazine's 44th Street offices, but that didn't stop him from becoming one of the twentieth-century Theatre's greatest playwrights.

Marc Connelly began his career as a reporter but found his true calling as a playwright. Short and bald, he co-authored his first hit play with the tall and pompadoured ***George S. Kaufman***.

Edna Ferber racked up Pulitzer Prizes by writing bestselling potboilers set against America's sweeping vistas, most notably, *So Big, Showboat, Cimarron,* and *Giant.* She, too, collaborated with George S. on several successful Broadway shows. A spinster, she was a formidable personality and wit and a much-coveted member of the Algonquin Round Table.

John Barrymore was a member of the Royal Family of the American Stage, which included *John Drew* and *Ethel* and *Lionel Barrymore*. John Barrymore was famous not only for his stage portrayals, but for his majestic profile, which was captured in all its splendor on celluloid.

The Marx Brothers: First there were five, then there were four, then there were three Marx Brothers — *awww, heck,* if you don't know who these crazy, zany men are, it's time to hit the video store or tune into Turner Classic Movies!

Also mentioned: *Neysa McMein*, artist and illustrator, whose studio door was open all hours of the day and night for anyone who wished to pay a call; *Grace Moore*, Broadway and opera star, and later a movie star; Broadway and radio star *Fanny Brice* — think Streisand in *Funny Girl*; *Noel Coward*, English star and playwright who took America by storm with his classy comedies and bright musical offerings; *Condé Nast*, publisher of numerous magazines including *Vogue*, *Vanity Fair*, and *House and Garden*; *Florenz Zeigfeld* — of "*Follies*" fame — big-time producer of the extravaganza stage revue; *The Lunts*, husband-and-wife stars of the London and Broadway stages, individually known as Alfred Lunt and Lynn Fontanne; *Tallulah Bankhead* — irreverent, though beautiful, southern-born actress with the foghorn drawl, who later made a successful transition from the stage to film — the life of any party, she often perked up the waning festivities performing cartwheels sans bloomers; *Irving Berlin*, *George Gershwin*, and *Jascha Heifetz* — famous for "God Bless America" and hundreds more hit songs; composer of *Rhapsody in Blue* and *Porgy and Bess* and many more great works; and the violin virtuoso, respectively.

A MOVEABLE FEAST
OF
MURDER

Chapter One

It was only natural that I should be nervous—all right, I panicked; after all, my Uncle Martin went down with the *Titanic*.

A February blizzard was raging fury over the East Coast as the *S.S. Roosevelt* was being tugged out of the harbor at Hoboken toward open seas. I shook from trepidation as I stood out on the open deck of the ship this midnight, the flurry of thick flakes, a disappointing substitution for confetti, changing to hard, biting pellets of mean sleet.

Mr. Benchley, collar pulled up and fedora pulled low over his brow to ward off the stinging assault, had accompanied me at my nervous desire to view, perhaps for the very last time, the island of Manhattan. We couldn't see much more than the blurred lights of the skyline beyond the ship's railing.

"To your right, you will see the Battery," bellowed Mr. Benchley like a tour guide, waving a hand through the howling gale and in the general direction of the southern tip of the city. He wrapped an arm around my shivering shoulders. "*Ah!* The Statue of Liberty; her flame lights our way out of the harbor, how thoughtful. Well, she's out there, somewhere in that general direction . . . ."

"I must have been mad, out of my mind!"

"Your usual self—"

"What could I have been thinking?"

The wind whipped us, and Mr. Benchley held onto his hat. "Oh, Lord! What a night to go out in a storm! It wouldn't be so bad if the crew wasn't yellow. You must write a short story about this. Wait! I have the first line: 'It was a dark and scary night . . . .' No, that won't do. 'It was a stark and starry night.' No! Let me think!"

"Don't, you'll strain yourself."

"Listen, why don't we do something useful to pass the time. Keeping busy will make you less anxious."

"A drink will make me less anxious."

"We'll begin by throwing overboard all the children's life jackets—won't the little tykes be surprised?—and then we can set about cutting the ropes of the lifeboats."

The blast of the ship's horn vibrated along the icy deck and thrilled through my body like the voice of Jehovah from out of the fog. I jumped, slid, and grabbed the rail.

"Mrs. Parker, I understand that you want to face death bravely and head on as it approaches, but let's let death sneak up on us while we're safe and warm inside," shouted my friend as he secured his footing and pulled me in toward the doors. "Too late to change your mind, my dear! We can't swim back now, much as you'd like; these are crocodile-infested waters, and you hate it when you get your hair mussed."

I started to laugh and a shiver quivered through me. I allowed Mr. Benchley to lead me in out of the storm, and the sudden absence of pummeling weather made my ears ring. I leaned against the door with relief, before the feeling of dread rose once more from within my lower regions. But, when the very weather-drenched Mr. Benchley looked at me and said, "Next time we go out for a midnight swim, bring a towel," I felt the fear abating.

As we walked along the interior deck toward the passenger cabins, I said, "Weren't there any cancellations? You don't have accommodations! Where will you sleep?"

"You'd think, sailing off in this tempest, people would remember the *Titanic* and call the whole thing off. But for our heroic captain and crew, people are beginning to believe the fantasy that the ship might actually make it across the pond—this time around."

I cringed, and then laughed. Gallows humor always perked me up.

"If I were a betting man, I'd wager our Captain Fried is due for a big loss. He can't sustain this winning streak," he said.

"We'll go down knowing we sailed with the savior of the wrecked English freighter the *Antinoe*," I stated, stoic and head held high for the fate that awaited this doomed voyage.

I needed a drink, and as we entered my cabin, to the joyful tail-wagging welcome of my canine companion, Woodrow Wilson, we threw off our wet overcoats onto the dozen bon-voyage fruit baskets sent by well-meaning friends. I pointed to a crate in the corner, behind my new steamer trunk, from which Mr. Benchley extracted one of the bottles of scotch we'd purchased from a bootlegger in Paramus on our way to the pier, and from which he poured two neat tumblers of the golden elixir.

After the flash-fire effect of genuine imported booze had warmed the cockles of my heart, I regained a modicum of sanity.

"I suppose I should feel safe. After all, we are aboard the ship whose captain was given a tickertape parade only a few days ago."

"I'm sure his Key to the City can get us out of any chance encounter with icebergs or tidal waves along the way," nodded Mr. Benchley, referring to the

gift presented to the captain of our vessel by May-
or Jimmy Walker three days ago at a banquet at the
Roosevelt Hotel to honor Fried and his crew. The res-
cuers were honored with a welcoming salute to "Hail
to the Chief," accolades, and hyperbolic speeches spun
out by every handy politician, as well as a concert at
Carnegie Hall, and an audience with the President. I
guess the Pope couldn't make it.

Knowing that an international hero was at the
helm did not quiet my anxiety. Of course I knew what
I was getting into. *I had boarded a ship!*—for a trans-
atlantic journey to France during a season beleaguered
with storms rocking the Atlantic Ocean, the worst in
recent years. Mr. Benchley had come along for the
ride to hold my hand, knowing my fear of the sea.
At least, that's what he told his wife, Gertrude, who
finally agreed that he could accompany me, only on
his promise to return home on the next ship.

My decision to leave New York for Paris had
been made only the week before, and over the next
six days I scrambled around making the arrangements, tying up loose ends, and saying good-bye to
my friends.

Ernest Hemingway had arrived in New York
two weeks ago. He came to sign with a new publisher,
Scribner's, who have agreed to publish his first novel,
The Sun Also Rises. Our mutual friend, Scott Fitzgerald,
now living in Paris, told Hem to drop in for lunch to
meet me and my friends at the Algonquin. He did

just that and we showed him the town—all the best watering holes. We hit it off. Hem talked about his life in Paris, and of the other writers and artists living and working there. It sounded like a creative paradise, a beautiful city where one could sit and write all day at a delightful, sunny outdoor café, sipping a *fine*. In the evening, one mingled with the best and brightest, artists like Picasso, Miró, Léger, Dali, and Man Ray, and the new writers, those employing a new style, James Joyce and Ezra Pound among them. When Hem mentioned that the exchange rate made it possible to live well on little money, and that liquor was legal, well, I thought a move could be the answer to my prayers.

For I had found it more and more difficult to do any serious writing. I have wanted to start work on a novel, but I seem to have fallen into a routine of doing everything else except starting on it. A clean slate, that's what I need; I love New York, but I've been getting weary of my routine, of being in a rut. I could do with a new environment for a while, one that would stimulate my creative juices. I will return home with a completed manuscript and rise up from poetess to novelist. It might take some time, but I will learn to speak French (with a lot of sign language), and perhaps I will find out exactly what a *fine* is and why I should be sipping it. So I booked passage on the same ship that Ernest was returning on to Paris. Mr. Benchley had tried to get a cabin in First Class, but landed on the waiting list. And as we steamed out into the Narrows, I told him that he was now officially a stowaway.

"I'll talk to the purser. There must be some sort of accommodation, even if it's in Third Class."

"You'll bunk with the crew, matie!"

"I suppose I'm destined to a week of swapping seafaring tales: the time that big white whale pulled my leg, and when I wrestled that fifty-foot octopus, the minnow I landed—"

"What about the mermaid you romanced off the coast of—"

"I asked you never to mention her name again!"

There was a knock at the door. I bade enter, and in walked Hemingway.

"You're just in time for a basket of fruit," I said. "Please take one away with you, Hem; they're cluttering up the cabin. And while you're at it, take Mr. Benchley away, too, please."

"I see he's cluttering up the cabin, too," said Hem, laughing at my friend, who had sprawled out on the bed. "I know there's no place else on the ship to put him, sadly. I'd take him in, but I've been told he snores and kicks in his sleep."

"Who told you such lies?" said Mr. Benchley, leaning up on his elbows.

"I'd rather not say."

I poured Hem a scotch. We were all a little drunk. We'd been partying all day with friends and my sister and her husband who'd come to see me off. An additional stop on the way to the pier to get a case of champagne had led to a roadside speakeasy where we'd had a very liquid dinner.

"I want to hit the sack. Just stopped in to say goodnight. We're all a little pie-eyed," said Hem.

"What do you mean *a little?*" objected my friend.

"Mr. Benchley always does things in a *big* way."

"That is so," nodded Mr. Benchley, swiveling his legs down from off the bed. "Very well, I'm off to see the purser," he said as he rose with a false dignity, throwing his coat over his arm and putting the soggy hat on his head. "Off to dreamland I shall go, if I can recall under which pillow I stashed my pajamas." He turned to look at me with scrutiny as he made for the door. "Will you be all right now, my dear?" The indignant drunk act was replaced by sudden sobriety. "If you like, I can ask the steward for a deckchair outside your door—"

I touched his arm and kissed his cheek. Endearing is my best friend and champion. His warm and genuine concern made me suddenly courageous. "I'm just fine, now," I said. "Woodrow Wilson will alert me if the ship takes on water. Good night, boys," I said, sending them out the door.

———◆———

I awoke with a start at ten o'clock; Woodrow, the scoundrel, laid sloppy kisses on my face. He flew off the bed when I shot bolt upright, and stood scratching at the cabin door. There was activity outside in the corridor and he wanted to investigate. The ship was rocking, but I'd heard no impact against the hull. I had fallen off to sleep from exhaustion a little before dawn, every creak and deep list of the ship wracking my nerves. I saw icebergs everywhere, phantom ships on the brink of collision.

A few minutes later, bundled up in my coat and scarf, we walked onto the deck, and as far as the eye could see there were the treacherous waters, great waves rolling toward us from a gray and undefined horizon. The storm had retreated, but visibility was low, and staring out into the filmy void I tried to shake off my fear, to embrace the mysteries of the great expanse, to conjure up visions of pirate adventures and Melville tales in an effort to calm my nerves. I must look toward the future; I was heading for a new life in Paris, and it excited me. There was hope for me, a fresh start, and I was suddenly high with expectations. Or, was it the salty air that made me feel heady? My face was damp from mist, which was not unpleasant.

I returned indoors, energized, to find the dining room, for I was suddenly ravenously hungry for breakfast, a meal I rarely ate. *Yes*, I thought, *I am changing my ways*.

———◆———

"Saltpeter?" said Hemingway, offering a small vial containing the stuff to Mr. Benchley.

"Are you making gunpowder for the troops?" I asked, sprinkling what was undoubtedly Morton's on my scrambled eggs.

"Got to keep the 'troops' from raising the flag, 'f you know what I mean," said Hem, with all serious-ness, his voice rumbling in his throat as he mixed the stuff into his oatmeal. "A sprinkle, Bob?"

"I can feel my sperm dying just looking at the stuff," replied Mr. Benchley, stirring a draft of gin from his hip flask into his orange juice. He popped two aspirins into his mouth and washed them down.

I stifled a giggle at Hem's assertion that he need-ed to keep his "troops" under siege—under wraps—out of the direct line of fire, or whatever *double entendre* suited the visual that flashed across my mind.

"I thought a ration of rum keeps the 'seamen' from raising a mutiny," I said. "What ever happened to self-control?"

Mr. Benchley said, "We are a generation that doesn't have self-control, didn't you know? It's gone out of style with high-button shoes and corsets. The term was banned from use to make room for the phrase, "No accommodations for you, sir!"

"Oh, my dear Fred, is that so?" I said, talking through the toast I'd ripped into. "Where did you sleep last night?"

"I laid my head on a sack of oats in a cubby in the stores."

"No!"

"*Ya-voll!*"

"A character-building experience, I should say," said Hem.

"That's what I told the harbor rat who stowed aboard and tried to wrestle me for a burlap blanket. I stood my ground, though, and now we are great friends. And I am on good terms with the rest of his clan."

"Cards after lunch?" I said, feeding a sausage link to Woodrow, who sat daintily on the chair next to mine.

"Need a fourth for bridge," said Mr. Benchley.

"We can play three-handed."

I returned to my cabin to unpack what I was too tired to get to last night, only to discover that my case of scotch had been stolen!

What fresh hell?

Nothing else had been touched. The remaining half-dozen bottles of champagne were right where I'd left them, next to a big gaping space where the case of scotch had been. How was I to get through the voyage on just a few bottles of champagne? I stormed down the deck to the purser's office, where I got little sympathy, a lot of head nodding, and a lecture after lodging my complaint. Why I bothered, I don't know. "The *S.S. Roosevelt* is an American ship of the United States Line, and abides by the U.S. prohibition laws, etcetera, etcetera."

Far from chastened, and dramatically chuffed, I marched back to my room, where Woodrow lay huddled atop the mess of clothing spilled out of my open steamer trunk. A glare from me did nothing to shift his position from off my lamé evening dress. He just snuggled down deeper, let out a sigh, and closed his eyes for a late-morning nap. My gay mood of just an hour ago had turned morbid.

Although I was still rabid and determined to ferret out the rat who stole my hooch, by lunchtime, with the news that there was an adequate store of gin and whiskey, the genuine articles of Napoleon cognac and Bordeaux, available through enterprising passengers for the purpose of providing such, my spirits were raised. Our destination was France, after all, and what was brought on board upon departure from New York was of no interest to American agents. Of course, it did race through my mind that it was probably one of these convenient on-board "bootleggers" who had stolen my supply in the first place and would sell it back to me at a premium, but what could I really do about it? There was still plenty of reason for a good time.

We played bridge with a man we picked up in the card salon. Although he was young, he possessed a rather forlorn, hangdog expression about him. I thought he was just lonely at first, but then, in spite of our joviality as we played our hands, I noted a protective reticence, as if he had buttoned close around him an old familiar sweater. Mr. Benchley had a way about him, with little said and no obvious effort, of drawing out even the most taciturn of characters until they were telling him their life stories and perhaps a few secrets. Mr. Benchley's interest would leave the storyteller, who may have previously thought his life ordinary and dull, with the newfound belief that he was really a most fascinating individual. And so, during a break, the young man told us that he had been wounded, nearly fatally, in Italy during the War. Hemingway was a Red Cross ambulance driver wounded in Italy. And to instantly bond the two old soldiers, they discovered that they had both been wounded at Fossalta di Piave and sent for treatment at the Ospedale Maggiore in Milan. As Hem always said, there were those who had fought in the War and were wounded and those who had not. You only trusted those who had.

And so, Mathew Hettinger, age twenty-eight, a native of Philadelphia, became a fast friend. That he was the son of wealthy parents, the third generation of a fortune made during the Civil War, did not cancel out Hem's respect. For Ernest Hemingway had been growing suspicious of the rich, even though so many of his fabulously wealthy friends had championed his work and helped to support him and his wife, Hadley, during the lean years in Paris. Mathew, traveling through Italy when war broke out, defied his father's order to return home to the States and enlisted in the Italian army, rather than go home and off to university. He told Hem about the beautiful Italian girl he'd been in love with, whom he'd married while on leave, and how he had been in hospital recovering from wounds, never knowing for many months that she had succumbed during childbirth along with his daughter. To Hem, these recollections made him even more romantic and attractive. And the revelation that Mathew Hettinger was a journalist, sent to Paris as a foreign correspondent for the *Detroit Register*, as well as an aspiring novelist sealed the deal.

A steward arrived in the card room with an invitation from the captain of the ship for our party to join him at his table for dinner this evening. I invited the men to come to my cabin for drinks, where we popped open a bottle of champagne to wash down a plate of hors d'oeuvres ordered from room service. Hemingway was excited at the chance to speak with our captain, being especially impressed by the heroic rescue of the *Antinoe* several weeks before. Two bottles emptied, the men went off to their cabins, except for Mr. Benchley, who didn't have a cabin as yet and went down to the purser's office to see if there was any news about where he would sleep tonight. He needed a permanent place to keep his steamer trunk during the trip, and certainly a room where he could dress in his evening clothes for dinner.

There was plenty of time for me to dress, so I took Woodrow Wilson for little stroll around the deck to do his business and to enjoy the salty smells of the ocean. The seas were calmer, and through a break in the overcast sky I could see the red strains of sunset streaking across the western sky. The vast expanse was awe inspiring; one certainly doesn't see the horizon while walking the streets of Manhattan. Our ship was a lonesome tub floating on an infinite pool. There was nothing to see any which way I looked, and as evening fell, the dark-blue waters grew black and foreboding, and the harder I looked into the great inky depths, the more mesmerized I was by the unfathomable mystery that surrounded me. It frightened me.

While my attention was arrested by the undulating waves, Woodrow was pulling at his leash. I came out of my morbid reverie and turned my attention to my canine companion, who was being entertained by a gentleman out on deck.

"Well, isn't he a cute little fellah!" said the tall, wiry gentleman with a New York accent, as he leaned over his cane.

He wore his leather visor cap and dark-brown corduroy suit with a scholarly air. It was a good suit, the cut very English, although it appeared to hang on him at the shoulders, as if he'd lost a lot of weight since its purchase. Why I should take notice of his clothes, I can't say. But there was something compelling about his countenance. Perhaps the very large, clear, and open moss-colored eyes out of which he viewed the world with an empathetic compassion? How could I know this? How could I size up a stranger so easily? I recognized something in him that had not so much to do with his outer, physical shell, but rather with that which emanated from within. I thought him immediately sympathetic, and for a woman who has grown more and more cynical over the years, and has shielded herself from the "slings and arrows" of supposed friendships with her own brand of piercing humor, I was strangely curious to know this man. I felt there was much to know.

The wind threatened his cap, and when he brought up a hand to secure it, I saw the long scar that streaked across his forehead.

"Terrier, is he?"

"Of the Boston variety," I replied.

"But of course he is," said the gentleman.

The wind was kicking up, and he grabbed his hat again to keep from losing it. He gave up the struggle and ran long aristocratic fingers through his hair, and I saw that the scar had scalped an inch-long line into his thick black hair. He tried to cover up the mean scar; it did no good; we both resembled victims of electric shock. Woodrow braced himself against the stiff gale. We made for the door leading into the ship, followed by Woodrow's newfound friend. Before I could ask his name or invite him in for a drink, he bade us good evening and walked in the direction of the first-class cabins.

Mr. Benchley appeared at my door, a bottle of scotch in one hand and two glasses in the other.

"Lookee what I found."

"Why, that looks like one of the bottles from my stash."

"Prob'ly, my dear Mrs. Parker!"

"So you are the scoundrel who absconded with my booze!"

"On the contrary, I just purchased this from a fellow down the hall. He probably did the dastardly deed, for all we know."

Mr. Benchley followed me into my cabin, and before I knew it he was stretched out on my bed unwrapping the chocolate from the box sent by a friend as a bon-voyage gift. "Delicious," he said, balling up the gold wrapper for a high toss into the wastebasket.

"Oh, get a room," I said, going to my steamer trunk to sort out the tangled mess of gowns. I chose a blue silk with Delmonte clips, and then went to sort through my jewelry drawer.

"Would if I could," said Mr. Benchley, taking off his shoes.

"Making yourself at home, are you?" I said. "Can't you bunk with Hemingway?"

"Out of the question," he said with a yawn. "He has the smelliest feet. But the purser promises he might find me a place with some Russian dancers from the Ballets Russes. Six high-steppers sharing a room in third class. I suppose that's better than accommodations with the rodent family. Does someone have to die for me to get a room?"

"What about the infirmary?" I asked.

"Those beds are reserved for sick people. I suppose I could pretend to be ill—claim seasickness, or something."

"I could have you committed, if you like. Mr. Benchley," I said, "you have the pathetic look of that proverbial lamb lost in the woods. I suspect a willing lady would take you in once she sees a few manufactured tears in your eyes."

I shuttled him out of the room, shoes in one hand, the scotch and drinking glass in the other. I told him I would meet him in the dining room at eight o'clock. He looked forlorn as I slammed the door in his face.

The S.S. Roosevelt

A view from the bridge

"Writers are either twenty-nine or Thomas Hardy."

Chapter Two

"Can't a chap get a drink around here?"

I turned at the sound of a sultry, British-accented voice, and was surprised to see a spritely young woman, pencil thin, in a shimmering little chemise of purple lamé. She had short, dark hair, slicked back, which was all the rage, and the boyish style made her look all the more feminine.

"I'm terribly sorry, Lady Twinton," said Captain Fried, as he stood up from his chair, as did the other men at the table at the newcomer's arrival. "This ship is dry, I'm afraid."

Our captain was a man of some physical distinction. Of course, there is always something distinctive about a man in uniform. The high color of his long, rectangular face might be attributed not only to a seafarer's life, but also to the invigorating effects of a glorious week of celebration. He was, after all, the hero of two continents. He had light, brownish hair that was graying at the temples, green eyes peering out from under heavy-winged brows. There was an air of amusement about his expression, if not of admiration, at the sight of Lady Twinton. And he was not alone, for the other men at the table, Mr. Benchley, Hem, and our new friend, Mathew, appeared to share the sentiment.

"I'm sure there are resources," said Mr. Benchley, looking at me as the source of Lady Twinton's future satisfaction. I let out a snort at his ingratiating manner. Men do get silly around attractive women. I wanted to say, *I have no intention of sharing my scotch with this pretty moocher!* But I kept quiet and the smile on my face as the waiter pushed in her chair and Mr. Benchley arranged her wrap over the back of it.

"Now, this would never happen in Paris, anywhere in France," said Hemingway. "You don't find nearly as many drunks in France as you do in the States; just goes to show you, make something illegal and it's suddenly in high demand. Try to change a way of life, and you wreak havoc, chaos, tyranny, fascism, and the abolition of civil liberties."

"I agree with you, Hem," I said. "But I'm *so* good at wreaking havoc, chaos, and tyranny, although I've yet to master fascism."

"Why the hell do you think I'm going to France?" said the Lady, who had obviously been sipping away for some time from some private stash. She leaned in, offering perky breasts for Mr. Benchley's benefit.

"It ain't for the crêpes suzette!" said an attractive woman, hovering somewhere in her forties. In contrast to the slangy comment, the voice was cultured and mellow. She had dark, classic good looks, patrician features, high cheekbones, full lips, and arched brows. Her dark, Marcelled hair glistened brilliantly in the chandelier light, fashioned in finger-waves across her sleek head. She wore a simple sheath gown of aqua satin that brought out the extraordinary green color of her eyes. She took a seat offered by the waiter and, with a lilt in her voice and an all-inclusive smile around the table, announced, "I'm Soledad Soleil."

Ah! The mystery writer whose amateur sleuth was an unassuming little shop-girl by the name of Harriet Morgan. Harriet's partner in crime solving was Jonas McGill, valet to the Duke of Twicksbury. Her books were funny, and I had already liked the author long before our meeting. She took a little flask from her purse and drained it into her water glass, having emptied the offending H_2O into the table's flower arrangement. Yes, I liked her very much.

"So sorry to be late," said another new arrival to our table. He was impeccably suited in evening clothes. I was blinded by the flash of brilliance that bounced off his sizable diamond studs when I looked up at the fellow. Early thirties, auburn-colored hair thinning at the crown, he stood there with one hand in his trouser pocket and the other leaning on the shoulder of Lady Twinton in the familiar gesture that spoke of casual intimacy. He pulled out from his coat an expensive-looking gold cigarette case, extracted a cigarette, and lit up by means of an equally extravagant gold lighter. "How are you, darling?" he said in the dulcet tones and fine elocution of a British thespian, as he leaned in to kiss the Lady's cheek.

"Dry, not a lick of it anywhere, and I'm damn thirsty."

"*Baby wanz ha bot-tle,*" I said in an aside to Mr. Benchley. We women had him book-ended at table.

"Ronald," said Lady Twinton, "meet the gang; the gang, meet Ronald."

Ronald shook hands with the men, reached for my hand, leaned over it and said, "Mrs. Parker, isn't it? It is such a pleasure to meet you, you can't know!"

"Oh, don't I?" I replied, drawling haughtily, sounding more like a Southern Belle than the English aristocrat I had intended to mimic. I felt my scotch was still threatened, thanks to Mr. Benchley's cavalier offer to share. I was like a kid with the key to a candy store, and I wasn't about to share my loot with the riffraff whose runny noses were pressed against the shop window. I don't know why, but I took an instant dislike to Lady Twit and her handsome beau.

"We serve an especially nice drink made with tea and fruit juices and a dash of bitters," suggested our captain. "We also serve carbonated beverages, coffee, tea—"

"Oh, I so wanted to have a good time," whined Lady Twit. "I suppose I'll have to make do with sarsaparilla."

"Never fear, dear lady," said Mr. Benchley, patting his hip flask.

She turned on him an arched brow and a dazzling smile, and with a gesture of conspiracy, squeezed his arm.

"I believe we will be great friends," she cooed.

Mr. Benchley blushed, the rat! But before he could reply, her attention was drawn to the entrance of the dining room, and whatever she was looking at turned her flirtatious manner into a look of sheer annoyance. I followed her gaze, to find the object of her contempt none other than the fellow Woodrow and I had encountered out on deck earlier. "I wish he'd just go away," she said.

"That nice fellow over there?" asked Soledad Soleil.

"Yeah, him . . . ."

"We met on deck this afternoon, but I never got his name."

"Gold," said Ronald, taking a seat. "Gold*blatt*," he elaborated, pulling his pant-legs at the knees as he sat and displaying impeccably white, pressed wristcuffs as he settled in. "But he goes by Saul Gold."

I knew that name, but I just couldn't place it. "Journalist?"

"Saul Gold," said Hem, attention drawn away from his discussion with the captain. "Poet, isn't he?"

"So he claims," said Ronald.

"Saul teaches at Columbia, and is a friend of Harold Ross's and Heywood Broun's. He's a fine writer," said Mr. Benchley, turning to look toward the entrance.

"Yes," said Hem, "I've read some of his poetry, now that I think of it. And he has a book that's come out. His work is dark."

"I'll say," said Lady Twinton, a comment laden with some sort of secret knowledge.

Hem's eyes settled on her, and he seemed to study her. I could see the details of his evaluation as his face changed expressions in rapid succession: A spoiled, rich girl, everything about her raised contempt in him. She was too skinny, brittle, and boney-chested, and all that was natural and genuine in her face was obscured with paint. Her clothes were expensive, but the simple cut and expert tailoring of the excellent cloth mocked the current trends in fashion with classic style. She was just too finished, too smooth, and she smelled of exotic, forbidden places where men secretly long to linger. She embodied everything he detested about the rich, and about the seductive, modern woman hell-bent on flaunting her sex. This tore at him. This challenged him. That he was nearly penniless, aside from the small advance he'd received from Scribner's against royalties for the publication of his novel, was embraced by him as some kind of virtue. Hem wore the smug moral superiority of the artistically inclined toward bourgeois lifestyles, having proudly endured the sufferings of icy garrets, worn shoe-leather, and the abject poverty of salad days. Gertrude Stein, his friend and mentor, fed this outlook when she told him, "You can buy clothes or buy art." Hem had one decent suit of clothes, purchased for the trip to New York, and the rest were little better than sorry rags, but he had yet to collect any art. No Picassos, no Miros—not even a sketch by his friend Léger. No, and he didn't like the rich, although it was the rich, the kind, wealthy people who befriended him and helped him through the hard times, paid for his fare, and provided help to his wife and his son, Bumby. He didn't like the rich. And he didn't like Lady Daphne Twinton. But that didn't make him apathetic. It made him interested.

"You know the man? Gold?" Hem asked her.

The Lady shrugged, "And I regret it, I suppose."

She didn't much like Gold.

"Well, we must ask Saul Gold to join us for a drink," I said to everybody at table, because I didn't much like the way things were headed. I saw more than dislike for the man in the Lady's and Ronald's response. It was an old, familiar look of disdain. Mr.

Benchley appeared oblivious to the subtext of their remarks.

So, Hemingway didn't like Lady Daphne and her friend Ronald because they were tactlessly rich, and the rich couple didn't like Saul Gold because he was a Jew.

"Sounds like a smart plan, Mrs. Parker, everybody," agreed Soledad Soleil. "You, too, Captain Fried, so we can personally toast your gallant rescue! My stateroom after dinner." And then, directed conspiratorially at me and Mr. Benchley: "How else are we to get through the night on this tub?"

Shrimp-cocktail glasses were replaced with soup and then plates of rack of lamb and the conversation split along several lines. Ronald and the Lady conspired with Mr. Benchley; Soledad Soleil, Mathew, and Hemingway listened with rapt attention to the adventures of Captain Fried at sea. I watched Saul Gold, standing near the entryway across the room, shifting his weight, smoking a cigarette, and appearing at a loss for what to do next. It was painful to watch, because he seemed so isolated. When he caught my eye, he nodded. I smiled back and with a raised eyebrow beckoned him to our table. But, he turned when the maître d' arrived to lead him to a table obscured from our view by a column. And as the orchestral strains of Mendelssohn wafted through the air, I left off wondering if there was something other than the fact that Gold was a Jew that had brought sneers of contempt to the faces of some of our dinner mates, because I was being drawn into the story of heroism at sea. I began to envision the great storm, two weeks before, a storm that followed a hurricane that had wracked the North Atlantic Ocean for twenty-two days. I was now, along with the men, completely entranced with the elements of the great sea rescue.

"From the Azores, as far north as Iceland, and west to the shores of Maine," said Captain Fried, "day and night, without reprieve, the gale raged on. We heard the SOS, and for a time we were uncertain from whence it came."

"I heard it was hours before your crew was able to effect a rescue," said Hem, his brown eyes catching the light and sparked with interest. *He is a handsome devil*, I thought, especially when passionately engaged.

"The storm was unrelenting, the sea, a churning caldron!" replied the captain. "We were a hundred miles distant, and had to guide the ship by radio compass. Still, it was not easy to find her with a drift of five knots as the day went on."

Mr. Benchley was as drawn in by the tale of adventure as was I. Hearing of the terror firsthand, I must have displayed a frightened stare, for Mr. Benchley said, "You see, my dear, you are quite safe, now."

"How is that?"

"Lightning never strikes twice, or something like that."

The captain continued, "—and it appeared the *Antinoe* was not alone in its troubles: The oil tanker, *Vacuum*, collided with and sunk the Norwegian freighter, *Solvang*, carrying a four-hundred-thousand-dollar cargo of sugar. Two disasters, back to back!"

"Never strikes twice, *hmmm?*" I said, throwing a face at Mr. Benchley.

"That crew, save one soul, was rescued by the efforts of the *Vacuum*'s crew.

"I should revise my statement," said Mr. Benchley, "Third time's a charm."

"You mean, three strikes, you're out!"

"Dance, Daff?"

I looked up to see Saul Gold, standing over Lady Twinton's chair.

"Thanks, no, I'm spent. Going to finish up my just desserts and off to bed."

"It's early, yet."

"So nice to see you," I said when Gold caught my eye.

"Mrs. Parker."

Mr. Benchley stood to shake hands, as did Captain Fried, Hem, and Mathew. Ronald and Lady Twinton just looked sheepish.

The steward appeared at the captain's side with a note, and after it was read the captain nodded at his crewman and then addressed Mr. Benchley. "We've accommodations for you, Mr. Benchley."

"Out of the cargo hold and into a cot in the infirmary?"

"A First-Class suite. Mr. Robins will have your luggage brought up as soon as the cabin is cleared."

"A kind soul has offered to let me sleep on his sofa? I'll be put out in the middle of the night, I fear, even though my snoring is no worse than a freight train barreling through the room."

The captain smiled winsomely. "No, no; It's your very own cabin."

"Excuse me, my dear," said Mr. Benchley, rising and touching my shoulder. "I shall return." He followed the purser out of the dining room.

I turned to Saul Gold, who hovered uncomfortably over the table, and bade him sit down at Mr. Benchley's vacated place. "I read a piece you wrote some time ago in *The Bookman*, about the synergy between Darwin's theories in *On the Origin of Species* and H.G. Wells's *Lost World*."

"*Hummm*," he nodded gravely, and then met my eyes and smiled wistfully, "I wish you'd forget it."

"Why?"

"It was tripe. Can't guess why they'd bothered to publish it. Wrote it after a nightmare where I was being mauled and then swallowed whole by a talking serpent."

"Some dreams are best forgotten, you mean?"

"Something like that, yes," he chuckled. He had a plain but pleasant face that was seen at best advantage when he smiled. But there was melancholy, too, which was only accentuated by the pitted scarring along his cheek—I'd seen this so many times over the past ten years, the results of shrapnel—and the scar etched into his hairline. His look was haunted; most men who'd known the travesties of the Front wore that expression. It hung about his eyes, earnest eyes, sad eyes. I recognized something else in his face, and I wondered if the elusive quality that I saw was the same that had caught the attention of Hemingway and Mathew when Captain Fried was called away from the table in the middle of his retelling of his adventures.

"Gold is a good poet, Dorothy," said Hemingway, with magnanimity, "rest assured. His images are *true*."

Gold flushed red, the lizard-shaped scar drained white, and I could see his embarrassment. He knew that he wasn't liked by several of the people at the table, and Hemingway's outright commentary brought to mind Hem's own discomfort with such obsequiousness. As much as Hem craved flattery, and he believed every flattering remark tossed his way, it only brought a strange sort of contempt for the flatterer. He thought it bad form to compliment, to acknowledge an artist's success or ability so overtly, telling me, when I had gushed about his short stories and his distinctive style, that our mutual friend, Scott Fitzgerald, in constantly voicing his admiration of Hem's talents, embarrassed him no end and made him feel cheapened somehow, his work less relevant. I got the point, of course, after he shot me down with complaints of Scott, so I don't tell him I admire his work anymore. With me, if I were told how wonderful I was, how marvelous my poems and stories were, I'd think the flatterer drunk or lacking artistic standards, that they probably liked A.A. Milne and thought him crafty. I would feel contempt for their shallow words and my own shallow attempts at reaching for "literature." Call me a malcontent, but most writers feel this way, shunning the praise for fear of ultimately being revealed a fake. But the paradox is, all creative people crave acceptance. On the other hand, a favorable review read in the privacy of one's home or an overheard remark of praise always suits me best.

Hemingway knew this, and could've guessed at Gold's reaction when he made his unsolicited assessment. Why did he say of Gold that he was *good* and his images *true* as if his critique was expected, if not to embarrass the fellow? Was there some professional jealousy here? I sensed no genuine admiration in the delivery of his flattery. This disturbed me, because Hemingway never struck me as anything other than a kind man.

"Why are you on this ship, Gold?" asked a rather tight Ronald. This was a frontal attack, and I tried to sort out the dynamics of the relationships among the people at the table, but I was at a loss in figuring it out. The remark had caused a rising tension that was almost palpable among the three—Ronald, Lady Twinton, and Saul Gold. Mathew appeared as perplexed as I, so he filled the dead air with nervous chatter, asking Hem about the Paris life. Hem ignored him for the drama unfolding right in front of him. So did Soledad Soleil. I got the impression that the two authors had taken out mental dictation pads and were poised with pencils to put down word-for-word what was being said. I know I had.

I interjected, "I've been asking myself that same question! Why am I on this ship?" I said, in an attempt to diffuse the bomb. I could see a fight about to start. But, who was going to throw the first punch? "There's not a decent bootlegger on board, and my little doggie has to stand guard over my stash."

"You've got nerve, you know," continued Ronald, ignoring me and pointing at Gold. "Nobody wants you here."

"Cut it out, Ronnie," growled Lady Twinton. "Just forget it, for God's sake!" There was no real conviction behind her words, just the lethargy of a drunk who couldn't care less.

"Ronald," I said, "tell me, are you going on to Paris after we arrive in Cherbourg?"

"Well, I've decided to avoid going home. England is cold and wet and unwelcoming, like my Daphne, here. Have to show my Daphne the sights, you know. Can't leave her for too long; she gets lonely without me."

"Shut up, Ronnie, you're boring when you're tight."

"But you do get lonely when I'm gone."

"Sure, sure, I'm lonely when you're gone." She threw a glance at Hem, and ran her tongue over her lips. Then she turned her gaze on Mathew, who looked entranced. "Give us a smoke, would you, Ronnie?" she said, keeping her eyes on Mathew as Ronald took out his flashy cigarette case and lit her up.

I was uncomfortable, to say the least, watching this obvious seduction of the men at the table. If I were to wash my lips with my tongue, I'd be handed a dinner napkin. "See you around," I stated and rose from my chair. It was a long moment before the men woke from hypnosis and rose from their seats to see me out.

Soledad Soleil gathered her purse and wrap. "I'm off, too. Have to think of six ways to murder a man."

"Wait, I'll take out my list." I said.

She giggled, "Whoever said writing mysteries wasn't fun?"

I waited for her to join me in exit from the room. The orchestra was now playing peppy dance music, tunes written by my Algonquin friends, Irving

Berlin and George Gershwin, and if the company had been more pleasant rather than rabid, and had Mr. Benchley been around, I'd've enjoyed tripping the light fantastic for a little while. But, I was not so very abandoned and left to my own devices. Soledad Soleil confided that she had brought aboard two cases of Irish whiskey and had an excellent bottle of Tequila as well, several limes in her fruit basket, and a pilfered salt shaker from the dinner table in her purse. I was liking the woman more and more as we glided out of the room to the upbeat strains of "Let's Misbehave." To my surprise, Saul Gold was on our heels.

"Come on, my stateroom is just around the bend, and there is room for all," said Soledad, moving forward to lead the way, and I liked that she had included Gold without a direct invitation.

As we entered the long block of staterooms and approached Mr. Benchley's, from a door beyond his room a little redhead of a man peeked out, saw us coming, and then retreated.

I heard the familiar voice of Mr. Benchley talking with a steward. He was getting settled in his new and quite lovely suite. I popped my head in to look at the spacious room. He returned a big grin when he saw me, and exclaimed, "Well, didn't I hit the jackpot?"

"I'll say! Who'd you have to kill to get this swanky flat?"

"I am innocent! It was a last-minute cancellation, and I don't have to pay a penny more than the ninety-dollar fare I paid for Third Class for this one-hundred-and-ninety-dollar First-Class stateroom with the extras you see here!"

"Well, well!" I said, nodding and pointing out the various accoutrements the room had to offer. "Complete with full-size bed, a fabulous view of the pitch-black night (it will be nice to see the sunrise at noon when you wake up), superior luxury furnishings—the sofa is covered in Dupioni silk, if you've noticed, and, of course, a complimentary fruit basket, I see."

"Gold," said Mr. Benchley, glimpsing the man peeking in at the doorway. "Come in, old sport! Now, where in heavens is my briefcase?"

"Well, set out your pajamas and toothbrush and join us for a drink, will ya?"

"Yes, Mrs. Parker," replied my friend. And then, with a phony, winsome expression, he said, "I will miss bedding down with my little rodent friends below decks, but the allure of Egyptian cotton sheets beats burlap pillowcases."

"Nice digs!" said Soledad, peeking around the door jam.

"Welcome to my humble abode."

"Join us for a drink, Mr. Benchley?"

"I'd be delighted, my dear Miss Soleil," said Mr. Benchley with a little half-bow. "After I've convinced our steward, here, to leave the fruit basket—I confess it was sent to the fellow who first reserved this room." He grabbed an apple from the top of the mound of fruit, polished it on his sleeve, and was about to take a bite when I interrupted:

"We are talking about honest-to-goodness Tequila," I informed. "Bring your Swiss Army knife. We need you to slice up the limes."

He pocketed the apple and turned with immediacy to the contents of his steamer trunk, pulling out drawers and retrieving various items. "I'll join you as soon as I've arranged this picture of my wife and sons, along with my knickknacks from the Nantucket Whaling Museum, of which I am a fan and contributor, and tack my banner from the Exhibition of 'Seventy-Six, which travels everywhere with me, over my bed—oh, hang it! I left my travel clock down in my old corner in the baggage hold! All right, I'll just pop down there and fetch it, and see if my briefcase is there, too. By the time I'm done I will most certainly be in need of a little refreshment."

"Well, I've lots of refreshment at my place, if you don't mind the linen-covered couch and the view of a lifeboat," Soleil said facetiously.

"She's one of us, Fred," I assured him, using the pet name I'd long ago adopted for him.

"I see!"

"So get along with your work, and we'll be in stateroom—"

"Stateroom two-sixty-five. Just a few doors down—for your convenience."

"Yes, and hurry it up, will you?" I added. "We are on a work mission."

"How's that?"

"A little game; we're considering various ways to kill a man."

"*Ahhh*, that's always a popular parlor game. Anyone in particular you have in mind?"

"Mistress murders lothario," tossed out Soledad.

"Slow, painful death, or fast and to the point?"

"Definitely slow. Painful is good—more sensational and sells more books. My readers are sadists, you know."

"For the bloodthirsty reader, *hmmm?*" he nodded, weighing the problem along with the ten-pound dumbbell in his hand. "Slow and painful . . . well, that's easy! She must smother him with love!"

Ladies' lounge

Dining room

Chapter Three

I decided to forgo breakfast the following morning. Anyway, I'd awoken at eleven, and my head was not exactly sitting straight on my shoulders. Much as I like tequila when I'm drinking it, it doesn't like me very well the next day. So I was not in the mood to take part in what was to be a morning ritual—Hem's flashy show of ingesting saltpeter. As the sun was shining, a welcome respite from the days of icy storms, I thought a stroll on deck with Woodrow might clear my head.

Bundled up in hat, coat, and gloves, I dressed Woodrow in his red-plaid sweater and braced myself against the unrelenting wind. But when we walked out of the door I was surprised to find the weather was quite mild, the breeze balmy rather than frigid. Scores of passengers were strolling the deck under a spectacularly sunny sky, while stewards were setting out deckchairs for those wishing to take advantage of the precious few hours of reprieve from expected stormy conditions. Woodrow led us to Saul Gold, occupying a wooden lounge and bundled in a wool blanket, a peaked woolen cap pulled low and shielding eyes that stared out into the hypnotically rolling inky-blue depths. The rumble of the engines and the constant wash of the ocean against the hull as the *S.S. Roosevelt* cut its path were somehow reassuring as we walked over to him. There was something vulnerable about the huddled figure; he looked small, and he wasn't a small man. He was rather tall and wiry when standing beside a more substantial Mr. Benchley. But he wore that wounded-warrior look, and I realized that he was indeed a wounded soul, having fought in the Great War and been damaged by gas that scarred lungs, shrapnel that tattered flesh, and the horrific visions of death that destroyed men's spirits.

Everywhere one looked one saw the ravages of the still-recent battle: on the streets of New York, in the small villages. Citizens of nations across the world were witness to the crippled and disfigured soldiers who had limped home. The trauma of the War was felt not only by the returning veterans, but also by those who had remained behind, who had lost sons, husbands, and brothers in the killing fields. Even when they weren't visible, like the raised, sinew-like marking that made me think of Halley's Comet streaking across Saul Gold's left cheek, the scars nevertheless were cut close to the bone, like flesh-piercing commemorative medals.

Ten million soldiers from all over the world, killed, twenty million wounded and maimed, and no one knows how many men, women, and children murdered in France; then the Armenian massacres, and twenty million more fallen to the influenza pandemic of nineteen-eighteen. I felt the hard jab of loss, and the even greater despair of my generation that things could never be the way they were before the Great War because something fundamental to our way of life had radically changed: A seismic shifting occurred while we were unaware, while we were fighting for something we didn't fully understand, and after it was all over, after we buried our dead and bandaged our wounded, we weren't quite sure how to proceed. The world conflict had served no one; no one was free from sinking into the quagmire. The War cut short the gentle breath of innocent youth, and what was once a simple path through life had become a complicated journey. For all our thrilling modern inventions, for all of our modern machinery intended to make our days easier, we had only burdened our existence and were left pining for the sweeter days, the simpler life before war exposed the sinister. Shit, we were all of us "the walking wounded."

Saul smiled when Woodrow's front paws touched his leg and he petted him with a gentle hand. "I've thought about getting a little friend like him," he said, and then he turned those dark, haunted eyes on me.

"Why don't you?" I said, taking the chair next to his, and looking out toward a never-ending horizon.

"I don't know if I'd be the best person to take care of a dog."

"The truth is, Saul, it doesn't really work like that. The dog takes care of you, you see. I just feed and walk him."

He chuckled, and continued to pet Woodrow. "I suppose that's the way it really is. Pure hubris to think otherwise."

"Woodrow makes sure I never oversleep, that I answer the doorbell, that I take my thrice-daily constitutional, and that I don't miss too many meals, of which he benefits from the leftovers. Best of all, he makes me laugh and not take myself too seriously. I couldn't get through a day without him."

Saul gave me an all-knowing look. We recognized in each other that we were both of us victims of dark thoughts, of recurring and troubling apparitions that stalked our nights.

"He takes his responsibilities seriously, does he?"

"It's really a mutual contract. Ever have a pet?"

"I had a pet squirrel when I was a kid. Don't laugh!"

"Who's laughing?"

"Well, I said he was mine. I liked to think he was. Sam—I named him Sam—lived in this vacant lot a couple of blocks from our tenement on the Lower East Side. It was just a dusty, crusty plot, a block square, where this rich man's mansion once stood that burned down before I was born. The neighborhood had gone downhill. The lot had this tall wooden fence all around it, with No Trespass bills pasted on. It was a sorry-looking plot, with the occasional rusty can and soda bottle woven down under overgrown weeds, and chipped brick and craggy cement piled at one end. But there was this mulberry tree, and when I sat under it in the summertime, it was like it was a little bit of country, away from the city and all the commotion of the streets. And because there was this big fence all around, you couldn't see the buildings nearby, just the sky and the clouds, you know? I liked to read there, under the tree, and there were birds, other than the usual pigeons, songbirds. And when the mulberries were ripe, it was the sweetest fruit I'd ever tasted. They were free and they were mine and nobody else's. I never felt so rich in my life, just me and my friend, Sam, whom I used to feed bits of bread and seeds and mulberries right from my hand.

"After winter, the next spring, when the trees were starting to bud, I left school one day to go over to my vacant lot to sit under my tree and feed my squirrel, and *goddammit*—the fence was down and bull-dozers had ripped the gorgeous tree up from its roots. My Sam, who was there only the day before—well, I couldn't find him. I remember running home in tears to tell my mother, who didn't think much about it. She said it was good; the lot was just a fenced-up eyesore, a place where kids could get in trouble at night, taking dope and knocking up the girls, and that the squirrel would just find another tree to make its nest, because squirrels don't belong to anyone in particular . . . . So, that was the only pet I ever had, Dorothy."

"I heard tell he relocated to the great elm in Washington Square."

He smiled, and then let out a hearty chuckle. "Well, then, it appears he moved up in the world."

While I pondered his tale, he called my attention: "There's Bob, doing what appears to be praying over a—what is that—?"

"Looks like a cigar box," I determined, and I called out to Mr. Benchley, who was standing solemnly at the deck's rail. When he didn't answer, I threw off my blanket and walked over to stand beside him as he mumbled what sounded like the *Pater Nostra*.

"Ashes to ashes, dust to dust—"

"What fresh hell?"

"*Shush*, Dottie; have some respect," he chided, while keeping his eyes on the cigar box. He completed his graveside eulogy, and then met my eyes. "It's Francesca and Antonio," he said, and then clarifying in the face of my frown, "my rodent couple from the nether-regions of this ship. I found them, dead."

"Rat trapped?"

"Certainly not! They must have gotten into something they shouldn't've."

"What else would you call a trap, but something you shouldn't get into?"

"And they smelled a bit . . . funny."

"You smelled a rat!"

"Make light of it, if you must," he said, slipping the box out over the rail and sending it into the sea. "Why, only last night, when I went down to fetch my travel clock, they were in fine spirits. After I fed them—"

"Quiet, they'll have you committed!"

"This morning, when I went back down there to search for my typewriter, I found them just lying there . . . ."

"All right, well, they died together, I'm sure that's how they wanted it to be."

"That's not funny."

"When you've had some time to think it over, I'm sure you'll see it my way. Say, shall we invite Saul to join us at cards? Five should give us a good poker game."

"Yes, let's," said Mr. Benchley, "He looks rather grim, if you see what I mean?"

"So it appears. You two have lots in common, I'd say."

"Is that so?" he said, as we walked over to Saul.

"You are both adopted of rodents as pets."

"What's that supposed to mean?"

"Never mind, I'm ready for coffee."

I left Mr. Benchley in the company of Saul Gold and returned Woodrow to my cabin, and then went in search of a pot of coffee in the dining room, on the way meeting Ronald, the Bad Boy of the British Upper Classes, who appeared sobered up if not a little hung over. The evening before I hadn't seen him approach the table, so I hadn't been aware of the serious limp or the cane he relied on. He turned an ingratiating smile and comment toward me as we now entered the dining room. "Mrs. Parker, once again I am graced by your presence."

"Hello, Ronald."

"Call me Ronnie, please, Mrs. Parker, everybody does."

"Except his servants, of course," came the dulcet tones of Lady Twinton, appearing suddenly at my side, taking my arm to lead the way. I was led to a table for four and we all sat down.

"The King calls me Ronnie."

"That's because your name is a mouthful," she said with a snort. "Marquis Ronald Everett Hampton-Crispin-Jones."

"The King?" I asked, disbelieving.

"And he's also the Duke of something-or-other, on his French mother's side."

"May I call you Dorothy?"

"Why not? Since me and the King can call you Ronnie."

"Ernest told me that your maiden name is Rothschild. That's quite a legacy," said Ronnie.

"Lot of good it did me," I chuckled.

"Can it, Ronnie; can't you see how embarrassing you are?"

"Go away, Daff. There must be some other fellow you can bother."

"That's no way to talk to your fiancée."

"*Ah*, yes, darling wretch, I almost forgot you are my intended," he said as he plopped into a chair and signaled for the waiter. "But don't you always forget you're *my* intended when you see a pretty face, my dove? Sometimes I think you only tolerate me."

"Mostly, I do," said Daphne, throwing off his attack to request a pot of coffee from the waiter.

I couldn't resist: "My, my, children, if you quarrel like this now, how will it be ten years from now?"

"I don't think that far ahead," said Ronnie.

"No, Ronnie doesn't think, period. He just broods."

"I suppose I will leave you then—"

"Please don't, Dorothy," said Daphne, touching my arm. "We are just getting our daily workout; our sparring keeps us on our toes. Keeps us from getting bored with each other. No harm meant."

"Yes, sorry, Dorothy, we are trying, I suppose, but our friends get used to it after a while. Let's talk about happier, more congenial things."

I wanted to say that I would never get used to their "sparring" because I had no intention of becoming their friend. For want of a polite reply I asked the mundane question, "Was this your first trip to the States?"

"Yes. We found it quite interesting, very entertaining, didn't we Daff?"

"Quite."

"Well, there we are, now. Glad we could entertain you," I said, gulping down the too-hot coffee, and then standing to leave. Ronnie jumped to his feet, well, he tried to, and asked me to stay so we could chat some more.

"Daphne, my dove, Dorothy must think we are incorrigible. We do love one another, you know. The way it counts."

"Yes, the way it counts," agreed Daphne, leaning over to plant a kiss on his lips.

I softened for a moment, considering the dynamics of their relationship.

"How long have you been together?"

"Not so very. We sort of grew up together, you see, so we were very familiar with each other. I married a chap—"

"My cousin!"

"Yes, Ronnie's cousin."

"And things didn't quite work out, so—"

"It's us now."

I didn't know how to make out his *things didn't quite work out,* but I knew I'd regret asking for clarification.

"When do you plan to marry?"

"Soon as the divorce comes through," said Daphne.

"I really must go, you know. Mr. Benchley awaits me out on deck, you see."

As I walked out of the dining room, I was trying to figure out how best to avoid their company during the rest of our journey, but I was met by Soledad Soleil in the hall. "Gird your loins, Soledad."

"I suppose I should heed your warning. Is it the Royal couple?"

"You are perceptive!"

"I'll order breakfast in my room, then."

"Sounds like a good idea. Will you join us for cards later?"

"I shall be there."

Just as we were about to part ways, there appeared an unexpected sight, and we stopped in our tracks to observe an ancient couple hobbling toward us. She was elderly and bent, which sent her stride out of kilter, and on pencil-thin limbs she appeared to fling from side to side like a tightrope walker. Yet, she soldiered on toward us. At her side, and supporting her weight from toppling to the floor, was an equally ancient character, bandying a cane in what appeared a coordinated rhythm to continue a forward-moving momentum. His leg clicked with each advancing goosestep. Had she not been so fragile, and he not so measured, and the roll of the ship not so prominent, one might think they were a couple of drunks staggering home at dawn.

The man was the more youthful in appearance, his profile regal and aquiline; despite the steely gray hair and the measured gate he had retained the strong and handsome features of his youth.

She was dressed in black, and topped with a head of thick, snowy-white hair, and her skin looked as tender and white as the skin of an onion. What really proved striking was the blue of the old woman's eyes against the snowy field of her face. When she stopped suddenly to cast a smile up at her younger escort, her eyes twinkled with youthful vigor, and in return she received a playful squeeze, which evoked a girlish giggle of delight.

Soledad and I made way for the couple to pass, giving them a wide berth with the hope that neither of us would get kicked by flailing limbs. They nodded at us and carried on into the dining room where luncheon was being served.

"That's the Duchess Sofia Louise of Russia, if you didn't know."

"Oh, my goodness!"

"A cousin by marriage of the Tsar's. She'd been in England during the Revolution, so she survived the slaughter."

"She is very frail."

"She is very old."

"And the gentleman?"

"Her companion, a Brit named Alfred Arbuthnot. He is devoted to her."

I went back out onto the deck and joined Mr. Benchley, who was snoozing in the deckchair I had occupied earlier next to Saul Gold. I took Gold's vacant deckchair and bundled myself up in the woolen blanket he'd left behind and closed my eyes.

It must have been the fresh, salty air, or perhaps it was the whooshing of the waves against the hull and the hum of the engines as the ship slipped through the surface of the water; maybe it was the flapping of the flags or the whipping of the lifeboat's rigging that lulled me to sleep, or the music of all of the sounds of an ocean voyage played together that slowed my pulse. Under that scratchy wool cover, my head tented against the constant gale, I felt an odd sense of peace. And I languished in that mood for some time, enjoying the sheer safety of my cocoon—as if a blanket could protect one from the powerful fury of the sea. But warm and safe and at peace I was, nonetheless.

I didn't know how long I had been asleep, but I was pulled out of my gentle doze by the familiar giggling voice of Mr. Benchley. I was too much out of the world to bother to see why he was laughing so, and once again sank down into my feathery slumber. Again I was awakened by more giggles and the words, "Behave yourself! . . . That tickles! . . . Your fingers are like ice! . . . Oh, you naughty girl! I must insist—"

What was Mr. Benchley up to, I wondered? Curiosity was winning out over sleep.

"Just dreaming," he replied to my swearing. "Time for my daily exercise!" he said, leaping out of the chair and beginning a series of jumping jacks, at which I just rolled my eyes and retreated once again under my tent. But, it was the peculiar hooting sounds that yanked me out from under the blanket yet again, and my perspective was thrown out of whack when I saw before my eyes a pair of size-ten Oxfords attached to brown Argyle hose below the buttoned cuffs of tweedy plus-eights that looked very familiar. The feet were dangling, tossing back and forth, and below them I saw that Mr. Benchley was no longer performing his

Canadian Air Force deep-knee lunges. I looked up and there he was! Mr. Benchley was levitating—in a vertical position! My mind put things right just then, and I realized he was climbing a rope.

What was he doing climbing up a rope? Where had the rope come from?

I threw off the blanket and got out of the chair to see what he was hoping to achieve in this madcap adventure. Truth is, Mr. Benchley doesn't usually engage in calisthenics—that is, he considers exercise a drain on his energy, and more than a short walk to the bar doesn't suit him at all. I called out to him to inquire if he'd lost his mind, but the only response I got were a series of whoops and hoots. It was then that I realized that my friend was being carried off and over the side of the ship by a rope that had him swinging and flying in the air like a middle-aged Peter Pan. I followed the rope up and saw that it was attached to the arm of a winch, the kind used to unload cargo.

Mr. Benchley was trying to keep his hold on the rope and to haul his weight up the line. But the man who was once the boy who was belittled in gym class wasn't succeeding. I started to scream.

The deck was deserted. It was the luncheon hour. A man jogging around the deck stopped, stood on a deckchair to grab at the rope, and crashed to the floor when the chair gave way. I continued to howl for help, and then a face peered over the rail above our deck. He disappeared for a time as I watched the rope suddenly descend to the water line; there was nothing else for me to do but scream some more.

Now my friend was being dragged in the violent beating of cut water like bait on a fishing line, his grip on the rope, tenuous. But it was the fast response of a crewman, whose attention was turned at the sound of the creaking winch, who finally came to the rescue, and with the help of several others managed to hoist Mr. Benchley back up out of the water and slowly into the air where he dangled before being gently set down on the deck above.

I raced to the staircase leading to the upper deck. There, a group of people were huddled over my friend. I managed to squeeze through, close enough to see a man placing a blanket over a dripping-wet, shivering Mr. Benchley, and encouraging him to drink from a flask. It was then that my friend passed out.

"Fred!" I cried. I collapsed at his side, and began slapping his face, and the gentleman checked Mr. Benchley's pulse and then put his arms around my shoulders. My world was falling apart.

"Come, come, my dear, you're shivering."

"But, he isn't—"

"He is just passed out, my dear. He will be all right."

"Are you sure?" I growled, grabbing the man's lapels, violently pulling him to me, face to face, and demanding the truth. I confronted brown eyes that bored into mine with an assured intensity.

"Yes, *yes!* He *will* be all right, believe me," he answered and held me to his chest as I burst into tears. He handed me a handkerchief, and then turned me toward my reviving friend.

"It's adding insult to injury, you slapping me like that, Mrs. Parker!"

"Oh, dear, precious Fred!" I said, collapsing on his chest, slobbering like a spanked child all over his shirt. And then seeing that he was all right, as the man with the brown eyes had assured me he would be, I lifted my head to scold: "What the hell were you playing at, you maniac!"

"I . . . was . . . ."

A little redheaded man in a trench coat and sporting a French beret and dark glasses passed by and looked at Mr. Benchley with inquiring eyes.

"You saw what happened, uhhh, Mr. —" I said, remembering I had seen him on the upper deck when I had called for help.

"Yes. I am Claude Dubois, Madame. Yes, I was walking along and heard a peculiar noise, and when I turned to look, I saw a rope with a big hook at the end descending to the deck below. I looked over the rail, and saw your friend rising up in the air. I called to a steward."

"We didn't lower that line!" shouted a crewman. "Why would we lower the line?"

"I didn't know—"

The commotion brought more people to speculate on what had actually happened, along with Captain Fried and other members of his crew to assess the situation. Mr. Benchley was by this time sitting up in a deckchair, the ship's doctor assessing for injuries after speaking with the gentleman who had first come to his assistance, a passenger who was himself a physician by the name of Dr. Hartley.

The ship's physician said, "Better get him out of these wet clothes."

"No! Don't say that!" said Mr. Benchley.

"Say what?" The doctor, not understanding, repeated himself: "You need to get out of those wet clothes."

"Yes, yes," I said. "We'll get him out of those wet clothes—"

"—and into a dry martini," said Mr. Benchley, relenting and warily quoting himself.

"I never wrote that line, you know. Some other smart-aleck wrote it, but I am forced to repeat it whenever I'm caught in a rainstorm or dunked in an ocean . . . ."

"This can be sorted out later," said the confused doctor.

"Come on, Fred; let's go."

I followed the entourage indoors as a shivering Mr. Benchley was assisted down to his cabin, babbling all the way about his experience becoming a new, exhilarating sport worthy of Polar Bear Clubs around the world. A steward ran a hot bath, which was my cue to return to my cabin to fetch Woodrow Wilson. Dr. Hartley and the ship's physician left the cabin with me. I thanked them both, and as I turned toward my room, Dr. Hartley said, "Are you all right, Mrs. Parker?"

I realized that I was still quite traumatized by the scene I had witnessed, and a cold shiver ran down my spine upon acknowledging the fact. Had it not been for the actions of some very quick-thinking people, my friend might have been killed. I felt wobbly-legged, even though the ship was steady.

I pulled myself together, looked into the soft brown eyes and told the doctor that I was just fine and thanked him for his prompt response in attending to Mr. Benchley. We parted ways, in opposite directions along the hall. Alone in my room, I looked at myself in the mirror and I could see why Dr. Hartley had expressed concern. I was a mess. My nose was red, cheeks blotchy; my hands were blue from cold and shaking. I threw off my coat and scarf, and belted back a tumbler of scotch. I combed my hair, washed the tear streaks from off my cheeks, and recovering, Woodrow and I walked down the hall to the dining room, where I spotted Hem and Mathew engaged in conversation and halfway through their meal.

The thought of sitting there chatting about poetry and writing and art didn't appeal to me at the moment. I wanted to see to Mr. Benchley, and I needed another drink, so I hailed a waiter in passing and asked that three luncheon trays be sent to Mr. Benchley's cabin.

Mr. Benchley buttoned up a wooly cardigan and sat down in an easy chair. Lunch arrived and we sat quietly for a while, eating, Woodrow at my feet contentedly licking off the remains of his Salisbury steak and mashed potatoes from his plate. As Mr. Benchley drank his hot consommé, I finally asked how he found himself dangling over the ship's side.

"Well, you know I was doing my jumping jacks."

"Yes,"

"And then I did a series of eight deep-knee bends—"

"All right."

"After that, I began the pushups—I only did twenty-five of them because the ship was rolling."

"Yes, all right, for God's sake: How'd you get caught by the rope?"

"Well, after ten toe-touches—you can't bend your knees, you know, or it doesn't count—I like to do a few pull-ups, or try to, that is, so I grabbed onto one of the horizontal lines securing a lifeboat, and when I came down from—I think it was the seventh one—well, I felt a drag, a pull on my elbow. I saw the rope, and I said to myself, 'By golly, you've been lassoed!' And I wondered if Will Rogers was aboard ship, showing off the way he always shows off, the big ham, with his rope tricks, and then before I knew it I was hoisted into the air."

"You weren't caught in a lasso."

"I didn't think so."

"A winch hook caught your arm."

"But how could that be?"

"That's what I'm trying to figure out."

"Why not ask the fellow who was watching."

"Watching? There was nobody there. I didn't see anybody!"

"Well, there was this fellow—beret, dark glasses—and then—well, then I got trussed up like a Christmas goose. That's all I recall," he said, pouring more scotch into our glasses, "except the part where I was waterskiing on my ass in subfreezing waters. Not a pleasant sport, I can tell you," he said, belting back the liquor in one gulp and then sitting back exhausted in the club chair. "Freak accident! But, I won't let a little thing like shark baiting ruin this trip."

Although his face was flushed from the effects of the hot bath after the dunk in the icy sea, my friend seemed rejuvenated, as is often the case when one escapes imminent death.

"Anyway, I'm ready to take away all your pennies at cards this afternoon, my dear."

———◆———

We were joined for card games by Hem and Mathew and then Saul Gold strolled in looking for a game. He took a seat next to me, and Mr. Benchley dealt the first round of cards. Mathew won the first hand and Saul the second. After a couple of hours we stopped for cups of "fortified" tea and a leg stretch. I was down six dollars, Hem had won the last three pots, and Mathew was looking rather green from his loss of two-twenty-five. Mr. Benchley was fifty cents in the hole. Soledad hadn't showed up for the game.

"I believe that old boy is wiping the floor with those men," said Mr. Benchley, looking over in the direction of another card game going on a few tables away. I turned to see four men deep in concentration over their cards, and recognized the elderly gentleman I had seen assisting the Russian Duchess into the dining room at breakfast time. His place at the table was piled high with chips. Just then, cards were folded, others revealed, and the old fellow swept in the stacks of chips from the center of the table toward his already-towering pile. I could see they were playing for high stakes, and it appeared that the other gentlemen were not taking their losses well; one man shot up out of his chair, and, by the look on his face, I feared he might decide to walk out on deck and jump into the ocean to end it all. From where we were watching it appeared the game was over, but Major Arbuthnot just sat there with his winnings as two of the three remaining and defeated men grudgingly stormed out of the room. The remaining man, a bald fellow who reminded me of our friend, Jimmy Durante (without Jimmy's comical smile, but due to his bulbous nose and stuck-out ears), leaned back in his chair, chuckled, and wagged a finger at the Major, before he got up casually, and with no hurry left the room. The Major signaled to a steward to help gather his chips onto a tray.

I hadn't noticed him before, but as I watched the two losers leave the room, the red-haired man who had witnessed my friend's aerial act this morning caught my attention when he abruptly popped up from his chair at a table where he had been playing a hand of gin with a party of two other players. He made fast apologies and hurriedly quit the room.

"Turgenev," said Hem, pulling my attention back to our game as he shuffled the cards to deal. "I started with Turgenev. Sylvia Beach—she's the woman who owns this wonderful bookstore, Shakespeare and Company—well, she let me borrow books on credit when I was strapped for cash. She lent me the Turgenev books and stories. He is a fine writer."

Hem was now engaged in the education of Mathew.

"I haven't read any Turgenev, but I like Dostoyevsky," said Mathew.

"I liked *Crime and Punishment*, but I couldn't finish *The Brothers Karamazov*. Maybe someday, I'll go back and read it," said Hem. "It was probably me. Something about me that made it hard to read, because I liked the other book. Chekov, you read Chekov?"

"Yes."

"Like him?"

"Chekov? Yes."

"Chekov's stories have the depth of a fine burgundy, and the clarity of spring water, though some of his stories sound like journalism. Some of the best writers start there, I suppose. If you want to write a book, start with clarity. That's the ticket. Find what is *true*. Why, I sometimes spend a whole day trying to write a true sentence."

Now, let me start by saying that I really like Hem. He is a most attractive and charismatic man who is quite charming and agreeable to spend time with. I really like the short stories he's had published, and I am assured by friends who know Max Perkins over at Scribner's that my friend Scott Fitzgerald was not mistaken in recommending they take on Hem's new book, *The Sun Also Rises,* for publication. But over the past few weeks of our acquaintance, I have heard him spout out some rather pretentious crap. Chalk it up to youth. He is only twenty-five years old. The idea that one sentence could be truer than another strikes me as preposterous.

"Are you saying," I asked him last week when we stopped in for drinks at Tony Soma's, *"true to the character,* when engaged in dialogue?"

"Not only then."

"When else?"

"The sky is blue. That is a true sentence."

"But it is not true," I countered, "if it is a rainy day and the sky is gray."

"Then it is gray, and that is true. It is when the writer lies, as most do, that the work becomes muddied."

"What do you mean *lie?* How does one write lies? When one writes a novel that is fiction, the whole damn thing's a lie."

"But, is it true?"

"I beg your pardon?"

"Is the lie stripped down to reveal a truth?"

"It makes a point; I try to show the real point of what is really being said under the guise of polite social conversation. The subtext."

"All right, what is really being *said*, then, is quite simple. And that is *the truth*."

"What do you mean, *stripped?*"

"Contrived. The similes, the adjectives. Cut them out of your prose."

"How do you express what a character is feeling, what the atmosphere is like?"

"Once I wrote a long paragraph describing how the rain fell over the city. That was how they used to write—the Henry Jameses, the Zolas—but I learned that what I wrote was not *true*. They were my lies. The only truth is: *It was raining.* Forget the adjectives. The less said the better."

"Are you suggesting that one should ignore how actions affect emotions, the state of mind and the quality of the setting?"

"Use the simple words like *good, true, fine, real, nice, cold, warm.*"

"Four-letter words, Hem."

"So they are," he laughed. You don't need more than those words to describe anything, really."

Some time later, after his book, *Sun*, was finally published, I noted additional four-letter words repeated in his standard vocabulary: *kill, hunt, fish, bull,* and *shit*—and a couple of others that Max Perkins insisted be purged off the printed pages and substituted for with a benign series of hyphens.

I thought of Fitzgerald, and how his style was so different from Hemingway's, about how his prose was filled with heartbreakingly visual imagery, his characters alive with color. Still, I thought I might learn from Hem.

"Tennyson, anyone?" cut in Mr. Benchley.

But before anyone could respond, a steward interrupted and handed Mr. Benchley a note.

"Oh, good, they've found my mandolin. There will be music."

"Alleluia," I said.

"It's been put in my room."

"Amen."

We played another hour, Mathew recouping his losses with a nickel profit, Hem handing over his earlier winnings to Saul Gold, who'd also taken Mr. Benchley's short-lived profit of four-fifty but then lost it all in one grand but obvious bluff to me, the winner of the afternoon, walking away with the grand total of nine-dollars-and-fifty-five cents!

"Drinks, my cabin before dinner," I said, as we left the card room. I went to fetch Woodrow so we could both stretch our legs in a walk around the deck. When we went outside, the sun had already set and a full moon had risen brightly in the cobalt sky. I spotted Soledad leaning against the rail, wrapped in luxurious mink, her head swathed in a pale-blue chiffon scarf, its ends floating on the breeze like ethereal apparitions. And by her side was the Dr. Hartley of the soft brown eyes, who had comforted me after Mr. Benchley's high-wire escapade. They were deep in discussion, standing quite close, and I didn't want to interrupt what might be the beginnings of a shipboard romance, so I turned to walk in the opposite direction. Woodrow would have none of it. Whenever he spied people he knew, there was a chance that they would bend to pet him, murmuring words of admiration. Woodrow was a very social creature, full of tricks and clever antics.He resisted my pull on the leash, so I lifted him up into my arms. Before getting very far, however, Soledad spotted us and beckoned us to join her.

"Dorothy, I'd like you to meet Dr. Richard Hartley."

"Hello, again."

"You've met?" said Soledad, and then, responding to Woodrow's demand for attention, patted his head. He gave her a paw to shake.

"I had the pleasure of meeting Mrs. Parker—"

"Dorothy, please—"

"—Dorothy . . . this morning, although under less favorable conditions."

"Moonlight and stardust are far more favorable, I agree, Dr. Hartley."

"Richard, please."

"All right, Richard it is."

"Richard and I go way back, don't we, darling," said Soledad.

"Oh, since the Ice Age, surely."

"We've slept together, you know."

"Bed partners, we!"

"*Très moderne.* I suppose I should be shocked," I said with a laugh. "But, you do make a dashing pair."

"That's what our mothers said—when we were babies."

"Our mothers were lifelong friends, you know, and they had plans for us to be together from the time we shared a crib."

"But, it didn't work out, did it, Sollie?"

"Alas, no, much to my regret."

"You say that now, my dear!" He turned to me and continued, "But she was always so damned promiscuous, you see; men worship her, and I just never stood a chance—"

"Don't believe a word of it, Dorothy. He threw me over—oh, yes, you did!—for a life of service."

"You make it sound as if I'm somebody's footman."

Soledad let loose a cackling laugh, and when

she threw back her head, the ends of the diaphanous scarf took flight in the wind. She was quite a beautiful woman, and the moonlight made her strikingly lovely, softening the sharp angles of her cheekbones and the determination of her chin. "I warn you, Dorothy: Be careful. He may appear harmless—"

"Really, Sollie, you are outrageous. What is Mrs. Parker—Dorothy—supposed to think. Now I haven't a chance to impress her with my charm."

"Oh, I'm not so sure," clucked Soledad.

She was right, of course. Richard Hartley was a charming man, I could see that even more now than when he rushed to our aid this morning. I could feel the pull of attraction. As I am susceptible to charm, I chalked it up to moonglow and the lunar pull of the tides.

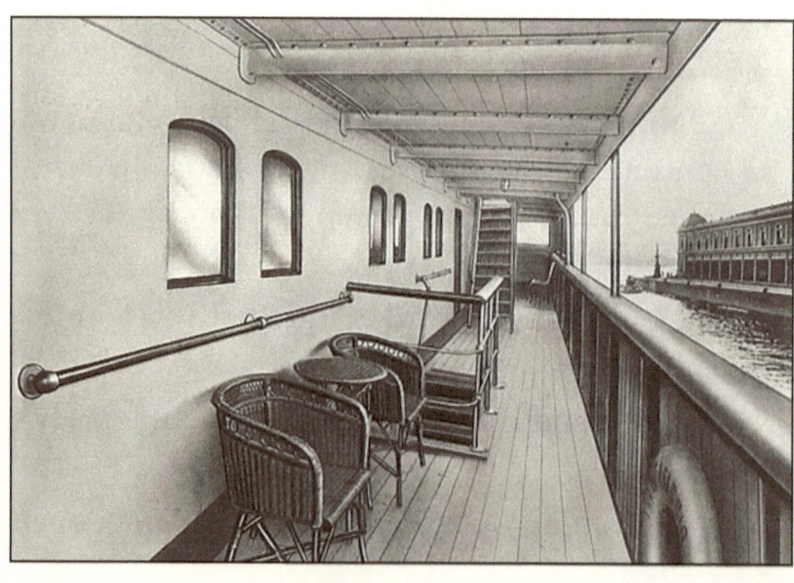

Chapter Four

Mr. Benchley, Hem, Mathew, and Saul appeared at the door of my cabin a half hour before dinner for their promised refreshment. Mr. Benchley and Saul were elegantly dressed in eveningwear, while Hemingway and Mathew dressed up their dark suits with black ties, and might've been mistaken for waiters but for Hem's old boots peeking out from under his trouser cuffs and Mathew's addition of spats over patent leathers. Soledad and Richard Hartley had accepted my invitation and I introduced Richard as the gentleman who'd come to our assistance earlier in the day, and lots of clever barbs were tossed around about how, once you save a life, you are forever responsible to the person you rescued from death.

"Of course, I didn't save him," said Richard. "T'was a crewman hauled him up out of the sea. I just looked him over, made sure he'd suffered no injuries, after the fact."

"And I was so looking forward to your indentureship. I could use somebody to watch over me and see to my dry cleaning!" said Mr. Benchley.

"Your dress is divine, Dorothy," said Soledad, admiring the one extravagance I had allowed myself when I went shopping for clothes for the voyage. A lovely little number called out to me. First, the color—a vibrant, blood-red silk velvet—then the sparkle—it seemed to shimmer on its hanger as I approached it, a provocative little light-dance that gave it life, and I was mesmerized. And when I tried it on, despite the fact that I was wearing dark stockings and my sensible shopping shoes, a glance in the mirror made me fall in love with myself. I had to have it. I have to admit that with the embellishments of jewelry and my hair under the control of a red embroidered bandeau, I clean up quite nicely.

I thanked Soledad for her compliment while admiring her pale-green silk frock, paneled along the sides with an intricate overlapping star-motif embroidery of blue and dark-green threads, and the matching bejeweled toque across her brow, cut in the shape of five points. She looked like a jaunty, modern Statue of Liberty.

"Poiret?" I asked.

"No. It's Nicole Groult."

A knock on the door, and a steward handed Mr. Benchley a note.

"Oh, good, they've found my golf clubs and put the bag in my cabin," he said, tipping the young man.

"Clubs? And where and when do you expect to—"

"Have you seen Versailles? What better place to practice my drive? From the Water Parterre, the Grand Canal and on toward the horizon—what a fairway!"

I considered the potential destruction to lawn and statuary, and then remembered who awaited our arrival in Paris. "I suppose if Aleck and Harpo could pierce the lawn with their croquet wickets, who's to complain?"

———◆———

"It took us three days, twenty-two hours, and twenty-nine minutes before the actual rescue. When the gale abated, we launched a lifeboat," recalled Captain Fried.

Dinner at the captain's table once again, but tonight included the Russian Duchess Sofia Louise and her companion, Major Alfred Arbuthnot, both of whose presence seemed to have the effect of subduing the quarrelsome tendencies of Ronnie, otherwise known as the Marquis Ronald Everett Hampton-Crispin-Jones, and his girlfriend, Lady Daphne Twinton.

I very much wanted to hear the tale of the Duchess's life in St. Petersburg, to be privy to the details of the attempted escape into exile of the slaughtered Tsar and his family, but there was really no chance of pursuing that at dinner, especially for the fact that Hem and Mathew pressed Captain Fried to continue the tale of his rescue of the *Antinoe*, interrupted the evening before when the captain had been called away from the table.

"So when I believed it safe to launch the lifeboat with members of our crew to effect a rescue, a violent gale caused a rogue wave to smash the vessel against the ship's side," continued the captain. His expression turned dark as he continued.

"We lost two men, two of our valiant crew— Boson's Mate Ernest Heitman and Crewman Uno Wirtanen, both twenty-eight years old. They could not be recovered."

Hemingway was enthralled by the sea tale of danger and heroism. And Mathew, a newspaperman, having read all the wire stories of that fateful storm and rescue, began to interview the captain. There was another story here. I could see the wheels turning in his head as the captain talked of other sea rescues in which he had played an instrumental role. There were his days as quartermaster aboard the cruiser *The Washington*. "During stormy weather out in the Pacific, a destroyer got adrift, having snapped a line, and then, as chief quartermaster of the *Tonapah*, I assisted a disabled submarine off the coast of Hatteras."

This man was courting disaster, I thought. *When would his luck run out and the ship he commands become the object of rescue? Please, God, please, not this voyage.*

"Then there was that fateful time aboard the *Minneapolis* in 'ought-six—we were on our way from Philadelphia to Havana . . . ."

Saul Gold suddenly appeared at our table and asked Daphne for a dance.

"Some other time," she said dismissively. "Captain Fried is telling us about his many escapades at sea, and it's just too fascinating to give up, you see."

"When can we—"

"Dance?" said Ronnie, half-rising from his chair like a wounded tiger about to pounce.

"I was speaking to Daphne. Daff?"

"You're tight, Saul," she replied.

"Yes, I'm tight, I'm sorry."

"I'm a little tight, too," said Daphne.

"Why not say what you *want* to say, Gold, right here, right now, so everybody can hear it?" There was real hatred and challenge in his voice. "Daphne has no secrets from me, now do you, darling?" Ronnie nuzzled her cheek and she made a small gesture to push him away.

"Captain Fried," Daphne prefaced, determined not to get caught up in a melee, "how old were you when you first went off to sea?"

"It was during the Spanish War—"

"Saul," I said when I looked at Daphne and Ronnie and Hemingway (who despised all weak men), and saw the sheer contempt on their faces. Humiliated, the raw agony Saul was suffering was unbearable to watch. His face grew dark. Of course, he had overstepped some arbitrary line, but he was driven with burning desperation and the cruelty with which he was handled made me angry.

"Let's foxtrot!" I said, as the orchestra had just broken into a peppy rendition of "I'll Build a Stairway to Paradise."

I got up and grabbed his hand before he could protest and he reluctantly followed me onto the dance floor.

"I apologize, Dorothy," he said, contrite now. "I'm a little tight."

I feared he would start crying, as all miserable drunks eventually do when they behave badly or find their loneliness unbearable. "Please forgive me. I made a fool of myself."

"What's to forgive? I do it all the time," I said, as he mindlessly led me around the dance floor.

"It was stupid of me to book on this ship."

"It's obvious you are mad about her."

"She *despises* me."

"I'm sorry, Saul."

"And I thought . . . I thought—you know? I thought she—why else would she have gone off with me those two weeks?" he continued, almost in tears, frustrated in his struggle to understand how things had come to this. "Why, if she didn't—*care?*"

There was nothing I could say to him. He was in love with Daphne, and Daphne had spurned him. I stated the fact as I knew it: "Well, she and Ronnie are engaged."

"I know that. She doesn't love him, though."

"And he knows that you—"

"He knows it all. She told him everything and they've had a good laugh about it, I'll bet. And now I see she's got eyes for your friend—"

"Mr. Benchley?"

"The handsome one, Hemingway."

Yes, I thought, *it doesn't surprise me.* I could see that queer, violent attraction made all the more acute for the conquering.

As Saul moved me around the dance floor, surprisingly graceful without his cane, his eyes drawn across the room trying to keep sight of her, I wondered what I could do to show him the futility of his determined pursuit of Lady Daphne Twinton.

What is it about some of us that we cannot let go when we've been let go of?

"I've money, now; I'm not poor anymore."

"Yes."

"I've plenty of money."

"I know, Saul."

"I thought . . . ."

"Yes, Saul, I know."

"Can't get a goddamn drink on this raft! I want a drink."

"All right, Saul, let's go get one; we both need a drink, don'cha think?"

As we started off the dance floor, Mr. Benchley met us with the cane Saul had left on my chair. Mr. Benchley had been keeping an eye on us as we danced; I'd glimpsed his face through the crowd. The three of us, and Richard and Soledad, left the music, the tales of heroic rescue, and a general malice as we walked toward Mr. Benchley's cabin.

———◆———

The next morning, around ten-thirty, with Woodrow in tow, I knocked on Mr. Benchley's door. He opened it, and through the crack I saw Saul lying on the bed, a blanket thrown over him. I had left Mr. Benchley's cabin soon after Saul had passed out on the sofa a little before midnight. Mr. Benchley eased out through the door as quietly and gingerly as a thief, and told me he had put him to bed shortly after Soledad, Richard, and I had gone. "He got up once, poured himself a scotch, and then went back to sleep."

We walked to the dining room for breakfast. No one from the evening before was present, which for me was quite a relief, so we sat at a small table and ordered coffee, juice, and rolls. The Duchess Sofia Louise entered on the arm of Major Arbuthnot, and their shaky advance across the room, legs and canes flailing about, brought to mind a smashed bicycle wheel, bent, with broken spokes jutting this way and that. Our eyes met, and Mr. Benchley stood to offer the couple to join us. After some adjustments, the two were seated and gave the waiter their orders.

"You should be commended, my dear," said the Duchess.

"I've never received a commendation!"

"All the same," she insisted, and the slight tremor that bobbed her little white head became a nod of approval.

I smiled back. She seemed to like me, not even knowing what I could really be like, so I found her charming. It's always easy to like people who like you. "Now, what would I do with a commendation?"

"We'll pin it on your dress," said Mr. Benchley.

"Like a corsage . . . . Now, tell me exactly why I should be honored?"

The Major finished stirring his coffee and laid down the spoon. "You were kind to that poor young man, you both were," he said, looking over at Mr. Benchley, "when others were rude."

"It is a sign of good breeding," agreed the Duchess. "We don't see much of that these days. Young people seem so . . ."

"So careless," said Major Arbuthnot.

"Why, your little dog, named after your dead president, has impeccable manners," said the Duchess. "Look how he sits there, like a little prince."

I refrained from being contrary. Woodrow wasn't just sitting there; he was biding his time until the waiter brought his meal of scrambled eggs and breakfast sausages. And the Duchess had yet to be present on the occasions when he would lift his leg on a potted plant.

But what they said was true. We were a *careless* generation. I think we have become so because so many young lives were sacrificed in the war, and no one who has survived has wanted to ever know sacrifice again. The prevailing philosophy is that life is too short not to live the years we have to their fullest. There remains a heavy pall of death in the air. It could all end tomorrow. It is fashionable to be outspoken, especially now that women have been unchained from lives of domestic drudgery, fashionable to discard the often crippling reserve of our Victorian parents, and to act in natural ways. Nobody seems to care any more about propriety.

But this elderly couple, relics from another age, were right: Carelessness in the treatment of one's fellow man can be cruel, and cruelty is never acceptable, never fashionable. And last night, cruelty reared its ugly head at Saul Gold.

The waiter returned with our breakfasts, and I was glad for the interruption because my face burned from both guilt and embarrassment at being lauded. As Woodrow plowed into his food, I started to change the subject—my curiosity was piqued; I wanted to know more about the Duchess and the Revolution in Russia and how she saw it all—when suddenly Richard Hartley appeared standing over me and asked if he could join us. His color was high, he was a little out of breath, and around his neck, tucked into his shirt, was a hand towel. When I asked if he was all right, he answered that he had just completed an exercise jog around the deck.

The waiter reappeared, and he gave his order— orange juice, coffee, ham, eggs, and sweet rolls—as he took the vacant chair next to Mr. Benchley's.

"It's a lovely morning out there," he said, after removing the towel from around his neck. "I should have asked for a glass of water," he said to Mr. Benchley.

Mr. Benchley reached out for his untouched glass of orange juice. "Have my juice, I haven't touched it and I'll take yours when it arrives."

"Thanks," said Richard, reaching for the glass, which my friend had moved for easy reach.

But, Richard must have miscalculated because the glass fell over, spilling the juice onto the table. He quickly threw the towel over the spill and was about to dab at the pool, when a hissing steam began to rise from off the cloth, forming an ever-widening hole through the linen.

"I know orange juice is acidic, but this is crazy!" said Mr. Benchley, moving back in his chair as we watched the slow burn advance across the table.

The Major said, "That's acid, my boy, and it's not of the citric variety!" Then, in a booming voice, "Waiter!"

There was much fuss as waiters all responded at the same time to the alarm in his voice, one helping the Duchess to her feet, the others carefully folding up and removing the smoking linens from off the table, along with the glass in which was still contained an ounce of the offending liquid. The maître d' took charge of it, and with righteous assurances proclaimed he would get to the bottom of how acid could have gotten mixed into a glass of juice. He then bounded out of the dining room and through to the kitchen to investigate.

"To think, dear fellow, that you might have imbibed the contents of that glass!" bellowed the Major.

"And I drank mine all up," said the Duchess, as we all began an exodus out of the room.

"Just an accident, I suspect," said Mr. Benchley, trying to keep everyone calm. He was shaken, I could tell, because he kept smoothing his trim moustache with a forefinger. And there was a frown on Richard Hartley's brow as he appeared to ponder that Mr. Benchley had had a close call.

"This is outrageous!" he whispered, and sprinted from the table and across the dining room where our waiter was being grilled by a furious maître d'.

"This is the kind of thing one expects in political intrigue," said Mr. Benchley.

"None of us is involved in intrigue," I said, assisting the Duchess on her left side as the Major supported her right. I was walking at an angle so as not to get kicked or tripped by flailing limbs and canes.

"I'm sure there's a simple explanation to it all," said Mr. Benchley.

"Right. Of course," I said sardonically, throwing a face at my friend. "There is always a simple explanation for murder!"

"It was meant for me!" wailed the Duchess, "There is an assassin on board!"

People at nearby tables and within earshot had been listening to us with alarm. The little redheaded man, the man called Claude Dubois, who had the cabin next to Mr. Benchley's, was seated alone at a table for two. He peeked over an open newspaper, and upon making eye contact with me, retreated back behind it like a turtle into its shell. Then he threw the paper aside and walked over toward us.

"There is something I can do, sir?" he asked.

"All is well, thank you, Mr. Dubois," replied Mr. Benchley as we moved on past him.

"I thought I escaped them all," continued the Duchess. "The first time, when I was in England during the revolt, and then again, in nineteen-nineteen, when they thought I was a threat to them. They want to be rid of me. My cousins' executions were not enough! What can one expect of devils who would murder children?"

The Duchess was angrily recounting her years of terror. She obviously had lived in fear that Soviet influence had far-reaching powers and that for as long as she lived she would be seen as a threat to the new republic. Her outrage seemed to increase her tremors. And then, suddenly, she caved in, as if losing all conviction. A steward appeared and relieved me as "crutch" for the Duchess. I am a small creature, and managing her weight, though slight, was difficult for me. I saw that her energy was spent, if not her spirit as well. "I want to go back to my room," she whispered as she was propped upright for the short walk to her cabin.

Mr. Benchley and I followed until they arrived at the room, and after offering to be of assistance, should any be needed, we walked out onto the outside deck for fresh air. In spite of the cold, the sun was shining. We walked along the portside toward the stern, where we found some relief from the buffeting wind.

"I find it hard to believe that the Soviets would see any threat from the ineffectual protest of an exiled tsarist. Why try to harm a little old lady?" asked Mr. Benchley.

"Perhaps she knows where the bodies are buried?" I said, knowing, of course, that nobody knows the burial place of the assassinated Tsar Nicholas II and his family.

"If it is true, what the Duchess said about an attempt on her life back in 'nineteen, it would have made some sense, because back then there might have been cause for the Reds to believe that the Whites could raise support to take back their country. Perhaps they feared her influence. But now . . . ?"

"I suppose it's hard for her. Her cousins all murdered, her way of life forever changed. You don't have to fight in a war to be affected by its far-reaching consequences."

The boom of rifle fire cut through the air, and the shout of *"Pull!"* brought another shot to ring out.

"Skeet shooting," announced Mr. Benchley in answer to my questioning look.

"Don't they know they are killing fish? The bullets have to land somewhere in the sea," I said.

"Now, Mrs. Parker, big fish eat little fish, so it won't make a dent, anyway."

"Pull!"

Boom!

"That is a feeble excuse for men to play with guns!"

We rounded the deck where at the stern several people were shooting, and I was surprised to see among the party were Hemingway, Lady Twinton, and Ronnie.

"Looks like Annie Oakley can handle a gun," I said, as Daphne Twinton yelled, *"Pull!"* and then blew apart the disk ejected into the air.

"I'll beat you yet, old girl," said Ronnie, and after he called out, he fired and missed. I could see the rigid determination even though his back was toward us. Hemingway shot clay pigeons to bits, one after the other, and Daphne never missed, putting Ronnie's nose out of joint. I thought for a moment that he was going to turn the rifle on her, because as Daphne aimed and fired, his own rifle was poised in her direction. I watched his profile, jaw set firm with anger.

I was paralyzed from the idea that he would shoot her, but then he suddenly pivoted around in our direction and lifted the shotgun up over our heads. I followed his aim across the sky.

I shouted, "No!" The shot rang out and the sea bird spiraled down into the ship's wake.

"Clay pigeon, you dolt!" yelled Daphne. "Not sea tern!"

It became obvious that Ronnie was tight: "There! Got the bloody bastard!" he said. "Kill the bloody scavengers!" And with the gun in tow, he walked toward us. He glared at Woodrow, who skittered behind Mr. Benchley's legs, and as he passed, mumbled, "—and all the bloody rotters that feed off the remains of the day."

"I see the Marquis Ronald is in his usual high-spirited mood," said Mr. Benchley, picking up Woodrow and petting his head with long, soothing strokes. A few passes at ear-kneading, which Woodrow so enjoyed, stopped his shivering. I wished Mr. Benchley could have soothed away my trepidations, but that would not have played well with Mrs. Benchley.

The crewman in charge of the shooting tried to catch up with Ronnie, who had absconded with the shotgun, and the two disappeared from view. I turned at the sound of gunfire to observe Hem and Daphne. The Lady Twinton continued her assault on the clay pigeons, while Hemingway, when not shooting, continued his very engaged, very attentive admiration of Lady Twinton.

We turned back from whence we came, I hatless and the stiff wind assaulting our faces. Mr. Benchley said, "Let's play a quiet game of bridge this afternoon."

As we left the outdoors for a calmer interior climate, a steward approached, carrying a canvas-covered tennis racket. "Sir, we've found your tennis racket," he said to my friend.

"I see! Good man! Now, if you can find where they hid my briefcase—"

"Why are your things scattered about?" I asked.

"There was a misunderstanding," replied my friend, and then addressing the steward: "Would you please put the racket in my room? Wait! Give it to me."

I said with a laugh, "Why? Do you want to practice your backhand hitting balls off the back of the ship? You'll lose your balls that way."

"Mrs. Parker! Really! I have no balls!"

"Just as I suspected . . . ."

"They're tucked away, shifted to the side, last I looked—"

"I don't need to know this—"

"—somewhere in my drawers—"

"Say no more!"

"—of my steamer trunk, back in my cabin."

"Just when you were getting interesting."

"I try never to be dull. No, I just realized that Gold is probably still sleeping it off in my room, no reason to disturb the man."

"You are a considerate fellow."

Richard Hartley caught up with us as we walked the long corridor to our cabins.

"There you are," he said. "I've been looking for you both. The captain was called down and they are looking into the juice incident. Can you imagine if either one of us had taken a sip, Bob?"

"I am trying not to imagine, Richard. I suppose Mrs. Parker would have had to see herself to Paris."

"Very funny, you idiot," I scolded. I turned to Richard. "The Duchess believes she was the intended victim," I said. "What, do we need to hire a food taster now? We escorted her to her stateroom. I suspect she has locked herself in for fear of Russian assassins!"

We all looked at each other for a long moment. Mr. Benchley asked in a casual tone, "What did you find out about what happened?"

"The waiter was in tears, as was the kitchen boy who set up the drinks—they swear it was all an accident, and that they had no idea how the acid got into the juice. I asked if the filled-up glasses were left unattended once they left the kitchen, but they assured me that the juice was served immediately."

"Were any of the other drinks from the tray tainted?" asked Mr. Benchley.

"Who can know for sure now? In the hysteria, the ones that weren't delivered were emptied down the sink by a busboy, and those delivered were taken away and dumped, too. Only a few people who'd been served drank theirs, and one woman became hysterical believing she was poisoned, too. I attended her immediately, but it was all in her head. I assured her that she wouldn't have had much time to raise an alarm had there been acid in her drink."

We walked toward my cabin to leave Woodrow there for his late-morning nap, and on the way spotted Mathew outside Mr. Benchley's door. He turned when we called to him, and came to join us.

"I was looking for Hem," he said.

"His room is down that way," I said.

"He's not there; I thought he might be with you, Bob."

I told Mathew that Ernest was playing with Lady Twinton. The look on his face changed from one of hopeful discovery to one of worrisome dubiety, resulting in my asking him if there was anything wrong.

"No, not at all," he replied, as if taken aback, before flashing a fast grin at us, and then he walked toward the doors leading out to the deck. He was a bad liar.

Lady Daphne Twinton

Gerald's Boatdeck

Chapter Five

Weather on the ocean descends the way stage scrims are lowered in a theatre. Fast. One moment it is all sun and balmy air, the next we are pitched into a raging storm. Such was the case soon after we sat down for our afternoon game of bridge.

I was coupled with Mr. Benchley against Soledad and Richard Hartley. It was good to laugh and enjoy witty conversation again after our morning escape with our lives, as well as the past several days of witnessing the tiresome sparring among the royalty at the captain's table. This was the first time during the journey I had really begun to relax. I liked listening to Soledad's sharp and clever observations about everything and everybody. This afternoon, Richard Hartley was a pleasure to be with: handsome, in an unconventional way, with those lovely, heavy-lidded, cognac-colored eyes — the light in the room set them atwinkle. His charm was a sharp wit combined with gentlemanly manners. He and Mr. Benchley were cut from similar cloth.

Across the room, the group of men who had been playing for high stakes the day before considered their hands. Alfred Arbuthnot was again sweeping up the chips, much to the frustration of his opponents. The same hefty fellow who had violently thrown down his cards the day before now repeatedly wiped his forehead with his handkerchief, and once, to the annoyance of the other players, had the bad manners to interrupt the game with an order to the steward to bring him a glass of ginger ale, into which he poured a healthy slug from the contents of a flask before meeting the bid on the table. I watched, suspecting that his too-obvious show of nerves was the bluff to take the hand, to make the others see his raise. It did not work. He lost to Major Arbuthnot.

Mr. Benchley followed my gaze across the room, took in the innocuous Major, and then nodded and flashed me an all-knowing smile that did little to inform me of his thoughts.

"Where's Hemingway?" asked Soledad when we took a break to order a tray of sandwiches along with beverages.

"Out fishing for a *true* sentence," I said.

"I doubt that's how he's spending his time," Soledad giggled wickedly. "I saw him knocking at Lady Daphne's cabin door after lunch."

"Selling Girl Scout cookies, I suppose," I replied.

"I thought I saw him climbing up to the bridge," said Mr. Benchley. "Perhaps he's at the helm—"

"I'll bet he is!" I said, throwing a knowing look at Soledad. "He likes to be on top!"

"—swapping tales of heroic rescues with our Captain Fried."

Soledad and I gave up the naughty insinuations, true as they might be.

"He is intrigued with him, too—our captain, that is," said Soledad.

"And Mathew?" I asked. "There's a young man intrigued with Hemingway!"

"Well, Hemingway is a striking character, I must say: handsome, manly, very sure of himself, very confident. I can understand Mathew's hero worship there," said Soledad.

"Emerson wrote, 'In the end every hero is a bore,'" Richard Hartley said with a chuckle. "And by the way, Sollie, you used to describe *me* as "very handsome, manly, very confident—"

"I doubt anything's changed there," I said, and then felt the heat rise to my cheeks.

I lowered my eyes for a moment from embarrassment, but my disdain for coquettishness forced me to face my companions. Richard held my gaze, and the look of admiration on his face forced me to comment yet again, as I was sure I was as red as a tomato. "Did you know—"

I was happily interrupted when the food arrived, and we set about "improving" our drinks and choosing our little sandwiches.

"What were you about to say?" said Richard.

Grabbing at straws I replied, "Just that our good friends, Aleck Woollcott and Harpo Marx, will be meeting us when we arrive in Paris."

"You mean the famous theatre critic?" said Soledad. "Why, his column is enormous fun. Richard, you know who he is, don't you? The fellow with the theatre column everybody reads? Why, I never read such hyperbole, mixed metaphors, and absurd similes as can be found in just one theatrical review by Alexander Woollcott!"

"Dear me!" I said, "For the love of peace, Soledad, don't tell Aleck that!"

"Oh, I shan't, I wouldn't, I promise. I've heard he is quite violent!"

"His remarks do sting, that's true. But, if he takes to you, the way he has to our Harpo and his brothers, he is a lamb and a loyal friend."

Mr. Benchley said, "Yes, Aleck is at times somewhat like a smiting god. He may smack you down now and then when you don't do as you are told, but his love is eternal."

"Someone once dubbed him 'vitriol and old lace,'" I said.

"I am looking forward to meeting him!" said Soledad. "I adore autocrats—they are so amusing!"

Soledad was like a refreshing breeze on this tub full of scoundrels. With her svelte physique, her lovely, fair skin, her glossy black hair reflecting the light, the generous red lips so quick to smile, I knew Aleck would also adore her.

And Harpo, the bad boy, would be all over her.

"I saw what you did!" bellowed a gruff, masculine voice, and we all turned to see the hefty man at the Major's table throwing over his chair as he pounded a fist on the table. Glasses teetered, cards and chips scattered. "You palmed that card!"

The Major leaned stiffly back in his chair, a look of horror crossing his face, before his features relaxed and a wistful smile settled in. "Gentlemen—" he began to protest in a low and soothing tone. But before he could continue, the man sitting to his right grabbed his brittle wrist, twisting it until the cards he was holding fell onto the table. The man who looked like Durante, who had the day before chuckled and wagged a finger at the Major's suspected cheating, walked over to the Major's table from across the room, where he'd been sitting in a club chair, reading. The players hovered over the frightened man, shouting accusations at him. The Durante lookalike stood behind the Major's chair and, after a warning glance, the other let go of the Major's wrist and turned over the cards he'd been dealt. One big cretin, who had remained seated during this inspection, rose up and roughly pulled the Major to his feet, making him look like a sorry old ragdoll and causing his knee-brace to click loudly, whereupon the others emptied his coat pockets before yanking off his coat. "Durante" objected, but was told to move aside. Although no proof was discovered to substantiate a cheat, that didn't stop their abuse. The violence with which the Major was handled was shocking to witness. Thugs—for the other men at the table were twice his size and half his years—molesting an old man!

Mr. Benchley and Richard bolted to their feet to go to his aid, while at the same time Hemingway and Mathew entered the card room, having heard the ruckus from the corridor. The sight of Major Arbuthnot manhandled by the brutish quartet sent Hem into a charge. He wasted no time in landing a right-hook to the jaw of the first accuser, sending the man spinning to the floor, and a serving cart crashing into a wall, the shattering glass and china ringing like wind-chimes on a stormy night. A dozen card players were trying to exit the room as the perimeters of the fight expanded.

Any ladies present in the room had been escorted out by the time Soledad and I were cornered. We clung to each other; we had no way of getting out of the room safely, no way around the battlefield without suffering injury, because in an instant, several other men who'd been playing a dull game of whist and gin threw down their cards and leaped, with newfound gusto, into the action and excitement that no mere card game could possibly offer.

Mr. Benchley was situated in the middle of the fray, ineffectually trying to make heard the voice of reason, which was ignored in the passion of the moment and the thrill of the fight. He ducked just in time to avoid a direct strike to his head. Throwing up his hands he watched in terror as he was charged at waist level and literally carried to, and then pinned against, the wall. The moment he was released by his attacker, who had bounced back from the impact, he grabbed a chair, lifted it over his head, and struck the fellow to the floor.

Mathew, knocked down, clobbered an attacker with a silver-plated carafe that had conveniently rolled into his grasp. Richard landed a punch in the gut of the man who had seized the Major.

Mr. Benchley helped the fellow he had crowned with the chair get up on his feet, asked him if he'd had enough, and, when the reply came in the form of a growling advance, made short work of the situation with a very successful block with his left forearm, followed by a side-handed chop to the trachea. "I won't ask you again," he said with a near-hysterical chuckle, "because I doubt you can answer."

The fight was winding down, but Hem was swiveling around, searching the room for more contestants to meet his fist. The men who had initially pounced on the Major were subdued, prone on the carpet, except for the hefty accuser, who was still standing, dazed and trying unsuccessfully to put one foot in front of the other in an attempt to quit the room. Hem, watching him with a hungry, joyful glint in his eyes, like a lion's for a gazelle, pounced on the man from behind; the two landed sprawling on the littered carpet, Planter's Peanuts raining down on them from the only remaining untoppled bowl of nuts.

Captain Fried appeared at the entrance door, and I could swear I saw a flash of amusement pass over his face as he noticed the overturned tables and the debris strewn all over the place. He assessed the scene of the crime, the disheveled figures that were responsible for the room's condition, and ignored their protests. He ordered the stewards, who had been attending the players before making a timely escape, to straighten things up, and sent a message with his purser to fetch the ship's physician to attend to any injuries. He nodded with a "boys-will-be-boys" look of approval before resuming a stern countenance, and then turned on his heel to attend to the business of sailing his ship.

Richard was being ministered to by an attentive Soledad, who'd opened a bottle of White Rock club soda to moisten her handkerchief and wipe away the blood and cigar ash that dirtied his face.

"Look at this," said Mr. Benchley, who had suffered a strike to his midsection and winced with pain when he bent to pick up his mangled tennis racket. "Look at what they did to my tennis racket." He held up the splintered remains of the handle, the woven catgut dangling off its face.

"It was Hem that done it," said Mathew, who had received the least pummeling; he massaged his shoulder, which he had used to block a box to his ear. When Hem looked over at him, he ceased the massage. I supposed he thought tending to his sore shoulder might be viewed as wimpish in the light of Hem's bloody face. "Hem has a powerful serve," he finished with obsequious ardor.

"Looks like I owe you a racket, Bob," said Hem with a hearty chuckle. He sighed, took a deep breath, forced it out with a loud *huff!*, and wiped his sweaty face with his shirtsleeve, looking all the worse for the gesture: blood was smeared down his cheek.

Hemingway was certainly in his element, his exhilaration evident, and he didn't seem to notice the bloody bruise on his forehead. The way he looked around the room at the damage and at the other men picking themselves up to stagger out of the room, I thought that he would have liked nothing better than for the wrangling to start all over again.

I don't understand men.

"This calls for a drink," said Hem, like the victor in celebration. "Who's got some booze around here?"

"I do," I said, "but do go wash yourselves up. I don't want Woodrow seeing you like this."

"What are we celebrating?" asked Soledad.

"Who needs a reason?" I replied.

"Life is good, Soledad," said Hem. "It is *good*."

Mr. Benchley's cabin steward, Rodney, now appeared and climbed over the wreckage carrying a briefcase, apparently oblivious to the state of the room: "Sir, we've found your briefcase. I was going to put it in your cabin, but there is a DO NOT DISTURB sign on the door."

"Why, yes, Rodney, just go in and leave it there. I'd left a friend sleeping late this morning, and he probably forgot to take the sign off the door when he left."

"Would you care for a cold compress, sir?"

"That might not be a bad idea, thank you, Rodney; I'll be in momentarily."

Mr. Benchley watched the steward leave the room, spritely gerrymandering around the broken chairs and mashed cocktail sandwiches.

"I wish I could take Rodney home with me. It would be nice to have a fellow like him: affable, considerate, not critical of the state of the living room," he said with a sweeping hand to indicate the ruination, "generally at my beck and call."

"You have a wife, don't you?" I scolded.

"Yes, of course, but a gentleman's gentleman rarely reproaches his employer. If Gertrude were here, of course, she would get me a cold compress, but the cold shoulder I'd have to endure for engaging in a good-natured free-for-all would prove much more painful. Do you think my rib is broken?" he asked me, lifting his shirt.

I jabbed the exposed flesh. He winced.

"Hey, where is our Major Arbuthnot?" asked Richard.

"I haven't seen him since the fight broke out," said Soledad.

"Wily little man." I said. "And I didn't see that fellow, looks like Durante, take any punches."

We picked our way out of the room.

As we walked toward our cabins, passengers unaware of the fracas backed away to let us pass, and I realized we must have looked like survivors of a train crash. That's when I noticed the collar of my navy-blue sailor blouse covered with an unidentifiable substance, probably clotted cream and strawberry jam—yes, clotted cream and strawberry jam it was, upon the tasting—and my skirt stained with some liquid that resembled chocolate milk. How Soledad had escaped unscathed was proof of her superior abilities, I mused. Or the fact that when the food was flying, she had taken cover behind me.

We parted ways, each to our own rooms, Mr. Benchley and I continuing on toward our cabins, when we spied Rodney backing out of the door that was still wearing the DO NOT DISTURB sign. He turned to look down the corridor, spotted us, and rushed up to Mr. Benchley's side.

"The gentleman is still sleeping, sir."

"My goodness," replied Mr. Benchley, "I suppose he needs the rest, after last night." He took the briefcase from Rodney and we continued on toward our rooms. "I'll be over for that drink, soon as I've changed," he said.

Before I turned to continue toward my room, I saw the now-familiar face of the little redheaded man, Claude Dubois, as he entered his cabin.

I had not yet unlocked my door when my friend beckoned me. As I approached I saw his distress, and when he let me pass into the room, there was Saul, still asleep under the bedcovers.

"So," I said, "let him sleep. He'll need the rest if he insists on chasing after Lady Daffy tonight."

"He's not going to be chasing anyone."

"Good. She's no good for him. He's seen the light."

"Yeah, right before St. Peter let him through the pearly gates."

"What! Are you trying to tell me—"

"Dead."

"Are you sure?" I said, rushing over to the bed and throwing off the covers.

"Quite."

Ronnie

A younger Duchess Sofia Louise

Chapter Six

"I got him into the bed at about two o'clock in the morning. He was so miserable, you see, and I hadn't the heart to send him off to his room. Frankly, I worried he might try to take his own life," said Mr. Benchley to me before the ship's physician and Captain Fried arrived at his cabin. Richard Hartley and Soledad, the last people to see Saul alive, other than ourselves, were called in to relate the events of the previous night.

"Drinks here after a late dinner—"

"We listened to the music piped in—"

"My steward, Rodney, brought in a tray of éclairs—we hadn't eaten much at dinner—and a pot of coffee. Saul didn't want to eat, and had had no proper dinner. He drank three or four scotches."

"We played a game of charades, but Saul wasn't concentrating—"

"He juggled oranges from the fruit basket, and tried to teach Soledad—"

"And we gossiped—you know—about celebrities and this and that and the other—"

None of us made reference to Saul's state of mind, and we weren't asked. From what the doctor could see, Saul Gold had succumbed to a heart attack.

His body was removed and Mr. Benchley assured that the room would be put in order. Evidence of Saul's last evening was strewn about the room: empty club soda bottles, a water-filled ice bucket, scum-ringed coffee cups, and chocolate-smeared flatware on doily-covered dessert plates. For want of something to do, Mr. Benchley picked up off the floor a rotting pear that had been bitten into and discarded, and the three oranges from last night's juggling entertainment. He tossed the pear into the wastebasket and the oranges into the fruit basket.

"Unless you wish other accommodations?" asked the purser, seeing my friend's dark mood and sympathizing.

"Are there any other rooms?"

"No. Not until we come into Ireland, where several passengers will disembark."

"Mr. Gold's room?"

"We can arrange that."

"No, never mind. I'll stay in here."

I fetched Woodrow for a walk, and Mr. Benchley followed me out on the deck, which was wet from the afternoon's storm. Now, after the fury had passed, there was a gentle, balmy wind enveloping the ship and the ocean lost its foreboding cast. At any moment things could change, I realized, sadly.

Alive one moment; dead the next.

We were both so stunned by Saul's death that we didn't speak as we strolled around the ship. The westering sun threw long shadows of the ship's funnel across the bow. The beauty surrounding us, the loneliness of the great expanse, suddenly made me feel small and frightfully vulnerable to its ineffable power. I wasn't so much in awe as I felt in jeopardy.

"There, there, my dear Dottie," said Mr. Benchley, putting an arm around me. He let me bawl against his shoulder, and the hand stroking my hair was meant to comfort, but only served to unloose whatever restraints remained on my emotions. Woodrow's whining distress pulled me out of my hole of despair, and Mr. Benchley's appeal brought me home: "My dear, we've survived storms, skirted icebergs; if you keep this up you'll flood the ship, and then where will we be?"

His handkerchief was again deployed to wipe my face and blow my nose. The honk made us both laugh and Woodrow leap up and down as if on a springboard.

The Major was standing near the rail, looking out to sea and smoking his pipe. I suppose he saw us pass by, so he walked over to us with his teetering gate. The contrast between his infirmity and his aristocratic good looks was striking.

"I'm terribly sorry to have caused such a ruckus, Mr. Benchley," he began. "I see you've been hurt, sir. Oh, dear, I didn't want that—Mrs. Parker, I hope you suffered no injury? Oh, dear, oh dear . . . ."

"Does it happen often?" asked Mr. Benchley.

The Major looked at him for a long moment before saying, "Pardon me?"

"You managed to escape unscathed this time, but I'll bet that sometimes you don't."

Another pause while he scrutinized Mr. Benchley, who kept a pleasant, if all-knowing smile on his face. He appeared to be weighing some risk.

"On occasion I have suffered the black eye or bruised rib," he said with a wry smile. "But I've learned to gamble at the more posh establishments, where any dispute is considered an embarrassment to the accuser."

He chuckled, and then, "I must be losing my touch, you know, for you to suspect anything from across the room."

Mr. Benchley, in the spirit of good-fellowship, said, "For years I've played cards with Alexander Woollcott and other members of the Thanatopsis Literary and Inside Straight Club. All I can say is, never play pinochle with Chico Marx."

"You won't—"

"Certainly not!" said Mr. Benchley, deducing what the Major was asking him *not* to do. "The boys had a grand time, and I was losing badly, so the interruption was well received!"

"Mrs. Parker is upset, though."

"Major," I said, "Mr. Saul Gold has died."

"Was he—?"

"Oh, no! He did not take part in the brawl. No; he was the gentleman who came to our dinner table last evening.

"Not the nasty—sorry—the man escorting that pretty Lady Twinton, I forget his name."

"No, but the fellow who asked her to dance."

"Oh, yes! Oh, my, oh, my!" he replied. "Scar across his head? Yes, yes! The man you were so kind to. We talked with you about him this morning! Oh, no . . . they were not nice to him; not at all nice to him. Of course, he was the Jew . . . . Such a row. Dead, you say? I'm so sorry. He was a friend of yours?"

"We just met him, here on the ship," said Mr. Benchley.

"One makes fast friends on crossings . . . . He seemed a decent sort."

"Yes," I said. "He was a writer of some note."

"How did he—"

"Heart attack," said Mr. Benchley.

Major Arbuthnot let out a sigh. "I see. Natural causes, then . . . . I suppose that is best," he said, leaning down as best he could to pet Woodrow. "I mean that it wasn't from any violence."

"No," I said

"Sad, still."

"Yes," said Mr. Benchley. "Very sad."

"Makes you think how one never really knows when, as you Americans say, one's number is up."

We returned indoors, Mr. Benchley accompanying me to my cabin, where he would have a drink and wait for Rodney to come and tell him when he might return to his room. We were passing by Lady Twinton's room when we could not help overhearing her voice, shrill and strained.

"And why shouldn't it mean something to me, why shouldn't it?"

"Why should it matter? I don't see why—" responded a male voice—no doubt Ronnie's for the lazy drawl.

"Everything's gone to hell!"

"Why do you persist?"

"I'll tell you why—"

"Pray, do, you rotten hussy!"

"What's the use! You haven't a soul! No soul! Not you! You're just a shell of a man—"

"But you like that in a chap, don't tell me you don't! It makes it easy for you if the chap has no soul to corrupt!"

And then his voice dropped an octave, and he hissed: "You like it when you can call the shots and poke your nasty fingers in a man's head and twist and mangle his brains; don't tell me you don't."

"Shut up! It's not like that!"

"Oh, I think it *is* like that!"

"Shut up! You disgust me! I hate the sight of you!"

"You hate the sight of me?"

"You drunken—"

"Look at yourself!"

"Let go of me!"

"Look at your face there!"

"I hate you, you cripple!"

There was a long silence, and Mr. Benchley and I looked at each other. It was so quiet that what was happening behind the door was either (a) they were so aroused by their fight that they were locked in a passionate embrace, or (b) one had stabbed the other with a paring knife. Then, again, maybe they were just refilling their drinks. Then:

"Don't touch me!" said Ronnie, his voice low and ominous.

"Ronnie—"

"Get yourself elsewhere, then, and see how it is!"

"Perhaps I will—"

"You'll not be away for long before you show your face—"

"Not this time."

"Until now, I've let you go off with this bloke or that bloody—"

"Well, why the hell not?" Daphne yelled with guttural wrath.

"You always slither back—"

An object crashed against the door, causing us to jump back and Woodrow to let out a yelp. We hurried on down the hall as another crash sounded.

"If they carry on like that now, what'll it be like after the wedding?" I asked.

"I don't really want to sit down to dine with them tonight, my dear. One could get impaled by flying steak knives. That's not good for one's digestion, you know. Dinner brought in would be a good idea."

"Ah! But the excitement of it all! What melodrama! Wouldn't miss it for the world!" I replied, as Mr. Benchley unlocked the door of my room.

I was being facetious, of course, but not entirely. I wanted distraction. I realized how hard I sounded, but I was angry and I couldn't pin the anger on anyone. Saul Gold was dead, and I felt like his death might have been prevented. I reasoned that that was crazy; he had died of a heart attack. But I wondered if it was not brought on by too much booze and a broken heart.

"Don't get me wrong, Fred: I'm devastated about poor Saul."

"I know you are."

"I just want to kick somebody, you know?"

"S'long as it's not me—or Woodrow."

Woodrow leaped onto the bed, yawned, circled three times, and settled in for a nap.

"Put down that briefcase, would you? You've been carrying that thing around for an hour. You might have left it in your room. You look like an accountant going off to the counting house or something. Pour me a tall one, would'ya? And forget the soda," I said, kicking off my shoes and throwing myself down on the bed next to Woodrow. "I need to dance a little, get smashed—or I think I shall die after all this!"

Woodrow, sensing my distress, tried his best to calm me with sloppy, wet kisses. Not as good as a cold compress, but I appreciated his efforts, nonetheless.

I sat up to take my drink, and said, "Am I horrible? Am I hateful?"

There was a knock at the door, and when Mr. Benchley opened it, in walked Hemingway and Mathew.

"What's going on in your room, Bob?" asked Hem. "They were carrying out your mattress."

The frown on Mr. Benchley's face, and the delay of the expected retort, prompted Hem to ask, "You wet the bed or something?"

"Not since Calvin Coolidge made a decision."

"What's going on? Why the long faces?"

"Saul's dead."

"Gold?" His hands leaped into his jacket pockets, and he just stood there, waiting for more, and when there wasn't any more, he said: "What about that drink you owe me, Dorothy?"

Mr. Benchley poured a couple of scotches and handed them to Hemingway and Mathew. His hand shook.

Mathew asked, "You mean he was killed in your cabin? Oh, Christ!"

"Have they arrested anybody?" asked Hem.

"Why do you think that—that somebody killed Saul?"

"Yes, Mathew. How'd you know that?"

"Well, why else would they be—"

"Yes, right, taking out the bedding . . . ."

"Well, let's face it: He wasn't much liked," said Hem.

"I liked him," I said, dangling my feet off the side of the bed.

"No one killed him," said Mr. Benchley, before I could tear out Hem's throat. "He just died. A heart attack."

Hem just stood there, a little dumbfounded, a great big buck, hands in coat pockets, looking like an adolescent. Somebody, one of my friends, had once asked me how old he was. I didn't know, "but then again, all writers are twenty-nine or Thomas Hardy," I said.

Mathew remained close to the door and dwarfed by his newfound hero. "Why don't you sit down?" I finally said.

My mood shifted. For some reason Hemingway's assumption that Saul had been murdered really irritated me and set me on the defensive. Whether it was because of the "Jewish" thing that had, in an unguarded moment, revealed his unsympathetic view of Jews, or the condescending comments made about

Saul's work and his obsession with Lady Twinton, I couldn't quite say. But, I just cringed when he said:

"I'm not surprised, really."

"Why is that?" asked Mr. Benchley. "Did you know he had heart trouble?"

"Well, he was gassed during the war, you know . . . . Hell, he was behaving like a sick calf over that woman."

Ernest Hemingway is a young writer who struggles with the construction of every sentence he writes. Now I wondered why he didn't choose the words he spoke with equal care. Because with every remark he made, whether intentionally patronizing or not (I could not be certain), I was growing more determined not to allow Saul Gold's legacy to be that of the man who died of a broken heart because of the rebuff of a posh floozy. Even if what Hem said about Saul held a fundamental truth—that he was morbidly obsessed with Daphne—the word *behaving* was belittling. There was censure in the sentiment. And referring to Daphne as *that woman* was an obvious pretense: I refrained from pointing out that Hemingway himself had been falling over his own feet chasing *that woman*. If he weren't careful, he'd be the next sick calf to succumb. But instead I said nothing.

Mathew was savvy enough to see that Hem had struck a nerve with me, and, despite his rigidly polite demeanor, with Mr. Benchley as well. Mathew offered

Hemingway a cigarette, and lit them both up, providing a moment for Hem to redeem himself.

"That's a damn shame," said Hem, blowing out a cloud of smoke, "a damn shame." And then he said with a concerned frown, "His wife will be—"

"She left him soon after he returned home from the War," I said, repeating what Saul had told me the night before.

Only a few hours before he died.

I didn't want to share the confidences he'd shared with me. I wanted to protect them. All Hem and Mathew needed to know was that he no longer had a wife.

It was obvious that my "cocktail party" was not going to be the gin-swilling laugh-fest the young men were hoping for. So when Rodney knocked at my door a few minutes later to tell Mr. Benchley that his room was ready, and he followed the steward out to go change into his dinner suit, the boys naturally made their exit, too.

———◆———

"It was during my time on the *S.S. Grant*, just after the Spanish War . . . ." Captain Fried was holding forth.

It was to be another gather-'round-the-campfire dinner, with roast beef and gratin potatoes instead of franks and beans, I thought, proving Emerson right, that all heroes become bores. But the captain's narrative was a distraction from the events of the day, so I didn't mind listening to his 1906 adventure, or the account of the rescue of 1911.

People glancing over at our table could see what appeared to be the members of a boxing club: Mathew, Hemingway, and Richard all bore testimony to their afternoon brawl in the card room. Their facial bruises had risen with red and purple distinction; the left side of Hemingway's upper lip bulged out as if he'd been stung by a bee. There was a bruise on his cheekbone. He wore his battle scars proudly and had enhanced the effect by slapping on a large plaster over his eyebrow since he'd been for a drink in my room. Mr. Benchley had acquired a lump on his crown, which appeared as a vicious blue carbuncle at his hairline. Occasionally, he would wince and groan at the slightest twist of his torso; Mathew favored his shoulder, Richard his bruised fist. Our Captain Fried must have thought their conditions punishment enough not to cluck or shake his head or in any way acknowledge the afternoon's melee. And I liked him for that.

The Duchess and the Major were having dinner in their staterooms, I was told. Thankfully, Lady Twinton and Marquis Ronald had not appeared at the dinner table by the time the soup was served. Even I had had enough of their kind of excitement for one day.

Hemingway, who was ordinarily enraptured with the captain's tales of sea rescue, was glancing over at the dining room's entryway every minute or two. And when the Lady appeared during the fish course, the captain could have been talking about his treacherous rescue of the rocket-ship *Cosmos* stranded on Mars, for all Hem seemed to care.

The waiter pushed in her chair next to Hemingway's, and the captain droned on with his recollections.

But Captain Fried was not insensitive to the guests at his table, and when the meat course had been served, he brought out a book that was tucked in his coat and turned to Soledad Soleil.

"Miss Soleil, I have long admired your clever mysteries—"

"You are so kind."

"They have accompanied me on many a voyage—"

"I'm so pleased!"

"Your little shop-girl, Harriet Morgan, is delightful and has the heart of a warrior. And Jonas McGill, the Duke's valet, an otherwise stuffy sort, is happily untwisted by her antics. Won't you sign your latest novel for me, Miss Soleil?"

"Soledad, please. I'd be delighted, Captain."

"George."

"Yes," she replied, her voice husky and full of promise. "Yes, George." Her smile dazzled.

She opened the front cover and turned to the flyleaf while the captain pulled out a pen from his coat and uncapped the nib. As Soledad inscribed the book, he took the opportunity of watching with evident admiration. She ended with a sweeping flourish, capped the pen, and handed it back to him. I could swear sparks flew when their hands met for an instant.

"Tell me, what is your next book, Miss— Soledad?"

"Oh!" she said, excitement trilling her voice, "It's about a murder aboard a steamship, entitled, *Death Sails the High Seas.*"

As soon as she spoke the title her smile dropped, as did the pitch of her voice. "Oh, dear. Oh, my . . . ."

To dispel his obvious attraction and, more immediately, Soledad's discomfort at having hit a nerve, Captain Fried turned to Hemingway and asked if he had read Soledad's mystery stories.

"*Uhhhh*," said Hemingway, taken by surprise, before recovering and flashing his brilliant smile. "I've not had the pleasure."

"You'll find them very amusing—very amusing, indeed," said Captain Fried.

"I've read Miss Soleil's books," said Mathew. "I like them. They reflect our society at the moment."

"Oh, yes, very," I said, looking over at Hem. "Soledad's Harriet is the new flapper type, and her valet partner is so ingrained with Victorian stuffiness that it makes for lots of fun to watch her un-stuff him. Once you've read one, you'll be hooked."

"They are really wonderful, Hem," said Mr. Benchley.

"Well," said Hem, "I like good books. I haven't read many mysteries . . . Dostoevsky's *Crime and Punishment* . . . and, oh, yes, I read *The Lodger*—"

"Yes, of course," said Soledad. "Marie Belloc Lowndes. She is a fine writer."

"Miss Stein let me borrow it," said Hemingway. "It was a good book—real horror, true and good. And the Simenon stories—"

"He's a crime reporter," said Mathew.

"That young man is a marvel," replied Soledad. "Why, he can put out forty, fifty, sixty pages a day. When I met Georges at the Café de Flores, not so long ago, he told me about a book he was commissioned to write. His character was to be a detective, and he was trying to decide what name to give him. I suggested *Maigret—Commissionaire Maigret*. I thought it humorous that such a prolific writer would struggle for so long over a character's name."

When the last drops of coffee were drained from Soledad's cup, Captain Fried asked if he could have the pleasure of a dance. That cued Richard Hartley to ask me for a twirl around the dance floor. Hemingway wasted no time in asking Daphne, who had not been participating during the dinner conversation, before Mathew or Mr. Benchley could beat him to it. But he needn't have worried. Neither competitor would be doing more than a two-step tonight.

"Are you all right, Dorothy?" asked Richard as the orchestra shifted from "The Sheik of Araby" to a perky rendition of the new Rogers and Hart song, "Mountain Greenery."

"Oh, yes," I replied, a little too listlessly. Richard met my gaze, and I realized he wasn't talking about how tired I was. "Oh, you mean about what's happened."

"Well, it is disconcerting, certainly." He smiled sympathetically. "I know you liked Saul. I did, too. He seemed to carry the world on his shoulders. A big weight on frail shoulders, if you know what I mean?"

"Yes. Exactly," I said, "and he bore that weight alone. You always bear the weight of life alone when you are not loved."

I regretted it the moment I had said it. *When you are not loved.* It sounded so *corny*, so *pathetic*, so Louisa May Alcott. The truth is that this insight was a little too personal for comfort because it was pretty much the condition of Dorothy Parker.

I decided to deflect Richard's response with: "Tell me about the paper you will deliver."

"It's a report of my findings on the treatment of infantile paralysis."

"How exciting. No, I really mean it! How wonderful to do work that can change the lives of so many people."

"It is rewarding when one finds a cure, certainly. Often one only stumbles upon one through a series of missteps. And it is frustrating, too, when all you can offer is treatment—a way for patients to cope with their misery."

Richard had been married once, before the War, but the marriage was quickly annulled. He didn't tell me why it ended when he'd mentioned it last night while we were laughing and playing and drinking in Mr. Benchley's cabin during the last hours of Saul Gold's life. I liked Richard. I liked his soft, cognac-colored eyes that looked upon the world and its many creatures with gentle compassion. He was quick to see the paradoxes around him, and where the absurdity and futility of life could make me suicidal it would merely make him smile.

Yes, I liked Richard Hartley. A *doctor*. My long-dead mother would approve.

Before I could consider the idea forming in my head, I saw Ronnie making his way through the tight hive of dancers. Hemingway and Daphne were only a few feet away from us. When he got to the couple, he cut in, in the rather rude fashion of a stumbling drunk. From the unguarded flash of disgust on Hem's face, I thought he was going to deck Ronnie, but a touch of Daphne's hand on his fighting arm brought him back from the edge. He nodded to his partner and, with jaw set, walked off the dance floor.

"I feel a rising tension," I said to Richard, watching Hem disappear into the crowd.

"Me, too," he replied. "But not how you think."

"My girdle must be too tight."

"No," said Mr. Benchley, like a phantom in my ear. "He's holding you too tight."

I turned to look at my friend, who was ridiculously keeping in step behind me. He pulled me around to face him. "I am cutting in, Hartley; go find some other darling girl to charm."

"Shall I knock him down?" joked Richard.

"Better not; he's got a glass skull."

"Phrenologically speaking, he's got the head of a criminal."

There was a commotion rippling along the dance floor, and couples were bumping into each other. "The many *ahh*s and *ouff*s and *I-beg-your-pardon*s and *watch-where-you're-stepping*s increased in volume, and then above the voices I heard Daphne let out a little yell and Ronnie's upper-crust voice ringing out with some slurred English, before Daphne cut through the crush and out past where we stood on the outer edge of the dance circle. She made for the doors with Ronnie in slogging pursuit. Richard, who was still on the dance floor, intercepted him and received a glancing blow to his face before Ronnie continued on his way.

"One fistfight a day is enough for me," said Richard with a hand to his forehead. "Let's get some fresh air," I said.

"Yes, I could use a cigar right now," said Mr. Benchley.

I gave him a knowing look.

"All right, then; I'll see you two kids later."

Richard fetched my wrap and we walked out onto the deck. A short distance away we saw Daphne, with Ronnie's arm around her shoulders. They were cheek to cheek and staring out over the silver streak of moonlight cutting through the dark expanse. We turned to walk in the opposite direction. It was cold, but the air was exhilarating, and in blue velvet and silver fox, with my hand in Richard's, I was cozy. Other passengers had the same idea, and we strolled along in silence; the swoosh of the ship slicing through the great black ocean and the steady hum of the engines were soothing. The great funnels sent out puffy white clouds that rolled away like forgotten memories dispersed among a vast universe of stars.

For the sky was emblazoned with them. I'm a city girl, and of course the best places in Manhattan to see stars are in Central Park, or down at the Battery, facing south into the bay. But, on this first clear night at sea, I was enraptured by the astronomical wonders to behold! The moon was full, and it was gently shedding its beneficent blessing upon us. I now understood the power of its brilliance—how, under its soft light, a dullard could turn into a poet or a sane man into a mad one, and, just for its own amusement, it could lift and lower the great oceans of the Earth.

"Look at all those stars!" I said, sounding like a schoolgirl. I thought "wonder" had long ago left my heart and been replaced with wary cynicism. "Look at those two, just below the moon! They are so bright!"

"Venus and Jupiter. The brighter one is Venus. And there is Orion, see? Over there, those three stars all in a row," Richard said, his arm around me, pointing up in the direction in front of my face for my eyes to follow. "See those? That's Orion's Belt."

"Oh, I know! That's from where the great Egyptian God, Osiris, watches over his earthly kingdom! And his wife, Isis—"

I didn't get to finish the sentence, which was fine with me, for I had no more knowledge of the Pharaohs to continue on anyway, when Richard moved me into a shelter from the wind and pulled me into a full embrace. His mouth was soft, and as he pressed against me he warmed the cold fox fur between us.

He smiled, and his eyes, dark with shadow, caught a moonbeam. And then, seeing it was all right, he pulled me closer and kissed me again.

I'd hit the jackpot! Smart, funny, classy, a doctor, and one hell of kisser! What did I do right?

"Are you wooing me?"

"You're wowing me," he said, before moving in for another kiss.

I was a little breathless. All right, I couldn't breathe. When he released me, his eyes searched my face, a finger lifting my chin toward the moonlight to better read my thoughts. His smile of amusement, of shy inquiry, remained. I just had to turn away. I was juggling conflicting emotions in my heart. I wanted nothing more than for him to make love to me, right there, right now, on the cold, shellacked wood of the deck—although a soft mattress would've been better— but as much as I wanted, *yes! so much wanted* to fall into his arms, onto the deck, onto a bed, and into love, I just *knew* that such an affair would be fleeting, and in the end . . . .

"Let's have a cigarette, shall we?"

"Yes, let's," I said, pulling the fox cape tighter around me, as if it could shield my thoughts and muffle the sound of my beating heart.

He pulled out his gold cigarette case from the inside pocket of his evening suit. I was about to say, "But we're supposed to wait until *after* the sex," but the words would have sounded fresh and common, like all the snappy retorts tossed about by my generation for the purpose of appearing modern and outrageous and, therefore, interesting. Not that; not now.

Instead of offering me a cigarette, he placed two of them between his lips.

We had the stars . . . . We had the moon . . . . We had . . . Mr. Benchley?

A disembodied voice sounded at my ear. "I'll have one, if you don't mind."

Damn! It *was* Mr. Benchley!

"Light it for me, would you, Rich? War's over; three on a match won't get us shot."

Richard looked at my friend like he'd encountered a lunatic, then chuckled and popped a third cigarette between his lips, lit them all afire, and handed ours over.

Very romantic.

"Thanks."

"*Yeah*, thanks," I said, while giving Mr. Benchley the Evil Eye.

"I knew I'd find you out here."

"Did you have to?" I said, and then, resigned, "What's up, Joe?"

Instead of answering, he lifted his head toward the sky and exhaled a stream of smoke. "My God! What a sky! Look at that moon!"

We'd been trying to! I wanted to say.

"Yeah, yeah, the moon," I said. "It's full."

"Well, ninety-two percent full," he corrected. "Won't be full until Saturday night, and then the tides will rise and the Dow will tumble."

"Thank you, Farmer Gray. Whaddayawant?"

"Oh, yes, well, I was about to tell you: There's something funny going on."

"You think so, do you?"

"It's my fruit."

"I don't follow," said Richard.

"My banana. At first I thought it was just *my* banana, you see—"

"Perhaps I should let you consult the doctor confidentially—"

"It's droopy and a strange, orange color—and my apples—they look like little coconuts without hair, they've shriveled so small and brown. As for the—"

"What? Are you nine? This doctor is not on call."

"In my cabin, you see, the fruit basket—"

"Oh, goody, more little Benchleys."

"It has this smell, not like your ordinary rotting fruit, but it somehow reminds me of Antonio."

"Who?" I asked a little too shrilly. "Oh, the rat."

"Yes. The fruit basket smells like Antonio. You need to see."

I caught Richard's eye before he could ask who Antonio was and why he smelled. "Don't!" I said, and with a frown he remained mute.

As the romantic mood had been broken, I acquiesced, and we followed Mr. Benchley to his stateroom.

As we entered there was a pervasive odor that I couldn't quite identify.

"Burnt almonds?" asked Richard.

"Yes, that's it," Mr. Benchley and I replied in unison, as Richard walked over to the desk atop which sat a sad-looking basket of fruit.

The banana was in a sorry state of decay, as was all the remaining fruit in the basket. Even the oranges Saul had used to juggle for our entertainment last night—although their skins were intact, the pulp within appeared to have collapsed, imploded, making them look like deflated basketballs.

"Cyanide," said Soledad, appearing at the open door and wriggling her nose.

"Yes," agreed Richard.

We examined the fruit basket with incredulity.

"They're full of cyanide," Soledad concluded with a nod.

"How can that be?" asked Mr. Benchley. "I'd never guess that cyanide could be a by-product of rotting fruit."

"It isn't," said Richard.

"But—how?—why?—I don't understand."

"Do you see that peculiar discoloration on the flesh of this pear, Bob?" said Richard. "That's because there was a hole there. Injection point. The same can be seen on the banana you were talking about. See the hole at the center of that black circle? They've all been injected with cyanide. It's degraded now, but the distinctive smell of the poison has leached through the skins of the fruit."

"A convenient way to kill someone," said Soledad. "I've used it time and again."

"*What*? Oh, in your mysteries, yes, of course," said Mr. Benchley. "I wouldn't think you'd be plotting against me. But, why would someone want to kill me?"

Had the matter been less serious I would have said something smart, but aside from ruining a romantic interlude, his life meant more to me than anyone's. I remained mute on that point, and then it dawned on all of us at once: Saul Gold had not died of a heart attack.

"It's all my fault," said Mr. Benchley. "I encouraged him to have something to eat because he hadn't had any dinner or the desserts brought to the room, so maybe after I fell asleep on the sofa he grabbed a pear. I picked up what was left of one from off the carpet when we found him. It never occurred to me . . . ."

He collapsed into a chair and covered his face with his hands at the horror of Saul's death.

"I feel so responsible for that poor fellow's death," said Mr. Benchley, staring out in space.

Saul died. How it came to be was unintentional. Right now all I cared about was my friend's peace of mind.

"You're not responsible," I said firmly, hugging him to me.

"That's right, Bob," said Soledad. "How could you know? The question is who sent the fruit basket?"

"I don't know. There wasn't any note."

"Anybody threaten you? Anyone want you dead?"

He thought for a moment, rifling through an inventory in his head.

"There was this bootlegger, a shady character. I insulted him."

I interrupted: "All you said was that he cuts his booze with water, and that he'll make a fortune when he learns how to cut the water. Hardly a reason to kill you."

"You don't know the bum. When he threatened to sue for slander, I reminded him the Volstead Act was in effect, so he promised to make me pay another way. Anyway, he didn't send the basket."

"How do you know?"

"When I was given the cabin, I was told that it was because another passenger had missed the boat, so they gave me his room. The fruit basket wasn't sent to me, but to him, I presumed. But as it was in the room, I was told to enjoy it. You know I killed Antonio and Francesca. I gave them the apple that I had popped into my coat pocket when I went down to cargo to find my alarm clock."

"Good thing, too," I scolded. "A good trade!"

"Thank you. I'm glad I didn't bite into it, but all the same, you are a heartless creature."

"Well, I'd rather have a rat like you for my best friend than—wait! The orange juice at breakfast!"

"What's this?" asked Soledad.

"At breakfast this morning. Mr. Benchley's orange juice. It was laced with a big heaping portion of drain cleaner, and the Duchess Sofia thought it had been meant to knock her off. Apparently, there had been past attempts on her life by the Soviet regime. Why they'd bother trying to kill an old lady, I have no idea. The juice was placed before Mr. Benchley, and you, Richard, know the rest of the story."

"The hole it burned in the tablecloth . . ." Richard explained to Soledad.

"All right, Fred, dear. You still have seven more lives."

"You fail to include our past confrontations with gun-toting floozies, knife-wielding assassins, and, of course, there're the four Marx Brothers. I'm running out of lives!"

Mr. Benchley, the voice of reason in my life, if not his own, was coming unhinged, sounding very much like a character from his own brand of humor writing, which had made him a very famous man.

Captain Fried and his chief officer arrived at the room and Richard told him of our discovery. I wasted no time confronting him: "Captain, what was the result of your investigation into the tainted orange juice?"

"Mrs. Parker, I assure you, I looked into the matter personally, and I have to say that it was sheer accident. A sink drain was clogged. A cook measured out the appropriate amount of drain cleaner into one of a dozen newly washed and ready juice glasses, one of which he had taken from a tray for the morning's service. He was quite contrite when he told me he had begun pouring the cleaner into the sink when the oatmeal he'd been preparing on a stove overflowed its pot and he put the glass back down onto the tray to attend to it. When he returned, the drain had been unclogged, and a helper had taken away the tray with the glass, which he then filled with orange juice for the waiters to serve at table. The helper never saw the drain cleaner in the glass when he filled the dozen or so of them with juice. The cook never had another thought about it until I came to investigate and he retraced his steps. He will be let go upon our return to New York."

"Please don't fire him. It was an honest mistake," said Mr. Benchley.

"I will consider your kindness, Mr. Benchley, but we do have standards."

"Captain, who was the passenger originally booked in this stateroom?" I asked.

"Yes, well, that is a question," said the captain with a frown. "The room was reserved for a Mr. Charles Latham; his luggage had been checked and brought aboard, but Mr. Latham had not himself boarded when we sailed. A wireless was sent asking what he wished us to do with his luggage, but the address we had been given for him in the United States did not exist, nor the telephone number."

"But, George," said Soledad, "the fruit basket."

"Yes, well, as you can see, there is only the stateroom number on the card, no name from whom it was sent."

"Then it is possible that someone on board right now could have poisoned the fruit, if it hadn't arrived already tainted," I said.

"But, why?" asked Mr. Benchley.

"Let's think this out," I said. The room contains all of the mysterious Mr. Latham's luggage, plus a bon-voyage fruit basket. He misses the boat, and the room is locked, is it not? Yes, and then the following evening Mr. Benchley is given the room. I presume only his steward entered here before Mr. Benchley occupied it?"

"Several stewards removed Mr. Latham's luggage, of course, and brought in Mr. Benchley's."

"Look," said Mr. Benchley, "I was in here with my steward when the men arrived with my trunk and bags and removed Latham's things. I would have seen it if anybody had injected my fruit. I took an apple from the basket, which turned out to be lethal to a couple of rodents, but I never bit into it. So I say the poison was in the fruit before delivery."

"Then," said Soledad, "*you* were never the intended victim. Mr. Latham was. And we now know the orange juice incident was nothing more than an accident."

"How do you explain my being trussed, dragged, and dunked? An accident too?"

"That," said Captain Fried, "I cannot explain. My crew assured me that on the final check before our departure, the winch had been secured. It may ring hollow, but all I can offer you are my profound apologies for all you have been through. Rest assured I will do everything in my power to make the rest of your voyage as pleasant as possible. Please don't hesitate to call upon me at any time, should you have any concerns. I will wire the proper authorities in France to investigate Mr. Gold's death. We will be arriving at Cobh the day after tomorrow, before pressing on to Cherbourg."

Richard asked if both he and the ship's physician could reexamine Saul Gold's body for the telltale signs of cyanide poisoning.

Captain Fried shot a wistful look at Soledad before he and the chief officer, carrying out the offensive fruit basket, left the room.

Mr. Benchley may have been momentarily touched by guilt, but he had not forgotten his manners.

"Please," he said from the chair where he was still sitting, "Please, Richard, would you pour us all a drink?"

"Yes, Fred, we'll all have a drink with you, and then we have some work to do."

THE SKIPPER WHO DID

Capt. George Fried, of the *President Roose-velt*, who has made his name famous.

Captain George Fried

Chapter Seven

"Captain Fried has eyes for you," I said.

Soledad smiled the smile of vanity, which on her was merely one of confidence with the opposite sex and she wore it most attractively.

"I'd say he is a perfect choice for me."

"How's that?"

"He's married, good-looking, an international hero, runs a tight ship, and is out at sea for twelve months of the year."

"*Ahhh*," I replied, "I see your point."

"I wouldn't have to listen to whining, jealous rampages or the demand, *Where were you all night?* The perfect man."

"But, Soledad, you are a genius! I should get me one like him."

"But, Dorothy, you have Woodrow, of course."

"So I do! And he does so like to cuddle."

"Richard has eyes for you, my dear. Oh, don't tell me you haven't noticed."

Daphne appeared, walking into the lounge. She spotted us and took a chair, falling into it as if exhausted. She didn't look at us or speak; it was as if we weren't even there. Her eyes were red, her mascara smudged, and she appeared to be quite drunk. Her usually sleek short hair was tussled and she looked young and vulnerable and miserable.

"Daphne?" I said, leaning in toward her. There was a dark stain running in a stripe down the front of her silk evening dress.

Looking up at me and then at Soledad and then toward the door from where she had entered a moment before, with a little frown as if trying to remember why she had come, she blurted out: "I liked him, you know? Gold. I liked him."

The feelings I had been harboring, the desire to scold her for her rude treatment of Saul during the days before his death, seemed to dissolve into pity with the power of her trembling voice. "We liked him, too," I said.

"He was a nice man. Treated me kindly," she said, nodding. "But he knew, he knew from the start what we were doing and that I was going to marry Ronnie."

I threw a glance at Soledad, who sat there watching Daphne with the faintest trace of a smile on her face. Like a python poised to strike.

I said, "Well, I don't know what to say about the whole affair. And I don't know if it's any of my business—"

"Ronnie, you see . . . well, he can't, you know."

I wasn't sure what she was talking about; about what Ronnie could or couldn't do. And then I figured it out. She must have seen it dawn in my face, and spurred on, she continued: "The War, you see; he was hurt in the war. At first they said he could never even walk again, and then when he did walk there was the hope that someday—well, he just *can't* is all."

"So you . . . ?"

"Yes—wherever I can find it, and . . . and Gold said he understood, but he didn't really, or he just didn't want to, I don't know."

"And he followed you on the ship."

"Yes, and I didn't know—Ronnie didn't know—that he was on the crossing. Ronnie doesn't mind, you see; he said he doesn't mind that I—because he can't, you understand, so it's all right for me to—but he doesn't like to have it thrown in his face," she rattled on now with an urgency that was more a plea for understanding than an excuse for her behavior. But it wasn't until she took a breath and spoke again that I truly understood her motive for approaching us.

"He didn't kill Gold. I can tell you that. He didn't kill Saul Gold."

"No one said he did."

"No, but he thinks you all think he did. And I think you think so, too."

Soledad broke her silence. "Until now, everybody's thought that Saul Gold died of a heart attack, you know that. But, you don't think so, do you? You think that Ronnie killed him, don't you? Don't deny your suspicions, Daphne. All this talk has been to defend Ronnie because *you* believe he actually did kill Saul."

"No!"

"No, Daphne," said Soledad with an air of disgust, "rest assured, your precious Ronnie did not kill Saul Gold."

Soledad got up out of her chair, with a demand in her eyes that silently said it was time for Daphne to leave. Daphne got up and moved in toward her with a plea in her voice.

"Then it was a heart attack, for real?" The relief brought renewed color to her cheeks.

"Oh, no," said Soledad, "he was murdered all right."

"But, who . . . ? I said it wasn't Ronnie who did it, it wasn't!"

"No, Lady Twinton, it wasn't your precious Ronnie killed Saul, the rarest of God's creatures, a truly good man."

"Do you know who did it? I liked Gold, really I did."

"Yes, I know who killed him," said Soledad in a whisper. "I'm looking at her right now."

Daphne's expression, bright with redemption, instantly changed into one of hopelessness. She turned to me as if to beg my rebuttal of Soledad's condemnation, which was harsh. I could think of nothing kind to say, nor did I want to comfort her. She may not have poisoned the pear Saul ate, but she had poisoned the man's spirit. And when I caught sight of Hemingway entering the lounge, and saw the way he looked at her, so interested, so energized, so enraptured at the sight of her, I could no longer stand to watch their little flirtatious dance, so I followed Soledad out of the room.

"It's time," I said, looking at my Cartier watch, a gift from Seward Collins, whom I had been seeing before I left New York. He was going to come to Paris next month, but I was not so sure that I wanted him to. (That is another story for another time.) "Let's fetch Mr. Benchley."

Soledad and I returned to our rooms to change into more appropriate attire. After all, we could not do our snooping wearing high-heels and silk frocks and fur coats. And so, dressed in skirts and cardigans, we arrived at Mr. Benchley's door at around two o'clock in the morning.

Mr. Benchley and Richard Hartley met us, each carrying a flashlight.

"Follow me," Mr. Benchley ordered, and we did so, single file, along the corridor, down two staircases, through several steel doors, and then past a convoluted series of utility-like rooms, built of steel and filled with stores of food and equipment. Another staircase, and we entered the area that stored numerous steamer trunks and other passengers' belongings.

"Here they are," said Mr. Benchley after flipping on a light switch.

There were at least a hundred crates stacked atop one another with Irish and French destination labels, and at least two dozen steamer trunks and fifty smaller valises stacked in the room.

"So how the hell are we supposed to find the ones that were in your room?" I asked.

"Check the luggage tags for a match of Bob's room number," said Soledad.

"And since the luggage had been sent down here two days after we set sail, it makes sense that they're on the outside of the stack," said Mr. Benchley.

"I believe I have found them, Bob. Matches your room number," said Richard.

"And those, I think, are the valises," said Mr. Benchley.

"Let's take a look inside," said Richard, after he and Mr. Benchley had pulled the trunk out to examine.

"*Shit!* They're locked, damn it!" I said.

Mr. Benchley flashed a look of disapproval for my "language." "We'll get into it," he said, removing his trusty Swiss Army knife and pulling out its toothpick.

"Stand aside, everyone," I announced. "Watch a magician at work."

"You've seen this act before, Dorothy?" asked Richard.

"Oh, yes, on numerous occasions Mr. Benchley has gotten us into, and sometimes out of, sticky situations."

"Well, said Soledad, "There's a little larceny in everyone's heart."

"There!" said my friend, releasing the flap of the lock. And with a little assistance from Richard they parted the two sides of the steamer trunk.

"What fresh hell!" I hissed when I saw the contents of the trunk. Nothing but old rags cushioning several very large rocks. "What kind of shit is this?" I yelled.

"Manhattan *schist*, I believe," corrected Mr. Benchley. "Manhattan's full of it. Let's see if there are any samples of upstate garnet in the valises—far more valuable."

Within a minute he had sprung open the cases to reveal more of New York City's bedrock.

"It appears our truant passenger was taking a little bit of home with him to France."

"I don't think there's anything illegal about that," I replied. "Remember, Count Dracula carried the soil from his grave in Transylvania in a trunk when he fled the country."

"I've told you time and time again not to read those kinds of books," said my friend. "Or if you must, at least draw the shades."

"Well," said Soledad, "this is most peculiar."

"It's weird, is what it is," I said. "I thought I'd seen everything, but this displaces Eva Tanguay from the top of my list."

"Not only do we have a phantom traveler," continued Soledad, "but his luggage appears to be a decoy as well. Very interesting . . . ."

"Perhaps there never was a fellow by the name of Charles Latham," I said. "There's nothing in these pieces of luggage connected with anyone."

"But if he does exist, well, where is he?" said Soledad.

"I think you might ask: What's happened to him?" said Mr. Benchley.

"Oh, Bob," said Soledad. "There's another trunk here. Your room number. I thought you said there was just the one steamer trunk."

"Perhaps I was mistaken. No, it's not mine. I'm travelling light."

I suppressed a laugh. He was toting to Paris a steamer trunk, two valises, and more sporting equipment than seen at the Summer Olympic Games in 'twenty-four.

The men set about pulling the trunk out from its nest, and again the Swiss Army knife appeared to do the trick on the lock.

"More schist, I'll bet," I said as they lifted the lid.

"No," said Richard Hartley, quickly dropping the lid back down. But before he did so there escaped a most foul odor. "Mystery solved, I should say. We now know what happened to the mysterious Mr. Latham."

"Oh, look," said Mr. Benchley, pulling out a case wedged between two trunks. "At last—I've found my typewriter!"

Authoress Soledad Soleil

Dr. Richard Hartley

Chapter Eight

I woke up around noon the next day, my ship's bed rocking to violent waves. The storm abated in the late afternoon, and Woodrow got his walk around the deck while my hair curled from the damp. Mr. Benchley and I played cards after we had dinner in my room. We weren't in a very festive mood after the past two days of consecutive deaths. Richard had stopped in for a drink before we called it a night.

At dawn on the fifth day of our crossing, the *S.S. Roosevelt* sailed into Cork harbor and docked at Cobh, a picturesque little village once known as Queenstown.

So this is the land from which had arrived the huddled masses, the wretched refuse, the homeless, tempest-tossed multitudes that stormed my city, my country, back before the new century. From this teeming Irish shore sprang the likes of Mary and Siobhan and Bridie and Colleen, young Irish lasses that I used to joke about my parents tearing from off the ships as they docked, "still bleeding," to come to work as housemaids. I could sympathize with these girls. My German-Jewish father's parents washed up in New York harbor in much the same condition from Prussia, after a thwarted revolution in 1848, from "the land of mud and flame," as I always called it. And there was our Mary, Siobhan, Bridie, and Colleen represented in the statue at the end of the pier, of Annie Moore standing with her little brothers, the first people to pass through the Ellis Island Immigration Center in 1892. And sadly, Cobh was the last port-of-call before the *Titanic* sailed off on its tragic maiden voyage into the Atlantic. Many poor Irish emigrants, booked in steerage, died that night.

It was damp and cold when I went out on deck with Woodrow; today the heavy fog that swept across the seaside village made me want to stay aboard our ship, even though my fellow passengers, Mr. Benchley, Richard, and Soledad, suggested we venture ashore. As reluctant as I was—I would have preferred staying cozily in my room—their argument had a point: We could have a pint at the little pub just a few steps off the pier, and Woodrow could benefit from a romp around the green and a sniff of the strange new land and generally engage in a little canine activity. I donned my wool coat and stuck a cloche on my head before venturing ashore.

Cargo was being unloaded, along with passengers whose journey was at an end, this being their destination port. A contingency of local police boarded the ship, and I assumed their appearance had everything to do with our discovery of a decidedly dead gentleman in the cargo hold, as well as the death of Saul Gold.

The ship would sail again at dusk, so we had plenty of time to see the sights, have lunch, and enjoy the really wonderful beers and ales Ireland had to offer. Hemingway and Mathew met us on the way down the gangplank.

We lunched in the rustic pub, all dark wood and whitewashed, and drank our fill—at least I did. One can imbibe only so much beer, unless your name is Hemingway. Then we all had shots of real Irish whiskey, a smooth treat after the rotgut found in most New York speakeasies.

By mid-afternoon the fog had lifted, if not the winter dampness. The spire of the Neo-Gothic St. Colman's Cathedral that towered over the village was now clearly visible and grandly impressive on its rise of land. We walked around its gargoyle edifice and toured the arched interior. And later, a walk through Old Church Cemetery, where many of the dead lie buried since the *Lusitania* was sunk by a German U-boat in 'fifteen. More than a hundred souls who washed ashore after the tragedy are buried here: men, women, and so many children. Coffins were laid side by side and were buried with great ceremony. Later, others from the disaster were buried here in individual graves as they were found after the initial onrush. Hem wanted to come here; I did not. I'd had enough of death. But there was a sort of beauty in the place, in its starkness and unbroken silence. The wispy-gray-clouded sky provided a somber backdrop to the heavy, piled-up stonework at the gravesite, like a monochromatic study in charcoal. It was a fitting tribute to their memory.

Where would Saul Gold be laid to rest?

———◆———

At dusk we sailed on toward Cherbourg. I left Woodrow snoring in my room to join the others at dinner. Upon my arrival, I found that our captain was not present at table, which delayed the questions I intended to pose and the answers he might give to update us about what the police were doing about the murders. We all wanted to know the particulars: Were they able to identify with certainty the dead man in the trunk? Was he indeed Charles Latham? It seemed probable that the fruit basket was meant for the man we found in the trunk, if he *was* Latham, and if so, had he died of cyanide poisoning? Or had he not been the intended victim, but an innocent bystander?

Richard Hartley suspected some sort of violent trauma, as he had seen a good deal of blood on the corpse before closing the lid on it. We had summoned the captain once again, without remaining for any further examination after we told him we had found the corpse while searching for Mr. Benchley's typewriter among the luggage. Of course, we didn't think it necessary to tell him we had broken into the other luggage taken from the room where Mr. Benchley was residing only to discover a load of schist. No one bothered to ask how we got into the locked trunk to find the body in the first place, so we didn't offer any explanation about that, either. Captain Fried had assured us that we would not be questioned by the authorities in Ireland, although he could not promise as much upon our arrival in France.

So far, there was the incident of Mr. Benchley's high-flying act on the deck of the ship, resulting in a brisk dunk into the North Atlantic—an accident; the "spiked" orange juice that spilled and burned a pattern through table linen resembling the Soviet Union—an accident; the poisoning death of a gentle man—an accident; and the discovery of a body in a trunk—which was no accident. Upon a quick inspection of the corpse by the ship's physician, Captain Fried had told us that no one could say for sure who the man was because there was no identification on his body; even the labels had been cut from his suit. The trunks and valises were bare of any identifying items, although we knew the rock specimens had originated in Manhattan.

Somebody had covered his tracks pretty well, and I figured there had to have been more than just one "somebody involved" to have carried off this plan.

And with the discovery of the corpse, I had come to the conclusion that everything that had happened to Mr. Benchley was definitely *no accident.*

But it made no sense. Robert Benchley had no enemies. He was considered the sweetest man on Broadway, known as S.O.B. (Sweet Old Bob). Even as drama critic for *Life* magazine, he had never been banned by producers from reviewing their shows. (The Schubert Brothers had tried and failed on numerous occasions to block our friend, Alexander Woollcott, from entering their many theatres after he'd panned too many of their shows.) And no actor ever suffered from a Robert Benchley review the way they suffered from my stinging and often career-ending critiques. Even when he didn't like a play, he never decimated it, and when he loathed a show he used humor, and never skewered the actors (the way I sometimes do). This led me to believe it had to be a case of mistaken identity. Some misinformed individual thought that my friend was really Latham, who had booked passage in that stateroom, the intended victim of a planned assassination!

It appeared to me, as I rested on the bed in my cabin after our sightseeing day through the Irish port and before our last dinner aboard the *S.S. Roosevelt,* that in order for the deliberate attempts on his life to have occurred aboard ship, the murderer had to be sailing with us. I could think of no one we had as yet encountered who might be the culprit. I thought about the people we had encountered: Soledad Soleil, a famous mystery authoress preoccupied with finding new methods for murdering her characters, and Dr. Richard Hartley, physician and medical researcher. What did I really know about either of them, except what they themselves had told me? They claim to have been great friends from childhood. Perhaps they were in cahoots with each other. That idea seemed rather feeble. Unless, of course, the Soledad that I have come to know is not the real Soledad Soleil, but rather a criminal posing as the writer. And until we can wire the States from Cherbourg, I cannot confirm whether it has been the real Richard Hartley making love to me under the stars . . . .

Mathew Hettinger—we had only his word that he was the son of a wealthy Philadelphian, wounded at Fossalta di Piave and nursed back to health at the Ospedale Maggiore in Milan—same as Hemingway. What a convenient coincidence. Was he really a journalist, sent to Paris as a foreign correspondent for the *Detroit Register*? I made a mental note to send a wireless to confirm.

Then there was Ronnie, the British terror, formally known as the Marquis Ronald Everett Hampton-Crispin-Jones, also bearing the title of the Duke of whatever, on his French mother's side, God help us! He could barely keep on his feet for what he imbibes, let alone string up Mr. Benchley—unless the drunk act was just a show. And his cousin's wife, soon to be his blushing bride, the Lady Daphne Twinton? *There's a piece of work,* I thought. Man-eater. But I doubted her *modus operandi* included anything more lethal than teasing a man to death.

I eliminated our Captain Fried and his first mate from suspicion, of course, and Major Alfred Arbuthnot, albeit he is a cardsharp. With his leg brace an obvious physical restriction, he'd be an ineffectual assassin; the clicking would forewarn any intended victim he tried to sneak up on. Anyway, his primary interest appeared to be the welfare of his companion, the expatriated Russian Duchess, who suffered from a sort of shell-shocked paranoia with the strange belief that she might still be considered a threat to the Revolution and a target worth exterminating after all these years. She could barely conduct herself from her stateroom to the dining room, a good fifty-foot sprint, let alone stuff a man into a trunk.

Were there any other suspicious characters lurking around who appeared inconsequential? There was the redheaded man, Claude Dubois, in the cabin next to Mr. Benchley's. He peeked out from the door of his room on several occasions when I had gone to see my friend, with nary a smile, only a sort of wary inquisitiveness, and he was on deck when Mr. Benchley took his flying leap . . . *hmmm*, I'd have to think more about that.

I tried to picture Mr. Benchley's steward, Rodney. Was he the killer type?

Mr. Benchley appeared among the passengers coming into the dining room with Hem and Mathew at his side. They took seats around the captain's table, before we were joined by Soledad and Richard. Soon the Duchess appeared with the Major, the crowd parting to accommodate their peculiar stride. The men stood as she was seated. She looked at the faces around the table. I could almost hear what she was thinking, the poor thing, as she appraised our party: *Who here at this table might be trying to kill me?*

I looked around the dining room with a similar kind of scrutiny, at the many strangers now eating and drinking on this last leg of our journey. Who among them were conspirators, murderers? The newlyweds? The maiden aunt escorting her adolescent niece on the Grand Tour? The many businessmen anxious to cut that Big Deal with their foreign affiliates? Perhaps that older couple, celebrating their twenty-fifth wedding anniversary with a trip to the city where they had first met? The vulgar Jimmy Durante lookalike? The Frenchmen returning home from the States? The soon-to-be-young-expatriates searching for greater artistic and moral freedom in Europe? Some of them were *poseurs*, pretending to be who they were not. Paranoia swept over me, and I began to see complicity in the faces of the waiter, the elderly woman laughing with her grandchildren, the professional tennis player travelling with his coach — and what about the ship's physician? He, more than anyone, appeared above suspicion, but had access to dozens of poisons.

As the waiter began pouring soda into our glasses, and Mr. Benchley improved his with a stream from his flask, a thought popped into my head and I froze.

Just then, Ronnie arrived and took a seat, and when Mathew asked the whereabouts of Lady Twinton, we were told she had a headache and was dining in her stateroom. Mathew and Hem looked disappointed, and that disturbed me for a second, but more unsettling was an urgent question.

I turned to Mr. Benchley and asked, "The booze, the scotch we bought? How many bottles have we gone through?"

"Why? Afraid there won't be any left for the boat train? We'll be in France, my dear; we can get all the scotch and champagne your little heart desires!"

"I don't mean that," I whispered a little too sharply, because my friend frowned. "Just tell me how many bottles are left from the seven you bought from the guy on board?"

"I just drained the third bottle we opened into my flask last night, so there are, let's see, seven minus—"

"All right, you failed math, now let's go!" I stood up, causing the men at the table to stand up as well, not an easy task for the Major. I grabbed Mr. Benchley's arm and he haltingly left the table, making his excuse, "Be right back; left a pot on the stove."

"What's all this fuss about our liquor supply? After all, if you hadn't taped your room's DO NOT DISTURB sign on the case—a warning to me, no doubt, as if I'd drink your whiskey!—why, if you ask me, it was daring a thief to steal it!"

"I'm not talking about my stolen stash."

"Hey! What's this all about? You look a little crazed—in fact, you look a lot crazed, if you really want to know."

"I don't really want to know!" I tossed back at him.

We entered his room and I went straight to the closet where he'd hidden his onboard purchases. Next to the three remaining bottles stood a bottle of Irish whiskey bought ashore in Cobh, one of two; the other was standing on his desk, already half empty since everyone came back to his room for a taste upon our return to the ship. I inspected the labels securing the caps and corks. I suspected that one of the bottles had been tampered with because the paper stamp over the neck looked torn, and there was a yellowish stain where the broken edges might have been glued.

"This has been opened," I said.

Now, the fact is that most disreputable bootleggers (and most bootleggers are disreputable) have been slapping counterfeit labels onto bottles of rotgut hooch since Prohibition began. And they've gotten pretty good at duplicating the real thing, on the packaging, that is. My problem now was that these bottles had been bought from one of the few *honest* bootleggers—I know, that sounds oxymoronic—and the bottles we had opened so far contained excellent Dewar's scotch, and a smooth Napoleon cognac.

Mr. Benchley took the bottle I held out to him and inspected it. "This hasn't been touched, dear. What's going on that you're so upset?"

"Poison."

"You're afraid the Dewar's is spiked with rat poison?"

"You're right," I said, looking over the bottle once again. The yellowish stain was simply the smear of ink. "It's just that I'm beginning to see murderers everywhere I turn. And all the things that were happening to you—well, I couldn't stand it if you were murdered to death."

"I appreciate the sentiment, my dear girl, and acquit you of just now murdering the English language!"

I wasn't sure whether to laugh or cry. I vacillated between the two.

"There, there, now, little Dorothy," said my friend, holding me to him and patting my head while I had a little cry and drool on his nice dinner suit. The handkerchief appeared at my cheek, and I took it, blew my nose, and then attempted to blot the dark, wet circle my tears had left on his satin lapel.

"I was only accompanying you on this crossing so you wouldn't be afraid for your life. And now, look! You're not scared of drowning any more, you're worried about little-old-me. Poor dear. I am touched."

"You certainly are!"

The way he had put it was like a backhanded compliment. It raised my ire: "Whaddaya mean, you only made the trip so I wouldn't be scared, you big oaf! You wanted to come for the fun of it!"

"Well, well, Mrs. Parker, you *are* out of sorts!"

"*Meeeee?*"

"You bray when you get cranky."

"I don't *braaaayy!*"

"Oh, no you don't! I know that game," he laughed diabolically. "You're worried about me, and getting angry at me is more comfortable than being worried about me."

I looked at him with crumbling daggers. "What's the use?" I said. "Whatever your real motive for coming along on this trip, I'm glad you're here, you big boob."

"Thank you for that, except for the 'big boob' part. Now, can we go back and dine? I'm starving."

"Yeah, yeah," I said. "You know I couldn't stand it if you starved to death."

Back at the dinner table, the cutlery was exceptionally violent: The Duchess wore a look of suspicion, pushing food around her dinner plate as if panning for gold; Ronnie kept his head down, solemnly folding and unfolding his dinner napkin, lighting one cigarette after the other, and more interested in his spiked ginger ale than in any conversation.

After a long silence caused by brooding about Daphne, Hemingway rallied to answer a question posed by Mathew, and he began to play the role of "Papa" (a nickname dubbed by himself and adopted by his expatriate friends, Sara and Gerald Murphy, after the birth of his son, Bumby), suggesting ways for Mathew to get published in the German periodicals, after having been rejected by the English, French, and American journals. Talking about writing always lifted his spirits.

Soledad reminisced with Richard about childhood events and people they knew back when, and then gossiped about the time she lunched with Agatha Christie, the successful new British mystery writer, and how she helped to un-knot a plot dilemma in Christie's novel, *The Mysterious Affair at Styles,* featuring Christie's new Belgian sleuth, Hercule Poirot. "She has a treasure-trove of poisons in her satchel of diabolical weapons!" she said with a laugh.

That statement instantly brought the Duchess to attention. The Major reacted with an abrupt clatter of his knife, which fell out of his hand and onto his plate.

Hemingway, puffed up with youthful arrogance after mentoring the young Mathew, turned to Soledad and said, "You know, I would find it difficult to write a mystery story. I can only write about what I know."

"Well, all good writing springs from an author's keen understanding and depiction of human nature, Ernest, and yes, it is best to write what you know. Of course, life is happening all around us and everybody has a story to tell, some more passionate and fiery than others, if you are willing to listen, so why be limited to one's own little boxed-up existence? After all, Dante didn't have to visit Hell to write *The Inferno*, now did he? All he needed to do was *imagine* it, along with the knowledge of, and insight into, man's propensity to commit sin. Murder and intrigue are all around us; even if we don't see it in our own lives, it exists. I may not have committed murder, etcetera, etcetera, if you know what I mean . . . ."

"There *is* murder and intrigue all around us," said the Duchess with a slow deliberate nod. "Evil exists; even if you don't see it, or want to see it, it does exist."

With profound seriousness Hemingway acknowledged her point before saying, "I am experimenting with a new approach in novel writing: the telling of the story in simple terms, as it occurred, stripping away the narrator's psychology and presenting the distilled essence. In this way, what is *not* said says more than what *is* said. A work of fiction must be judged by the excellence of the material that the author *eliminates*."

A frown flashed over Soledad's smile. "Gertrude Stein?"

"Excuse me?"

"American woman, looks like a man, lives in Paris?"

"She has lovely eyes."

"Yes, I'm sure she does. I'm not being deliberately coarse; just didn't know how else to describe her and I didn't want to use the word *lesbian*. There, I've said it. But Paris has been liberated on that front. She has a salon, am I right? She's a writer, too, I believe. I'd love to meet her."

I glanced at Richard, who was trying to suppress his laughter at Soledad's futile attempt to repair the damage from her initial description of Gertrude Stein. I, too, was curious to meet the lady who had championed the likes of Picasso, Cézanne, Braque, Rousseau, Derain, and Matisse, and whom James Thurber, a friend of *New Yorker* editor E.B. White, calls "one of the eminent idiots" of the new automatic writing style. "It is a marvelous and painstaking achievement," Thurber wrote, "in setting down approximately eighty thousand words which mean nothing at all."

To distract us from his discomfiture at having been caught quoting his own mentor's philosophy right after playing mentor to Mathew, Hem said, "We can call on her. Mathew, Dorothy, Bob, would you like to meet Miss Stein, too? I will arrange it."

After an "improved" club soda in the lounge after dinner, Soledad, Richard, Mr. Benchley, and I retired to our rooms to pack our things for the early-morning arrival in Cherbourg. I took Woodrow for a final stroll on the deck. The waves were kicking up, rocking the ship. No one was about; it was late, after midnight, and the party over.

The moon was one hundred percent full this evening, according to Mr. Benchley's almanac forecast, and its light shimmered across the water. I walked toward the bow of the ship and narrowed my eyes against the wind to look out over the horizon, faintly visible now by the lunar light. Soon the continent would appear. France! *Tomorrow*, I thought, *I will begin a journey on a new adventure.* I will adopt a new way of living, of working. Although it frightened me a little to be alone in a foreign land, I felt a heady exhilaration. Ahead lay the opportunity to live a different kind of life from my old one in New York City. So many discoveries awaited me, and the excitement trumped any fear I had been harboring about the move. My regret was that Mr. Benchley would be returning home in a couple of weeks, and I would so sorely miss his easy companionship.

After a few minutes, my face and hands buffeted by the cold wind, I turned to head back indoors.

It was the sound of voices that stopped me. They were coming from the other side of a lifeboat, which obscured my view of the speakers. The waves were loudly crashing at the hull of the ship, and maritime hardware, pulleys, ropelines, lifeboats creaked, and the hum of the engines muffled the conversation. I tried to maintain my balance as the ship rolled.

"They found him . . . floating in the East River, shot . . . head, execution style. I got the wire an hour ago. It's Latham; it's confirmed. They left nothing to chance, did they? They were going to get Latham before or after he boarded ship. These people don't take chances. Had their men on board ship known Latham was killed, there might not have been this mess to complicate matters. It's Yezhov in the trunk. Yezhov was working for the other side."

A wave crashed against the hull and I couldn't make out the other man's response.

"I see it this way: Latham discovers Yezhov is at cross-purposes, kills him, hides him in the trunk—temporarily. But Yezhov's cohorts seized Latham before he was to sail. If they couldn't grab him before he sailed, they had a backup plan: the poison, and whatever other dandy methods they could scheme up. It was a case of mistaken identity with that fellow, Benchley, who took his stateroom. He looks a little like Latham, too, from what I've heard of Latham's description. So, Latham never had a chance to dispose of the body. And Yezhov's confederates don't yet know their man is dead. They pick up Latham on the street, the way they often do, and the luggage sits in his apartment. But before they get a chance to search Latham's place, the trunks are gone, taken from his apartment to the pier; probably Latham had arranged the transport days before. But now a more serious question arises: Did they find what they were looking for? Either they found it on his person, or they tortured him into handing it over, or their man on board, who didn't yet know that Latham never made the ship, found it hidden in Latham's luggage. Knowing Latham, there's *another* possibility: There was no longer anything he could pass on to me, because he had memorized it and it went into the East River with him. I must change the plan."

Frozen against a wall, I waited, listening for more, praying that Woodrow would not give us away. After a long silence, and waiting for what seemed forever out in the cold, we continued on around toward the doors leading inside. I was frightened of being seen coming in from the deck on the chance that one of the men would think I had overheard their conversation. These men sounded ruthless, and I wished I hadn't been privy to their schemes. Once indoors I walked briskly down the corridor and knocked on Mr. Benchley's door. When he didn't answer, I knocked again, and he opened the door, dressed in pajamas under a silk dressing robe.

I barged into the room and shut the door, leaning my back against it. He looked at me as if I were mad. Before he could make a snide remark I pressed an index finger to my lips, and turned the lock.

In a whisper, I said, "He was found in the East River, but he didn't have it on him. Of course he may have memorized it and now it's gone—in the East River, that is. A person named Yahoo or something double-crossed him, and so they picked Latham up on the street before he could dump the body, and then they killed him, and the man on the ship doesn't know that yet, at least he didn't right away, maybe he does now, though, but the trunks were already gone to the pier . . . and now they have to make a new plan."

"Would you repeat that?"

"Are you kidding?"

I didn't think I could repeat anything I had said. I had just been parroting what I had heard, unable to figure out what all the words meant because everything was out of context. Who was Yahoo? A doltish person in *Gulliver's Travels*? What dolt would name a kid Yahoo?

"Who's a Yahoo?"

"Maybe it was Yatzee."

"*Hah?*"

"The guy working for the other side."

"Other side of what?"

"How the hell am I supposed to know?" I hissed. "But he's the one who had Latham picked up on the street, the way they do. Only Latham didn't give it to them. At least they don't think . . ."

"Give them what? And who is *them*?"

"*It.* Whatever *it* is. And *them* is the other side!"

"Not to sound argumentative: the other side of *what*?"

"It is something he memorized."

"Who?"

"Latham. And *it* is what the other side wanted. Unless *it* was discovered, so then they wouldn't want *it* anymore, because they would already have *it.* Thing is, he didn't dump the body."

"Whose body?"

"His body."

"Makes perfect sense."

"It does?" I asked, a little amazed I had gotten through to him.

"It's my turn to say *are you kidding?*"

Mr. Benchley poured himself a measure of Irish whiskey, and when I asked for one, he refused. "Sit right down here, my dear, and write down what it is you want to say, in the order it must be said. If I can make heads or tails out of your essay, I will present you with a gold star and I will pour you a drink. Right now, I need you sober, or I'll go out of my mind!"

I did as he asked, recounting the conversation I had heard, and found that in the writing, I communicated the main points:

> _Latham, the man who had originally reserved this stateroom, had discovered that an associate, with a name that sounded like Yatzee or Yahoo, was really working for The Other Side. (This sounds like espionage!)_
>
> _So, Latham kills Yahoo, in his apartment, I gather, hides him in a trunk, temporarily, and goes out (who knows why? Ran out of smokes?), where he is abducted from off the street, and probably tortured to hand over It (something he might have memorized?), and then he's shot in the head—by The Other Side—and dumped in the river._
>
> _Meanwhile, The Other Side doesn't know that Latham killed Yahoo, and that Yahoo's body is in a trunk in Latham's apartment. And before The Other Side can conduct a search for It at Latham's place, the luggage and The Trunk containing Yahoo's body (which Latham never had a chance to dispose of because he got picked up on the street), is taken, by prearrangement, to the ship._
>
> _Now, there must have been a plan to ensure Latham was killed. If they didn't get him before he sailed, their confederate would_

kill him aboard ship—hence, the poisoned fruit—and then search for It, hidden among Latham's things. But, the person working for The Other Side who was travelling aboard ship didn't know that Yahoo and Latham were killed. Problem is, everything went wrong: The on-board confederate apparently wasn't informed of Latham's murder, or assumed Mr. Benchley was either Latham or Latham's replacement.

To sum up, Latham's dead; Yahoo was the man in the trunk; there are bad guys and good guys on board ship; I have no idea what It is, or whether It has been found or went swimming with the fishes.

—Dorothy Parker

P.S. They said they need a new plan.

I handed my affidavit to Mr. Benchley, who sat down to read it. After a minute, he looked up at me and then back down at the paper. After he had reread it, with a sigh and a very serious voice, he said: "I think we've gotten ourselves into a heck of a mess, Mrs. Parker. A dangerous one, at that." And then he asked, "The voices you heard, did you recognize them?"

"Yes," I said. "One of the men."

I didn't want to say it, because it might be true. I argued with myself that I could be wrong. But Mr. Benchley kept looking at me, like he knew I was struggling with a decision. I turned away and just said it: "One man's voice was Richard Hartley's."

Annie and her two brothers

St. Coleman's Cathedral

Chapter Nine

The next few hours were a waiting game. I couldn't sleep. Sometime around dawn I fell into a fitful slumber, the tragic face of Saul Gold and a laughing, diabolical Richard Hartley plaguing my dreams. After a nightmare where Richard had flung me over the rail and into the sea after making love to me under the full moon and stars atop the deck of a listing *Titanic*, I awoke in a sweat.

Quickly, I washed and dressed, packed away my things into my valises and steamer trunk, and went on deck to walk Woodrow. As I looked out toward the bow of the ship I could see land, and knew that very soon we would be docking in Cherbourg. Several passengers were out and about watching our advance toward the continent, so I felt a sort of safety in numbers, although I couldn't wait to get off the ship and onto the train to Paris so that Mr. Benchley and I could finally free ourselves from this death-cruise to Murder and Mayhem.

When Woodrow was ready we walked to the dining room, where I downed a cup of coffee and grabbed a cinnamon roll and a plate of bacon and scrambled eggs and several breakfast sausages from the buffet and retreated to my room. On my way I had to pass by Mr. Benchley's stateroom, and the door was open as porters were carting off his trunk and sports paraphernalia from his room. I said hello, and we agreed to meet near the ramp as soon as the disembarking was underway, and Woodrow and I walked on to our room.

I didn't want to see Richard. I knew there was little I could do to avoid him, if just to say good-bye. And then I remembered that he would be travelling to Paris on the same train we were, and my heart sank. Perhaps Mr. Benchley and I could somehow forget the boat train and hire a car?

"Shit," I said, distracted for a moment from my plan, as I bent down to place the breakfast plate of eggs and meat for Woodrow's breakfast. "Fred left his briefcase here." He was carrying it around the afternoon we found Saul dead, just after his steward, Rodney, had tried to, but couldn't, deliver it to his room. I ran out of the door and looked down the hall, but it appeared that my friend and his luggage were long gone. I figured there was nothing else to do but carry it off myself, but a few minutes later, when the porters arrived to remove my trunk, I decided to let them take it. To prevent any confusion, I crossed out

Mr. Benchley's room number and wrote in my own, so that all the pieces from my room would be set together for retrieval.

Now, how to get the hell off this tub without bumping into Richard?

It didn't matter how often I tried to hide behind this pole or that, slithered around one wall or another, ducked down, turned around, and generally looked like there were ants in my pants, I couldn't avoid the man. As Mr. Benchley and I were walking down the gangplank, after thanking Captain Fried for "our pleasant journey," Richard and Soledad called out to us from the foot of the ramp, so there was no way to pretend we didn't see them. Now we could all board the train together after producing our passports for the local French authorities. Hemingway and Mathew had retrieved their baggage and walked off to a café for a drink with Ronnie and Lady Daphne.

When I looked back for a possible retreat I saw that the Duchess Sofia and Major Arbuthnot were behind us, the redheaded Claude Dubois following them. I caught a glimpse of "Jimmy Durante," a plaster across his forehead covering his fight injury, waiting his turn to walk down the ramp.

What was very peculiar was that there were no police awaiting us for questioning. Even stranger, no one approached us at all, neither at the dock nor as we went through customs. I held my breath when we were asked to produce our passports for the funny little man in uniform, who looked me up and down a few times, too often for good taste, and wriggled up his nose with the universal expression of distaste at the sight of Woodrow, who wriggled his snout right back at him. Mr. Benchley and I were told to move on.

Our luggage was carted over to the boat train station, a few feet from the docks. It wouldn't leave until all the passengers from the ship on their way to Paris were boarded. That gave us an hour to spare, so after sending off wires to friends and family back home, telling them we had arrived safely after an uneventful trip—we are such liars—and one to Heywood Broun at *The World* to check on the credentials of Richard Hartley and Mathew Hettinger, we all went into the crowded station café, inviting the Duchess and the Major to join us. We squeezed through the chatty crowd and settled them at a table for two, and Mr. Benchley fetched drinks from the bar. Soledad, Richard, and I stood beside the table; Woodrow was taken from my arms to be held by a very affectionate Major Arbuthnot. We talked "dog" while we waited for our beverages, the Duchess wistfully recalling the half-dozen wolfhounds of her youth in Russia, and the Major giving us a brief history and lineage of his family's hunting bitches. While they spoke, I watched Richard, and followed his glance at the door of the café as new customers entered. I recognized a newlywed couple from our crossing and one of the men who had joined the card room fight. There were two young students who had travelled third class, but although we hadn't seen them on the ship, their presence on it was marked by the luggage tags dangling from their duffle bags. After the redheaded Claude Dubois, wrapped in a trench-coat and sporting his usual beret and dark glasses, walked in, Richard seemed to lose interest in who else was coming into the café.

So, it was the little redheaded Du Bois who was in league with Richard Hartley.

No. His accent was French. The man talking with Richard was American. All I could hope for was that they were the good guys. And then a thought flashed through my mind: *What if all the players were bad guys?*

———◆———

The boat train journey from Cherbourg to Paris was an express train, and the fare was included in the cost of the crossing. It was to take fewer than seven hours, and according to the schedule we expected to arrive in Paris at around 5:30 P.M. if all went well and there weren't any delays, cows on the tracks, that sort of thing.

Richard had bought a compartment for an additional fee, which he insisted we share with the Duchess and the Major. Seven hours with Richard

Hartley would be too much to bear, I thought, and I was glad when Hemingway and Mathew, travelling in a third-class car, came by and popped their heads in the door, after we'd been travelling for an hour, to ask if we wanted to join them for a bite to eat. I proclaimed that I was starving, even though I had little appetite, and I immediately rose to follow the boys. Mr. Benchley and Soledad decided to come, too, but Richard said he'd join us soon and remained behind. Outside in the corridor, Claude Dubois leaned against the wall smoking a Gitane, pretty much blocking the way and making passengers squeeze around him.

I turned back to look at the Duchess, who appeared exhausted, the book she was reading now on her lap as she stared out at the rolling countryside.

"Woodrow and I are going to the dining car. Would you like some lunch?" I asked. Just then the train lurched, and I had to grab the doorframe. I realized such a walk for the couple could prove injurious, so I added, "Better still, would you like for me to have a porter bring you something on a tray?"

"That would be lovely, Mrs. Parker," said the Duchess. "You are very kind."

The Major said, "Can Woodrow visit with us while you dine? He's such delightful company."

"Yes, please," said the Duchess.

I left them in Woodrow's care, and proceeded down to the dining car, where Mr. Benchley and Soledad had taken a table. I slipped into the banquette, across from Hem, Mathew, Daphne, and Ronnie, who was already pie-eyed and not very happy to be sharing his intended with the other men. The charged atmosphere around them was palpable. There was a growing hostility between Ronnie and Hemingway. I feared a cockfight brewing.

We ordered lunch and wine was set on our table. Mr. Benchley had no need of his flask for the first time in six years, so he openly ordered a whiskey on the rocks with a great sense of freedom in the act, knowing the liquor would be of a good quality and, above all, safe to drink.

He was expounding on the scientific fact that whiskey had to be served on ice in order for the flavor of the various herbs instilled in the liquor to be released when splashed over it, when Richard appeared and slid into the vacant seat next to me.

"You are awfully quiet today, Dorothy," said Soledad. "Ever since we left the ship."

This took me by surprise, and I looked across the table at Mr. Benchley and Soledad, avoiding Richard's eyes, not knowing what to say.

"Let's count our blessings," said Mr. Benchley.

"That's not a nice thing to say," I replied with a fake pout, not taking it to heart. He was just babbling, reaching for something to say to relieve my discomfort at being around Richard. It is always difficult to make small talk when you feel at odds with a person.

"Well, you know that old expression," said my friend. "When you can't say something nice about somebody, say nothing."

There was an implicit warning message in his voice: *Watch what you say. We don't know what kind of criminals we are dealing with.*

"I must warn you, my dear: Keep that up and your career will go down the tubes!" said Soledad with a spritely laugh.

"You are right, Soledad, you are right. What will my public think now that I omitted to sprinkle a bit of verbal vitriol upon the inflated head of the customs official who sneered at Woodrow?" And then, to respond to Mr. Benchley's warning, I added, "Well, dear Mr. Benchley, I am holding my tongue for the time being, as we are in rather close quarters, and I'd hate to see the innocent whiplashed."

"Dear God, Dorothy!" said Richard with wide-eyed concern. "What *is* the matter?"

"Don't look so shocked; I didn't use the *F* word."

"Not yet, at least," said Mr. Benchley.

I reined in my words. "I didn't get any sleep last night."

"Excited about starting your new life?" asked Richard.

Hemingway's voice boomed across the short aisle, which was followed by Daphne's throaty laugh.

I looked over at them and watched Ronnie fiddling nervously with his knife and fork. Forgetting for a moment my own dilemma, because I realized Ronnie's behavior appeared more sinister as Hem's and Daphne's intercourse grew more animated, I called over, "Hey, you over there, who wants to play a game of gin in the lounge after lunch? Ronnie? Do you play cards?"

He looked at me like I was mad.

I *was* mad all right! I was angry, and it was for all the betrayals I had endured at the hands of men. I'd thought Richard was different, and, after last evening, after hearing the conspiracy in his voice as he whispered about some kind of plot, I now suspected him of being a criminal. And I have so admired Hemingway's talent, and his dedication to his art, writing something fine and good while supporting his little family. Now that I could see that his attentiveness to and obvious fascination with Daphne was a betrayal of his wife and child, I realized that the only thing he was dedicated to was himself. I was mad all right, mad at men. And mad at myself, too. Through too many failed relationships I'd let my love for a man interfere with my work. At last I could see that now, and admit it, if only to myself.

This would have to change; romance was fleeting, and what really mattered, all that was truly lasting at the end of your life, was the work you left behind.

"Oh, Hem, there's a little boy a few compartments down from ours who looked so familiar, but then I remembered where I saw him—in that photograph you showed us of Bumby. But, of course your little boy is with his mama, so it couldn't be Bumby at all, now, could it? Will we get a chance to meet Hadley and Bumby in Paris, Hem?"

"Let me see that photograph, if you don't mind?" said Soledad. "If you have it on you."

"He always carries it, don't you Hem?" I said as lightly as I could. "I wish I had a little one like him. Such a darling!"

Hemingway opened his billfold and removed the picture to hand over to Soledad.

"Oh, he *is* a little darling, isn't he?" she exclaimed. "And is the woman with him your wife?"

"Yes, that is Hadley," he replied soberly. "They are vacationing in Schruns. I'll join them in a week or so, after I show Dorothy and Bob the sights."

"Well," I said, "as I will be staying on in Paris, I will have the pleasure of squeezing those pudgy little cheeks, I am sure!" I added, "I've a little gift for him in my valise, Hem. I couldn't resist it—just a toy. All children should have a toy now and then, don't you think? 'Cause when a boy grows up, he can't have toys anymore."

The danger I'd felt had passed—Ronnie appeared calmer, even if he was staring out of the window at the rolling countryside; at least he no longer had a knife in his hand. I steered the talk to all things Paris: What best hotel in which to reside? Or should I find rooms in a house? Could I borrow his typewriter while he was away in Schruns? Until I bought my own? Will we get together with Scott and Zelda tomorrow? Oh! The Murphys will join us? "I can't wait to meet them, Hem. He's an artist, a painter, I know. And Sara Murphy is a great beauty, I hear."

Soledad said, "I've seen Gerald Murphy's marvelous paintings."

Hem said, "He doesn't paint anymore. He has given it up."

"What!" said Soledad, "But, why? Has he been ill?"

"No, just come to his senses."

Daphne wanted to leave the table, so Ronnie had to get up for her to pass. She said nothing as she rose and walked out of the car. Hem slipped the photo of his family back into his billfold, and when he went to return it to his inside jacket pocket, I glimpsed the vial containing saltpeter he would make such a show of sprinkling on his food, and wondered if he had been so crude as to do so in front of Ronnie. For a moment, looking at Ronnie, sitting there slumped, drunk, and miserable, I empathized with him. But, only for a moment. For he had money, position, power. Much more than many thousands of wounded veterans had to return home to, whatever the injury. And then I realized that he was suffering something far worse than the physical pain and limitations of his war wounds— that he was consumed with love for a woman who didn't love him, a woman he could never totally possess, and that is a kind of slow, wretched death.

We had been walking back through the many passenger cars from the dining car when the train slowed to a crawl. As Mr. Benchley held the connecting door I heard Woodrow's familiar bark of distress. I rushed past my friend toward the compartment. But before I could get there, Claude Dubois rushed the door and then Richard pushed me aside to follow him in.

I could see a violent struggle through the glass.

And then everyone involved became still. Two figures, men in brown overcoats and fedoras, their backs to the glass door, ordered the others in the compartment to stand back. I was unable to see their faces, but as I moved forward to enter I caught sight of the barrel of a gun, heard a strangled cry from the Duchess, and found myself frozen in place. I stopped Mr. Benchley's progress with a firm hand to his chest, right before the brown-coated figures furtively opened the compartment's exterior door. One man leaped out onto the tracks. Woodrow, having grabbed the other man's trouser cuff, was doggedly clinging to him in spite of the man's efforts to shake him off.

The report of the gun shocked us violently and I heard a wounded cry.

Had they shot Woodrow?

I screamed as I watched the murderer jump out of the exterior door and onto the tracks.

The train was picking up speed. All hell broke loose as Richard and Claude flew out after them. The fluttering tails of a brown overcoat flashed across the compartment window.

And then, from outside the train more gunfire made our hearts jump.

The Duchess's cry rang out like a million shattered dreams. I rushed in and took her in my arms as Mr. Benchley pulled Woodrow out from his retreat under the Major's legs, placing my shivering pup on the seat beside me. Woodrow was unharmed, merely startled and shaking, although there was a gaping hole in the floor. And then Mr. Benchley sprang into action, reviving the Major, who had been knocked cold where he sat, with a drag on his flask, as Soledad begged water from a porter for the Duchess. Several porters appeared to attend passengers crowded into the hall. Hysteria heightened with each round of gunfire. They feared for their lives, for their children, for their money and jewelry; the Americans envisioned a train robbery as in the days of the Old West. Was this still commonplace in the savage regions of France? Had anarchists put a bomb on the train? What fate awaited us all in Paris? The news spread quickly that the engineer had been fooled into stopping the train, which already had been travelling at a snail's pace through a section of conjoining rails and signals on its way through Caen because of a stalled vehicle obstructing the tracks.

I looked up to see that Richard had returned to the train and was standing over me; Claude Dubois was behind him in the corridor.

"You have some explaining to do, Dr. Hartley, or whoever you are!"

———◆———

"They won't try again soon," said Richard Hartley. "Not too soon, anyway."

"But, why?" I asked. "Why kidnap an old lady?"

"I suppose we were wrong to think the old gal paranoid," said Mr. Benchley.

"I just don't understand," I said. "The Tsar and his family are gone, and you haven't answered my question: How is she a threat?"

An hour after the attempted kidnapping, the Duchess was sleeping in the compartment, the shades drawn, thanks to a light sedative administered by Dr. Hartley; the Major's injury was assessed as negligible.

He sat with an icebag on his head with Claude Dubois and Soledad on guard, while Richard, Mr. Benchley, and I sat talking in the empty dining car. The men in the brown coats had escaped capture by means of a getaway car.

After a moment Richard continued: "It's complicated. And I don't like having you dragged into this."

"Well, we are, and Mr. Benchley has had a few pretty close calls. Does what's happened to him and this man Latham have anything to do with the Duchess?"

"Nothing whatever to do with the Duchess!"

"Then, for goodness sake, what the hell is going on, here?"

"There are some things I cannot tell you that have to do with our country's national security, do you understand?"

Richard just looked at me, waiting for my response. I wondered what he was thinking, what he was trying to hide from us, what else he was going to reveal, and what he was not about to reveal.

I couldn't reply to his question, because I *didn't* understand. There was a challenge in his eyes, I saw, when he wouldn't look away. He was either lying to us or holding something back—something he'd decided from the beginning of our talk that we were not to know.

And then Mr. Benchley soberly asked him, "Whom do you work for?"

"All I can tell you is that I *am* who I say I am: a doctor and a medical researcher. I can tell you little more than that for now."

"And the man, Latham?" asked Mr. Benchley.

"Give it up, Richard," I said. "I heard your conversation with that man last night out on deck. Who was he?"

"What do you think you heard?"

"All of it." I replied, and told him the contorted gist of the conversation.

"Latham . . . was murdered."

"Yes, so I heard you say. I heard the whole conversation, out on the deck, under the stars, Venus and Jupiter, under the one-hundred-percent-full-moon. Who was he, and what did the man named Yahoo 'walk into'?"

"Yezhov," he corrected. "His name was Yezhov, and he was a Soviet spy. Latham worked for us."

"Us?"

"American and free-European interests. U.S. Intelligence, all right? Oh, Dorothy, Bob, you've really stepped in it!"

"So now that we have stepped into the crap, you need to tell us what's going on," I said.

"These things are dangerous for you to know!" said Richard, practically hissing a warning. "All right, but be careful and keep this to yourselves, for God's sake. I don't fancy finding your bodies stuffed in a trunk." He took an impatient breath.

"Latham probably discovered, somehow and too late, that Yezhov, who was supposedly working for U.S. Intelligence, was actually spying for the Soviets. Yezhov proclaimed he had escaped a labor camp through Persia. But there had to have been something more than just the discovery that Yezhov was a Soviet spy for Latham to have killed him. In most cases, a revelation like that can serve a purpose; rather than eliminate a mole, it's better to keep a man like Yezhov close, feeding him false information to take back to the enemy.

"As Latham had had contacts in the States and throughout Europe, he must have discovered more than Yezhov's betrayal. I know not what. Latham and I were supposed to meet on the ship. I received a coded wire from my superior earlier on the day we sailed, which suggested a transfer of vital information, but as you know, unbeknown to us, he was killed before we could meet. Yezhov must have been caught out by Latham—by something he said or did that gave him away or threatened Latham's plan. No doubt there was a confrontation, and Latham made the split-second decision to kill him. Whatever our man Latham discovered and planned to share with me is gone with him now. I thoroughly searched the luggage he sent to the ship—by the way, the rocks in the luggage were for show, to put weight in the bags, and so was the reserved stateroom for show. He never intended on sailing. It was all a diversion. He wanted it to appear that he was on the crossing. He was only to deliver to me whatever it was he had found before midnight, before we embarked, whether by word or through some physical exchange—as I said, I don't know which—and then he intended to quit the ship before departure."

"Then you knew there was a body in the trunk when we went to the baggage hold?"

"I was as surprised as you were. I had no idea about Yezhov, and when we found his body, I knew nothing about Latham's having been murdered at that time. I had wired my man when we sailed to say Latham had missed our meeting, and to ask if there had been a change in my mission. I received no immediate reply until a return wire stated that Latham's body was discovered in the East River. The coded wire came almost immediately after we discovered Yezhov's body in the trunk. I knew nothing about who the dead man was. I'd never before seen Latham or Yezhov, so I really didn't know who was in that trunk.

"As for the Duchess, she is considered an 'enemy of the state.' They want her because they believe she has raised sympathy and financial support to take back her country. They will take her back to stand trial or hide her away where her voice will not be heard."

"Meanwhile, a series of events has changed everything. Where my original mission was merely to deliver the Duchess to a safe house with the assistance of French agent Claude Dubois, I was instructed at the last minute to also receive information Latham wanted delivered to a contact in Paris. Then, when Latham failed to show, I was wired to await further instructions, and in the interim continue with the original mission of coordinating the protection of the Duchess Sofia. After we discovered the body in the trunk, I later made a thorough search of the bags—their linings and seams—looking for hidden and recessed compartments, hoping to find whatever it was that Latham had hoped to give me, thinking it might have been sitting in his luggage all along. It wasn't."

"Why is the Duchess travelling under her real name? Why not a false one?" I asked.

"The Duchess Sofia Louise was booked on five different steamships, and several trains to Canada and the West Coast. It's hard to disguise a person of her countenance and social standing. She was brought onto this ship a full day before we sailed, as cargo, and had not left her room until the day after we sailed and I had done a check of all the passengers on board. But I must have missed uncovering a communist agent on board, after all.

"Now, I must insist that you not tell anyone about what has happened on the ship. Captain Fried and the ship's physician were taken into my confidence before we sailed. No one else but we three, the captain, the ship's physician, and Soledad Soleil, know that Saul Gold was poisoned. It's for your own protection as well as for the sake of others that you must keep this to yourselves."

Mr. Benchley got to the heart of our immediate concern. "All right, our lips are sealed. But what happens to the Duchess now? Does she go into hiding as planned?"

"In light of what's just happened, there is all the more urgency to get her to a safe house, although I'm reluctant to bring her to the one we had planned. Its location may have been compromised. I'll have to find someplace else, and quickly—someplace they won't think to look for her while I make permanent arrangements. And from now on, you and Dorothy have no further contact with me. We met casually on the crossing. We say goodbye at the station, 'Have a lovely trip,' and all that, and that's all anybody who might be watching you will ever know happened between us. Do I make myself clear?"

"I think I know where the Duchess could stay for a day or two, a place that has no connection to her past, and as you have never had contact with the persons I'm about to suggest, there is no link to them."

"Bob, did either of the kidnappers see you or Dorothy during the scuffle?"

"I don't think so," he said. "Their backs were to us when we arrived at the compartment, and then they jumped off the train by way of the exterior door."

"I'm concerned that you two might be made pawns in this game."

"How? The kidnappers didn't see us," I said. "Don't worry, we'll do as you say."

"Good. And it's best you never know the American agent I had the conversation with out on deck, so don't try to figure that out, Dorothy."

"Do you think there are other Soviet agents on the train," asked Mr. Benchley, "or on the crossing with us?"

"On the crossing, yes. He's been arrested." said Richard.

"Who?" I asked. "Would we know him?"

Richard said, "No. Stop asking me these things. Just help me get the Duchess to a safe house."

With that he ended the conversation.

———◆———

"Who's that fat man walked right out of Lautrec's 'Aristide Bruant' poster?" asked Richard when we pulled into the Paris Gare Saint-Lazare.

I turned to see the haughty and hefty Aleck, wrapped in his usual costume of black cape, red scarf wrapped around his many chins, and slouchy black felt hat.

"Yes, that rotund fellow," he repeated, "standing alongside that slow-witted young boy making faces and waving an American flag?"

"Why, that's the famous Alexander Woollcott, and the idiot is his unofficially adopted son, Harpo Marx."

"Woollcott! My goodness . . . ."

"Yes, the Devil himself."

I looked at Richard's wonderstruck face. "Why, you're speechless," I said, "and you have yet to be verbally garroted."

Mr. Benchley said, "It's all been arranged; she should be safe there." He took Richard's hand to shake and slipped a door key into his palm.

"Goodbye, Bobby."

"We are in Paris, now: It's *au revoir!*

"Yes, *au revoir!*"

And with that, Mr. Benchley hopped off onto the platform to greet Aleck and Harpo and to attend to our luggage.

"This is where we part ways, Dorothy, for now," said Richard.

Our eyes locked, and I saw his regret. It matched my own. He moved in closer. I tilted my face for a kiss, but a voice broke the spell. Richard turned to attend to Duchess Sofia, who was accompanied by Major Arbuthnot and Claude Dubois. I acknowledged them all with a little nod, and then they disappeared into the crowd.

I had regrets, *so many regrets*, as I watched them blend into the crowd.

I scrutinized the many faces on the platform, looking for sinister or unnatural behavior. Everyone was suspect; anyone could be a Soviet agent. A scuffle caught my attention. It was an arriving American from our train loudly accusing a young man of lifting his billfold.

"Dorothy, my dearest wretch!" boomed the familiar voice of Alexander Woollcott. I turned to see my friend, his arms extended for an embrace. "Little Acky's here!"

I was sucked into his arms like a long-lost child, even though it had been barely a month since we last lunched together with our gang at the Algonquin.

"How was the crossing, my love?"

"Rough," I said. "The only thing I could keep on my stomach was the first mate."

"Did you bring the maple syrup?"

"Yes, of course, a quart, and your pepper jelly, two cans of corn chowder, your special-formula toothpowder, and an entire grocery shelf of Ritz crackers."

I turned to greet Harpo, who, in imitation of Aleck's bear-hug, pulled me into his arms. He drew me back to take a good look at me and then pinched my cheek. (No, a lower cheek.)

"We're in Paris, for cryin'outloud, not in Rome, you two-bit masher, you!"

When he pinched again, I affectionately slapped his hand and then his face. We laughed, and then he slapped my hand and then my face. "If you want a slap-out-slam-down fight, Harpo, I'll introduce you to Ernest; he's always game."

"Where is the Wunderkind I've heard so much about?" asked Woollcott.

I looked around. "There," I said, pointing as I called his name. Hem looked over at the sound of my voice, smiled, and waved. He and Mathew were chatting with a handsome couple who looked as if they'd walked out of a magazine fashion page. I could make a good guess as to who they were. Judging by their elegant deportment—she blonde and graceful, he tall, slim, and possessing an easy, dignified bearing—they had to be none other than Gerald and Sara Murphy, American expatriates living the artistic life in France with their three children.

Mr. Benchley had come to know them well. Gerald was heir to the Mark Cross empire, and a brilliant artist of the new abstract style who'd designed spectacular sets for Diaghilev's Ballets Russes, alongside Picasso, Braque, and Derain. Influenced by the Dadaists, four of his monumental works depicting the precise interior workings of machines hung in exhibition at the Grand Palais beside those of Léger and Bonnard and Goncharova and Max Ernst.

He and his delicately beautiful wife, Sara, left New York for Paris a half-dozen years ago to lead unconventional lives in the pursuit of artistic endeavors. Unencumbered by the demands of conventional American lifestyles, they sought a freer environment where they might work shoulder-to-shoulder at whatever they chose to create, whether it be a garden, a home, or a canvas. It was an idyllic plan, and from what I had heard from Mr. Benchley, Aleck, Donald Ogden Stewart, and other mutual friends, they had since been enjoying a charmed existence in Paris and at their summer home, Villa America, on the Côte d'Azur. What was admirable about them was how they embraced, encouraged, and very often financially supported so many striving artists and painters and their families, including John Dos Passos, Archibald MacLeish, Fernand Léger, Pablo Picasso, and Ernest Hemingway.

But, I thought as they walked over to us alongside Hemingway and Mathew, *with the size of their incomes, a charmed life is easy to buy.*

I realized sometime later, though, that they gave so much more than they received from their patronage, when I considered their great affection for the Fitzgeralds. Gerald and Sara Murphy served as the loving and patient parental figures the younger couple so needed in their often-turbulent and undisciplined lives.

Hemingway made my introduction, and I was immediately drawn to the Murphys' gracious manners. But although Mr. Benchley had told me lots about Gerald's artistic and scholastic achievements—he was voted Best Dressed at Yale and a member of DKE and Skull and Bones—I was a little put off by Gerald's upper-crust Standard American speech—rich people's high-falutin' speech. All right, *cultured* speech. In my experience people who spoke like this were generally bores. For, when Gerald said, in dulcet tones, "This is the *first* time we meet, Mrs. Parker, but I have *heard* such wonderful things about you from Bobby and Aleck, that I feel we are already friends, 'far 's I'm concerned," I thought the word *first* should have had an umlaut in it!

I introduced Hem and Mathew to Aleck and Harpo. Harpo behaved himself and Aleck sized up the brawny Ernest.

"Where's the Lady and her rich tramp," Soledad asked Hemingway, appearing from behind a baggage cart loaded with a dozen Louis Vuitton steamers, shoe cabinets, and valises.

"Daphne and Ronnie are checking into the Gallia. We'll probably see them tomorrow."

"Can't wait," replied Soledad, dripping sarcasm in her vividly purple paisley coat and matching hat, trimmed all around with yards and yards of black mink. "I'm at George Cinque, Dorothy."

I introduced Soledad to my friends and the Murphys.

Aleck, eyes wide with wonder at such a glamorous sight, was, for once, flummoxed by her shamefully flattering greeting: "Why, you're the man everyone in America talks about!"

Harpo pulled a face, flapped his tongue out like a dog, panted, circled her wagons, as predicted. She left to follow her trunks.

We all soon parted company—Aleck and Harpo with me and Mr. Benchley to our hotel, Hem and Mathew to the Hemingways' rooms on the rue Notre-Dame-des-Champs, where Mathew would have a bed for the night, and the Murphys to their small *pied-à-terre* on quai des Grands-Augustins, which had a wonderful view of the river and the Tuileries, and where they had agreed to install the Duchess and the Major on Mr. Benchley's request.

As soon as all of us were settled in our rooms we would meet at Michaud's for supper.

I once read in a travel brochure that Paris has been dubbed *the city of lights* for a couple of reasons.

During the Age of Enlightenment it was the place to be—to be enlightened, that is. Later, Paris was one of the first cities to convert from gas to electric lights, so again it was the place to be for "illumination." Nothing beats the glaring brilliance of *The Great White Way*, of course, but this city had a particular beauty all its own and was unlike any American city I had ever deigned to visit.

Looking out from the taxi windows, as we barreled along wide thoroughfares and boulevards, I marveled at the size and expanse of its monuments: Napoléon's Arc de Triomphe dwarfed New York City's Washington Square Park memorial to George Washington, and the Louvre sprawled on for acres, much larger than our Metropolitan Museum of Art on Fifth Avenue. And the fountains! All lit up at night! Spectacular!

Aleck relished the role of tour guide, pointing left and right from one landmark to another for my edification. He instructed the driver to take a different route: "*Suivez le Boulevard Haussman jusqu'au Champs Elysées et puis allez au Place de L'Etoile.*" He told the driver where to slow down, and after we drove past the Tuileries, to move on with the little tour.

"I have made plans for us to tour the Louvre—"

As we drove under the brilliantly lit arch, Aleck instructed the driver to circle another boulevard toward the river. And what should my eyes behold as we approached the bridge, the Pont de l'Alma, but the graceful ironwork candlestick of the Eiffel Tower, ablaze in all its glory!

"—and if the weather holds, we'll take a stroll through the Luxembourg Gardens after lunch. And on Monday we might venture out to Versailles—but the big event is l'Académie des Cinq Arts Festival of Fools on Tuesday night to ring in Ash Wednesday. What's the address of the hotel, Bob?"

Once off the major avenues, the taxi twisted around a labyrinth of narrow streets, bordered with buildings of old stone blocks, a style unlike anything I'd seen in Manhattan, where all is brick and mortar and brownstone and concrete over steel guts. Court-yards everywhere, louver shutters and balconies and wrought-iron grillwork dressing their edifices. And everywhere, cafés and restaurants, one after the other, a yellow glow washing out onto the cobblestone streets, each distinctive and alive with music and crowds of neighborhood patrons looking for a laugh, a drink, and a friend after a long day's labor. This neighborhood was loud and vibrant; the yells of frustrated arguments, cheers of happy greetings, screams of stubborn children and reprimanding parents rang out from windows and sought escape into the night sky above the city but were trapped in the narrow passages to reverberate in echoes.

From some of the cafés tables and chairs spilled out onto the pavement. Aleck told us that the weather had been unusually warm for this time of year, when it might otherwise have been cold and damp and rainy. I had to laugh when I saw a sign over one establishment. "Les Deux Maggots!" I said, interrupting Aleck's five-franc tour. "Imagine naming a café such a thing!"

"The title of a play from last century," said Aleck.

"Typical French humor," said Mr. Benchley, "but then, the French language is, in itself, an exercise in humor."

"What are you talking about, Bob?"

"Well, think about it, Aleck: The French have the vowels *a*, *e*, *i*, *o*, and *u*, and the three accents, the acute *e*, the grave *e*, and the circumflex *e*—all of which are pronounced *ong*. And so: *a* equals *ong*, *e* equals *ong*, *i* equals *ong*, *o* equals *ong*, and, of course, it goes to follow that *u* equals *ong*. Lots of vowels equals one *ong*!

"So," I asked, "I should forget about how the language is written—is that what you say—and I should just learn to throw in the *ong* sound in between the consonants?"

"That's about the gist of it, Mrs. Parker. But there are a few phrases that you must learn by heart to survive in this city, so, *ecoutez!* Repeat after me:

"When you want breakfast you ask the waiter, '*N'avez-vous pas des griddle-cakes?*' You are asking him, 'Haven't you got any griddle-cakes?'

"When you take a sip of demitasse, you could say, '*Appelez-vous cela coffee?*' In English you would spit and yell, '*You call that coffee?!*'

"When the waiter scowls at you, you say, '*De tous les pays goddams que j'ai vu!*' which, of course, all tourists have learned to say, and means: 'Of all the goddam countries I ever saw!'

"And you'll hear this spoken by Americans everywhere you go: '*Quelle espèce de dump is this, anyhow?*' Which will be on the tip of your tongue a dozen times a day, and means: 'What kind of dump is this, anyhow?'

"'*Ici est où nous used to come quand j'étais ici pendant la guerre.*' Now, with a limp and a cane and a scar, it will buy you a wish and a prayer. It means, 'Here is where we used to come when I was here during the war.'

"When you are feeling a bit lonely you might say, '*Je n'ai pas vu une belle femme jusqu'à présent!*' In English it means, 'I haven't seen a good-looking woman yet!' Oh, yes, for you, my dear lady, throw in '*le bel homme*' for '*belle femme.*'

"And when all else fails, strike out with: 'What's the matter? Don't you understand English?' Which in French is pronounced, '*What's the matter, don't you understand English?*' Now that's enough for your first lesson, Mrs. Parker. I see we've arrived at our hotel."

We got out of the taxi and Aleck paid the driver, who then saw to our hand luggage. Our trunks would arrive later, so we walked into the hotel's little lobby.

Harpo, who had remained silent throughout the ride, now looked up and down and all around the shabby interior and said: "*Quelle espèce de dump is this, anyhow?*"

Harpo hit it on the nose. The hotel was a dump, all right. Thank you, Ernest Hemingway, for arranging our stay here at *Chez Le Crappé.* Tomorrow morning we would look for accommodations that offered hot running water, heat, and, if we were lucky, bathrooms with porcelain fixtures, instead of the rank-smelling apertures at the end of each floor that were nothing better than foul outhouses brought in and placed on each landing, just disgusting holes in the floor. I didn't realize that this was the norm for bathrooms throughout the city, and later, upon my inquiry, I was told, "*Boot, tzare ahh no sooch ting as de plumb-iere in Paree.*"

There would be no bath tonight.

After pulling up the bedsheets to check for bugs—I didn't see any in the lumpy, stained mattress— I washed my hands and face using the pitcher and bowl provided. I changed out of my navy-blue travelling suit and quickly threw on a simple wool shift, which I dressed up with strings of crystal beads. I fixed my hair and strapped on a pair of leather pumps that could handle the cobblestone streets. From one of my hatboxes I took out a chocolate-colored cloche adorned all around its hatband with floral sprays constructed of cleverly twisted colors of contrasting felt and ribbons. After I'd added mascara and a bright lipstick, Woodrow and I knocked on Mr. Benchley's door to tell him I was going downstairs to the lobby to meet the awaiting Aleck and Harpo, so he should move his carcass. Gay Paree awaited me!

The photograph in Hemingway's wallet

Bruant or Woollcott?

*Gerald and Sara on the beach at
Villa America*

Chapter Ten

I watched with hypnotic fascination as one of the men at a nearby table poured a couple of fingers of green absinthe into a glass. Balancing a flat, perforated spoon across the rim of it, he placed a cube of sugar on the bowl. From a small pitcher with a long and narrow spout, very, *very* slowly, with a steady hand, he began to trickle water onto the sugar cube. Drop by drop, the sweetened water dripped through the holes of the spoon to combine with the green liquid in the glass. Swirls of opalescent mist turned the mixture opaque white. After the long ritual, he raised the glass to sip.

We were in a café a couple of streets from the fleabag hotel, killing time and knocking back some good booze before our dinner hour. The air was heavy with the eye-watering reek of Gitane cigarette smoke, stale booze, and unwashed bodies. A sad-looking little man playing an accordion occasionally crooned the words of the song he was playing in a deep nasal tone, words my high school French was insufficient to interpret. The conversations were loud and animated, and at times I wasn't sure if they were passionate arguments or simply excited revelations. Occasionally, laughter broke out. Once, a man pounded on the bar and with sweeping gestures yelled something passionate at *le barman* before storming out of the café.

All sorts of characters walked in and out of the place, and most times the waiters greeted the customers with warm congeniality and delivered plates of oysters and mussels and crusty bread and cheese and liters of white wine. We appeared to be the only Americans here, and we were looked over—Aleck's costume and Harpo's crazy facial gestures, notwithstanding, Mr. Benchley and I were decidedly American tourists to the eyes of the regulars. This café catered to the laborers and vendors of the neighborhood, and the many veterans of the War proudly wearing Croix de Guerre ribbons or the yellow-and-green Médaille Militaire on frayed and dusty lapels. Through observation, one could guess at the professions of the clientele from their utilitarian garb and soiled hands and faces, the very poor by the worn collars and cuffs and patched coats. In New York, the standard dress at a nightclub often belied the small income of the lowly clerk or housemaid. But here, within ten minutes of each arrival, the trials of their workdays appeared to abate with the help of drink and convivial conversation. This type of gathering is of universal appeal, and such is the case in neighborhood speakeasies in American cities. The clientele may vary, but as I was seeing here, watering-holes around the world serve well for shedding the day's hardships while offering a palliative for pangs of loneliness.

I was enjoying my first taste of night in the city, trying to absorb its atmosphere and observe its people, while half-listening to Aleck's continuing oral exegesis on "how to behave with the French."

"I used to come here during the War," he had prefaced, "with Frank and Ross and Jane."

Frank is Frank Pierce Adams, the famous columnist, Ross is Harold Ross, the publisher of *The New Yorker*, and Jane is Ross's society-columnist wife. They are our friends and fellow Round Tablers.

"*Ah!*" said Mr. Benchley with self-congratulatory cheer in his voice. "One of the phrases I taught you in the cab: '*Ici est où nous used to come quand j'étais ici pendant la guerre!*' Just throw in the extra names wherever you see fit."

"Shut up, Bob; I was telling Dorothy never to smile at people or look at them directly in the eye, if you can avoid it. We're not in New York. They will think you are an imbecile."

"That's right," said Harpo, "or they will think you are looking for sex."

"That's true, Harpo. I've told you to stop smiling," said Aleck. "The Parisians think you are mentally deficient *and* a pervert."

"Yeah, but I'm getting plenty of sex!"

Harpo received the bone-crushing Woollcott glare, which was magnified tenfold by Aleck's thick spectacles.

"*As I was saying*, don't *ever* apologize to anyone, Dorothy," said Aleck, ignoring Harpo, who sat there cross-eyed with a silly grin on his face, counting his fingers. "It's admitting culpability and a sign of weakness. And, if someone knocks into you as you're walking along the street, don't expect a '*pardon.*' And don't *you* say it, either. It's bad manners."

"Yikes!" I said. "You mean, if someone slams a door in my face, I can't call him a shit?"

"Now, that won't happen. A Frenchman will always hold the door for the next person. It is requisite good manners, even if it winds up that you are forced to trot the distance of a football field to reach it. Then, you have to hold the door for the next long-distance runner, or you are thought a brute."

"When I used to come here during the war," he continued, "I always — "

"Ah-*ha!*" interjected Mr. Benchley, "You see how useful that phrase has become? Why," Mr. Benchley barreled on, putting to rest Aleck's lecture, "the first time I came to Paris *après la guerre* as a correspondent for the *Dairyman's Age and Trade News* to cover the peace conferences in 'nineteen, I was barred because I didn't have a passport."

Mr. Benchley ignored the loud *harrumph!* expelled by Aleck.

"I had no documentary record of ever having been born, and, in view of this serious deficiency in my credentials, I was held by the officials to be a *de facto*, but not a *de jure,* member of the human race, and therefore not entitled to a passport to leave the country, because, according to the law, I had never entered it.

"Furthermore, I made the mistake of smiling at one official, hoping to win him over, and he charged me with 'obscene behavior toward a government agent.' When I begged his pardon for my misadventure, he said my apology meant that I had indeed confessed to perversions of a sexual nature. When he opened the cell door for me to enter, I said, '*Merci*,' and then returned the gesture, and united through common pleasantries, together we spent the night in jail playing pinochle and talking about old times."

"All right, Bob; you've made my case," said Aleck, resigned to the madness, "if in a rather peripatetic way."

We had another round of drinks and then it was time to leave for the restaurant. We walked out onto the street, and turned toward the boulevard, Harpo taking my arm. He was telling me his thoughts about the women of Paris, the places he had visited with Aleck as his tour guide that he found most exciting—the Moulon Rouge to see the big show, and best of all, his visit to Notre Dame.

"A very famous church. You didn't get baptized, did ya?"

"I know, I'm Jewish, but I feel a kind of sympathy for Quasimodo, you know? I might pretend to be a fool, but he was the *original* village idiot."

"Harpo! I didn't know you've read Victor Hugo's book," I said.

He stopped short, and threw me the oddest look. "Who said anything about reading any old book?"

"Well, you said—"

"Lon Chaney played the part in the picture show."

Harpo and Aleck are an odd couple. Aleck, who considers himself an intellectual, believes that Harpo Marx is the most brilliantly funny man in the world. On stage, Harpo can do no wrong; his comic off-the-top-of-his-head improvisation, along with his brothers' antics, is flawless. It was Aleck who discovered the team of Vaudevillians when he decided to review their first Broadway show, *I'll Say She Is!*, when no other first-string critic would bother to waste an inch of column space under their bylines for a show with the cast of an old Vaudeville act. His effusive raves in the *New York Times* drove in the crowds to fill the seats of the theatre, and the Marx Brothers became the toast of Broadway. ("Add a little cream cheese and lox, and we taste as good as we look.")

Aleck, often the pedantic curmudgeon, becomes less officious and more lighthearted when Harpo is around. Harpo in turn is getting an education. Aleck has figuratively adopted Harpo, the Upper East Side kid who had no formal education and usually has no idea what the man is saying when he bandies about his ten-dollar vocabulary. Aleck's affection has always been reciprocated. For Harpo, that he should be included in, and accepted by, the notable friends of my little circle who meet every day for lunch at the Algonquin Hotel dining room, is a source of amazement. Like Aleck, we all love Harpo's unaffected charm; you never know what he will do or say, and there is an edge of excitement in that. There's always pure, good-humored fun when he's around.

"Oh, look!" said Harpo, pointing to a man on the other side of the street, standing in a doorway and lighting a cigarette.

"Hey! Hey, there, Jimmy!" he called out with a wave of his arm, but the man walked away and around the corner.

Harpo turned to me and said, "What's he doing here? I didn't know he was in France."

"Who? Someone I know?"

"Sure, someone you know. Jimmy! Jimmy Durante!"

———————◆———————

"Well," prefaced Mr. Benchley when we were out of earshot of our friends, "if that man is following us, he's not following the Duchess Sofia."

"He's following us, hoping that we will eventually lead him to her. We have to keep away from the Murphys' apartment," I said. "How much did you tell Gerald and Sarah about the Duchess and everything that's been going on?"

"Just that she was the intended victim of a kidnapping by Soviet agents, and the location of her safe house had been compromised, so she needed somewhere to stay for a couple of days until things could be sorted out. They were more than willing to help. As a matter of fact, Gerald suggested that Richard and Claude drive her down to their Villa America tomorrow."

"That sounds like a good idea," I said, as we entered through the deco glass doors of the Café Michaud on the rue des Saint-Pères.

The restaurant was crowded with diners, and people were milling about the entrance and the bar, waiting for tables, so there was a festive mood alive with chatter and movement as the maître d' welcomed the new arrivals and bade farewell to those departing. Waiters scurried to and from the kitchen with platters of *marennes*, flat and orangey-colored oysters, and steaming tureens of soup, and trays stacked with *crabe Mexicaine* and fried potatoes and tournedos with Béarnaise sauce. The sommelier poured out first sips of the Châteauneuf du Pape or the Pouilly-Fuissé for discerning diners. The steaming parade of food made my mouth water. I spotted Hem at the bar with Mathew. As we were inching toward them, Gerald and Sara arrived. The maître d' saw the couple's arrival and with obsequious attention had us seated within a minute at a table along the wall, from whence I could see all the action.

Mathew talked about his new assignment as foreign correspondent for the *Detroit Register* and how much he admired Aleck and Harold Ross and Frank Adams and Heywood Broun's columns, and gosh, he'd love to meet those famous fellows someday.

He had once seen the five Marx Brothers and their mother, Minnie, on the Vaudeville circuit when they played an Albee house in Detroit and thought them very funny. Harpo brought us up to date: Gummo had retired from Showbiz and Minnie was too busy managing the boys' careers to be onstage anymore.

Aleck turned to Gerald and said, "So this is the young man you were telling me about, Gerry?"

"Yes," replied Gerald, "this is our boy, Ernest; friend of Scott's, too."

"I understand your book will be published. Sorry I missed you in New York. Did Bob and Dorothy show you a good time?" he asked in all seriousness as he hungrily devoured the menu with his eyes.

"Did we, Ernest?" I asked.

"You bet! I'm returning the favor, showing Bob and Dorothy around."

"We shall later discuss the itinerary," said Aleck, possessively.

Soledad appeared, dressed in a lovely fuchsia velvet dress under a dolman-sleeved black satin coat. She was on her way toward our table when she suddenly turned and greeted a family dining a few tables away. After a few minutes, she arrived and Mr. Benchley held her chair.

Aleck's eyes lit up at the sight of the beautiful Soledad; Harpo crossed his and grinned. She laughed as lightly as a dinner bell, and Hemingway looked at her with newfound admiration. He said, "That's Joyce, Joyce and his family you were speaking with at that table over there."

"Yes, Ernest, James Joyce and his wife, Nora, and their children, Giorgio and Lucia."

"I didn't think—I mean, I didn't know you were friends."

I could see that, for Hem, the mystery writer had just climbed five rungs up the ladder of literary importance.

"Yes, well, we made each other's acquaintance in Trieste before the war," she said, looking over to the table where the man with the thin face and thick eyeglasses was engrossed in cutting his chops. "I was on honeymoon with my first husband, Arthur, who later died at the Somme. James taught me a little Italian." She chuckled. "He just asked if I had come to Paris to resume my Italian lessons. You know that Italian is the only language they speak at home? He's almost mastered Russian, he told me."

"Joyce, did you say? The man who wrote the book that was banned?" asked Aleck. "A polyglot, too?"

"He's a Mormon," whispered Harpo, "who writes dirty books?"

"Yes," said Soledad, in answer to Aleck's question. "But Sylvia Beach has since published it herself."

"Sylvia's a good friend of mine and Joyce and Ezra Pound, you know; I'll bring you to meet her at her bookstore," said Hemingway.

We placed our dinner orders, Aleck instructing the waiter in flawless French that his tournedos of beef must under no circumstances be too rare or lose all color.

"*La viande doit être rose mais pas trop saignante ou je vais le rendre. Cinq douzaines huîtres à partager. La soupe d'abord, un consommé de boeuf et après des poireaux à la vinaigrette. Aussi, apportez-nous une bouteille de vin blanc pour le faire descendre; et pour la viande donnez-nous un bon bourgogne.*"

I nodded to the waiter and pointed to Aleck. "I'll have whatever the big man's having."

Gerald and Sara talked about their participation in l'Académie des Cinq Arts Festival of Fools, scheduled for Tuesday night, and insisted that we all get fitted for costumes. Aleck assured the Murphys that he had taken charge of the wardrobe we were to wear. When Mr. Benchley was informed he would be costumed as King Louis XVI, he stated unequivocally that he would not wear a wig that was in any way curled like Lillian Gish's hair, let alone dance tights.

"Who will you be dressed up as, Gerald?" I asked.

"Sara and I will be dressed as *what*, not *who*: automobile engine parts."

"Oh!" cheered Soledad, "don't you just love it? How inventive! I am so dull to appear as Oscar Wilde!"

"You'll be dressed like a man, in trousers," noted Hem. "Why Wilde? Why not George Sand?"

"I don't smoke cigars," she tossed back, and turned to Aleck. "And you, Monsieur?"

"Moi?" said Aleck. "Catherine the Great."

"Oh, jeez . . ." I said. "Yes, I can see the resemblance. What horror have you planned for me?"

"Little Bo Peep."

"Not on your life."

"You'll be adorable."

"Shit."

"He wants me to dress up as a court jester," said Harpo.

"It's in your nature," said Aleck.

Harpo jerked his thumb at me. "Dottie said it."

After two hours of eating and laughing and gossiping, Gerald picked up the diner bill. "Where shall we go now?" he asked. "Let's go to a club."

"A jazz bar," suggested Soledad.

Harpo said, "Let's stop in at Bricktop's. There's a little dancer there—"

"Yes," agreed Soledad. "It's quite a gay club, and we should all be gay tonight for Dorothy's first night in Paris."

Hem wasn't enthusiastic. He begged forgiveness for declining, but he wanted to go home. He encouraged Mathew to go on with us. Tomorrow we would "lunch with the Fitzgeralds," and he wanted us to meet Gertrude and her friend Alice, so he would pick us up at our hotel at noon. Mathew looked torn, but Hem pressed him to join us, "if only to see the less salubrious haunts of the city." So we all piled into a cab and were on our way.

Aleck said that when Cole Porter first saw the incomparable Ada Beatrice Queen Victoria Louise Virginia Smith, better known as "Bricktop," perform in her club, Chez Bricktop, he was overwhelmed by her long, beautiful legs. She had "talking legs and talking feet," he said, and asked if she could dance the Charleston. She did. And then he asked if she could teach the dance to him and his friends. She did. Night after night, Cole brought his famous friends to her little club, including the Murphys, and they in turn brought more friends. Soon, the failing enterprise of a few months before became the most exciting cabaret in Paris.

When Harpo was introduced to the red-haired, freckled-faced American Negress, he was so tickled that he poured his highball over his head to cool off.

And the club was hopping, all right. The band was pumping out a hot little number when we walked in, and people were dancing and chatting away, and it was so jam-packed with color and loud with laughter and drunk with cheer that if you took a stick to it, the little room would have exploded like a Mexican piñata. I just loved it!

"This *is* a surprise!"

I turned at the sound of the familiar voice to see the familiar face of Zelda Fitzgerald coming in for a hug. The glass she was holding spilled a little bit of champagne on my sleeve, which Woodrow, whom I was holding, mopped up.

"It certainly is," I said. "Ernest said I wouldn't see you until lunch tomorrow."

I waved to Scott, a few heads away. He was talking with Mr. Benchley.

"Zelda, I want you to meet Soledad Soleil. We met on the boat."

"Oh," said Zelda, looking at Soledad with squinty eyes as if trying to place her face. "I know the name, and I know I've seen your picture in—where?—*Vanity Fair?* Or was it *Town & Country?* One of those horsey magazines like *Thoroughbred Monthly*—I know! You're that mystery writer. Yeah, hello."

She cut through the queue lining the bar, and yelled at *le barman* to break open a bottle of champagne. Then she turned and asked, "How was the crossing? You survived a week with Hemingway?"

"Murder and mayhem," said Soledad, but Zelda had no idea how true the statement was.

"Where's the son-of-a-bitch, anyway? I don't see him," she said, patting Woodrow's head.

"Ernest went back home after dinner at Michaud's. He didn't want to come."

"I should say not! Too many homosexuals around—he doesn't like fairies, you know. Did he tell you he used to carry a knife for protection, just in case he was accosted by a fag?"

"Not yet," I said.

"Well, he'll tell you about it someday; he likes to tell that story."

"I think he was just tired and wanted to go home." I said.

"Tired, shit! He's gone home to write down everything you all said during dinner before he forgets, so he can make a book out of it. Watch out what you all say to him. *An original voice*, my ass!" She said it as if she were quoting a review.

There was no place to sit, but a waiter carried over a tray of glasses filled with champagne. We each took one, and then Zelda yelled out over people's heads for Scott to bring the gang for a drink.

"Have you read Hem's new book?" I asked.

"The one he went off to New York to sell?" She took a sip from her glass and then offered the rest of it to Woodrow as she continued, "The one about bullfighting, bull-slinging, and bullshit?"

Soledad and I looked at each other and burst out laughing. Zelda didn't appear to find what she'd said particularly funny, and I saw that she was not joking. She didn't like Hem, even though her husband considered him a great writer and tried to help him and generally thought the world of him. And from what I gathered from spending time with Hem, he didn't have much use for the flapper type; they were all style and no substance as far as he was concerned, and Zelda was the embodiment of today's popular feminine image. She had once said to me, back in New York after the birth of her daughter, Scottie, that she wanted the child to grow up to be a flapper, "to be free and know her own mind, and live a happy and gay life."

I looked at her now, after not seeing her for a good three years, and was sad to see a little of her youthful bloom had faded; the lines around her mouth that once had appeared only when she smiled were now embedded and visible when her face was at rest, and the skin around her jaw hung a little slack. I thought she was playing too hard, running too fast, and drinking too much. Zelda was not a great beauty, but there was this aura about her, an excitement—she vibrated enthusiasm. With that level gaze of hers, blue eyes fixed straight at whomever she was addressing or listening to, one couldn't help but be drawn in. Her spontaneity was charming, too. She never bothered with much small talk; it was always the bigger things, ideas, and points of view that she set her thinking to. I liked her directness; I liked the way she showed no fear in what she said or did. The surprises she sprung weren't founded on an ability to be witty; they were the results of a deeper intellect and were sparked like spontaneous combustion in her mind. Sometimes, from out of the blue, she'd say things that would make you wonder to what far-reaching place her mind had wandered. If you didn't know her well enough, you'd be a little shocked. If you had spent a lot of time in her company, you would just smile and let the strange comment go as the result of too much champagne and not enough sleep.

The music changed tempo and then Bricktop began to sing "Embraceable You" in French. She and her dancers did a Charleston, and the club was smoky and hot, and there was no place to sit, and I couldn't put Woodrow on the floor or he would have been trampled in the crush, so I held him sleeping in my arms. The men all bought cigars, which were the signature smokes of *la doyenne* of café society, and went out to the courtyard to light up. Soledad, Zelda, Sara, and I followed.

"Where are you staying?" asked Scott.

"Fleabag Central," I replied.

"Oh, it's not that bad," chuckled Mr. Benchley. "Toughens the spirit, you know?"

I countered his remark. "For a man who's lived with crabs and bunked with rats, fleas ain't so bad, I suppose."

"Let me guess," said Zelda, "Hem got the rooms for you."

"*Zel-da!*" jumped in Scott, "be a honey, will you. I'm sure Ernest thought—"

"Yeah, yeah, well, I don't know what the hell he was thinking. You must check into the Ritz. Scott, in the morning we'll send the chauffeur over there to get their trunks—no two ways about it, now, Dottie, I won't have Woodrow infested." Zelda bent down to pet Woodrow, who was lying on the walk, asleep on his back. "What's wrong with the little thing?" she said when he didn't respond to her touch. "Is he *dead?*"

"He's drunk!" said Scott, and he was right. "Tell me you didn't pollute the little lad with—"

"So he had a drink, what's the big deal; at least he's happy."

Once again I scooped up Woodrow into my arms. His snoring made everybody laugh. And when Harpo suddenly emerged from the club he thought we were laughing at him.

"It's Woodrow; he's drunk and he's snoring like your uncle!" said Scott.

"My uncle? Uncle Jake warned me never to do an act with a kid or a dog. They get all the laughs."

"Harpo," said Zelda, "don't you think that Al Jolson is just like Christ?"

"Oh, brother!" said Scott.

Harpo stared back at Zelda's penetrating eyes, and decided to contemplate the absurd comparison that came from out of the blue, because in some portion of Zelda's intoxicated mind this was a serious consideration, and Harpo was never unkind.

"They have a lot in common; they are both Jewish and only-begotten sons, who love their mammies. And they both command an audience, so they have a lot of fans." And then, as an afterthought, he added, "But Jolson can sure belt out a hell of a great tune."

"On the contrary, Harpo, my boy; Jolson is not an only-begotten son. He does, indeed, have a brother."

"Shut up, Aleck," replied Harpo.

The Murphys, Soledad, Aleck, and Harpo got into Scott and Zelda's chauffeur-driven car, and the rest of us crammed into a cab to follow them to the next nightspot.

But, there appeared to be a diversion. The Fitzgeralds' car made a few unpredictable turns, and we entered the rue Notre-Dame-des-Champs before slowing to a stop at the curb.

Scott leaped out of his car as Zelda hung out from the window yelling at him to come back. But after a few indistinguishable words to her, Scott turned and walked through the courtyard of number one-thirteen.

Mr. Benchley asked the taxi driver to wait and we all got out of the cab and walked to the car. Zelda practically flew out of the automobile and after Scott, and then Gerald Murphy slowly stepped out through the street-side door and walked around to meet us.

"Scott wants Ernest to join us," he said, pulling from his coat his cigarette case and offering it around. He watched Zelda as she grabbed onto Scott's arm, pleading with him to return to the car. I heard the doorbell and the concierge's window brightened slowly as a lamp was lit—the yellow glow of gaslight. Gerald said no more, but I could see the trying of his patience in his demeanor, his eyebrow raised, a hand slipped into his coat pocket, as he just stood there, watching. The only thing that revealed his tension was the rush of smoke as he exhaled.

Sara and Soledad stayed in the car, chatting with Aleck, who wouldn't budge his ponderous physique from a comfortable position unless it was absolutely a matter of life and death or on the request of a rumbling stomach. Sara leaned out of the car window to say, "Scott, dear, I don't believe he's home—or perhaps Hem's asleep. You can see the apartment is dark."

Mathew said, "He's probably sleeping—that's what he said he was going to do when he left us after dinner. I should stop Scott from waking the concierge. Hem gave me the key to the front door."

But it was too late. Woodrow was awake, and the effects of the champagne he had imbibed were wearing off because he began pulling at his leash toward the ruckus playing out between the concierge, Scott, and Zelda.

"Now, listen, you!" Scott barked at the night-robed woman of uncertain years. "I demand to see him. What have you done to our friend?"

"Scott! Don't be an ass; the man's not home," yelled Zelda.

Gerald pitched his cigarette to the ground, stamped it out, and walked over to Scott. "Get into the car, boy; everyone is waiting on you. *Scottie!* Ernest is not here, and you are behaving abominably."

The concierge made shooing motions at the couple, obviously not understanding why the man was yelling at her with such force. She didn't understand a word of English. With a scowl, she stuck out her lips and told him where to go, by the sound of it, and then, shaking her fist, she backed up into the entryway and shut the door in his face. By this time, several windows around the courtyard over the sawmill had been thrown open and there began a series of taunts and threats and jeers. A dog started barking and from the rooms inside the building I could hear a baby crying and the voices of others shaken from sleep.

"Hem!" shouted Scott, "come down here right away. We need you to settle something. That fellow up there—" he shouted, pointing at a scruffy-looking bald man in his union suit who was hanging out over the little balcony on the second floor, "he has insulted me!"

The man was about to climb down from the balcony when his wife started to yell at him to come in. She, too, began to curse the couple in the courtyard.

Harpo, who'd joined us at the curb, said: "This is just like back home on East Ninety-Third Street! Only they're yelling in French instead of German!"

Mathew walked to Scott's side and told him that he thought maybe Hem had gone out, and that when he and Hem had settled in after their train ride Hem had gone out to use a telephone, and Mathew figured he was arranging a meeting. This explanation, and Gerald's hand on his shoulder, appeared to placate the insistent Scott, who then turned back to the car with a new plan to track down his friend. Zelda trailed behind him, spent from the game of tug-of-war with her husband.

After our first bar stop in search of Hemingway, Aleck, obviously tired of the pointless mission, begged to be excused to go back to the Hôtel Crillon, where he and Harpo were staying.

Harpo said, "See you all tomorrow," when we hit the second bar on the Hemingway search. Within the five minutes we were there he was deep in conversation with a girl who had let him light her cigarette. The Murphys took our cab, to be dropped off at their apartment. So Woodrow and I, Mr. Benchley, Soledad, and Mathew hopped into Scott's car to continue the search for the wayward Ernest Hemingway.

We found him at the third stop: the Dingo Bar.

Hem was at a table with Daphne, and at first I thought they were alone, until Ronnie emerged from the crowd with a woman who had a haggard air about her. She was very rough looking, and her black hair was lank and, on closer view, oily and needed washing. Her eyes were rimmed with dark lines and her mouth was a red slash and her skin had an unhealthy-looking pallor. She was very thin, and her arms were bare; she wore an orange blouse, which was none too clean, off the shoulders to show her brittle shoulder blades, and a tight-fitting black satin slit skirt. There was no doubt of her profession. When Ronnie sat down she took his lap.

"You see?" said Scott to a weary Zelda, "I told you he'd be here."

"You didn't know nothin' like that," she replied, deliberately fracturing her English. "Why do you want to spoil a perfectly lovely night?"

When Hem saw us, he didn't even look non-plussed at our unexpected appearance, notwithstanding a couple of hours ago he had claimed exhaustion. He simply stood and grabbed available chairs for me and Soledad to sit. Zelda made a beeline to the bar.

"We met up at Bricktop's," said Mr. Benchley, by way of explanation of the inclusion of Scott and Zelda.

A table cleared, and Mr. Benchley and Mathew brought over a few more chairs. Zelda returned from the bar, and when she was offered a chair she told Scott to sit and then mimicked the girl on Ronnie's lap by sitting on Scott's. Her arms around him, she pecked his cheek.

"I was looking for you," said Scott. "I wanted you to settle something."

"What's that?" asked Hem.

"It was important; I don't remember now."

Hem introduced Scott and Zelda to Daphne and Ronnie and *Pipette,* who claimed, too readily, that she was a cashier—not that anyone asked her; she probably offered the information so we wouldn't presume her a prostitute. I supposed cashiering was her day job.

She trumped Zelda's kiss on Scott's cheek by planting a full one smack on Ronnie's mouth. Daphne didn't seem to give it a thought, and if she was miffed it was probably because her cozy *tête-à-tête* with Hem had been interrupted.

"Can't a chap get a drink around here?" she said after draining her glass.

"What'll you have?" asked Scott.

"Thanks, a brandy and soda."

"Right you are; I'll fix that right up."

Scott didn't budge. Well, he couldn't; Zelda kept her stranglehold around his neck. "Bobby, tell the waiter to bring a bottle of brandy and a siphon of soda, would you?"

"What will you have?" he asked Zelda.

"I'll stick to champagne; what about you girls?"

We agreed that was best, and although Pipette spoke not a word of conversational English, she did say, "hansum mon, hansum mon" repeatedly to Ronnie, her eyes widening greedily when she saw the bottle arrive and a glass flute placed before her.

Zelda said, "Have you ever seen Sara Murphy sip champagne?" She lifted her glass and imitated Sara's cultured tone: "One must look *to-ward* the heavens, as the glass touches the lips."

After a few minutes Daphne announced, "I need to bathe."

So do I need a bath, I thought. From this company I felt soiled and oily, like Pipette's hair, and it wasn't just the result of a long exhausting day hopping from a boat to a train to a dozen nightspots. Woodrow and I needed a bed, even if it were a bit lumpy. Zelda had stopped talking altogether and spent the time we were at the Dingo watching Hemingway with her hawk eyes, which was a bit unnerving. I expected her at any moment to fly at his neck and say something like, "What makes you think you're such a hot shit?" Woodrow, who'd been snoring on my lap, poor dear, opened one suspicious eye. He would never trust

Zelda again. He'd have a hangover in the morning. At around two o'clock we called it a night.

As we waited for the chauffeur to bring the car, Soledad looked at me and said in a whisper, "There's no love between Zelda and Hem."

"Well, he called her crazy, and Scott foolishly told her, and Hem says she deliberately interferes with Scott's work. No love between them."

"That Ronnie, what *does* she see in him?"

"She'll move on, soon as she's licked all the gilt off his ass."

"I was talking about what *Daphne* sees in Ronnie, Dorothy, not that sad little 'Puppet' sitting on his lap," she corrected.

"Aren't they the same?" I replied, realizing that some behavior transcends class. "And I *was* talking about Lady Daphne."

———◆———

I was in a tranquil glen surrounded by woods. I heard the buzzing of bees around my head and the twitter of birds in the low bushes. There floated on the breeze the high-pitched melody of a Pan flute, and I marveled at the specter of the satyr emerging through the line of trees. The yellow eyes of the creature bore into mine; a shiver ran through me when I heard its goat-like bray . . . . The bee buzzed dizzily around the clover, and then landed on my nose.

I awoke with a start, having smacked myself awake. No one else could have struck me, I realized, as I looked around the shabby room, because I was alone, except for Woodrow sleeping at the foot of the bed, and the horsefly that was still screaming and whining around my face.

I was in my seedy hotel room, which, with the sun streaming in, was a bit cheerier than in the shadowy night. And yet the dreamscape lingered after I sat up and threw off the covers. The music of a Pan flute persisted, as did the *baa*ing of goats. I rose stiffly from the bed and Woodrow followed me to the window. I pushed aside the tired-looking curtains, pulled open the French doors, and stepped out onto the little balcony for a better view of the courtyard below. At the pavement was a goatherd with his flock, playing his flute as women from the surrounding houses, carrying empty pails, gathered in the yard and began milking the goats while chattering happily. Such a thing as this I had not seen since I was a very little girl, growing up before the turn of the century on the Upper West Side of New York. At that time the land was still a landscape of farms and shanties bordering rectangular tracts where brownstone houses had begun to fill Manhattan's grid plots all the way up to Riverdale. I watched with fascination the country ways in a modern urban setting. And then I lifted my eyes to the view beyond the roofs across the yard.

The rising sun brushed the city into a golden sfumato landscape. The Seine, a short distance away, shimmered. The fragrant spring air was balm for my spirit, and the warm, yeasty aroma of baking bread wafted seductively along the breeze and lent a feeling of well-being. I wanted to run outside and see and explore and eat the warm bread and capture the heart of Paris for my own. So this was why Hemingway had put us here in *la dump*: to see his glorious city at its best advantage. I couldn't fault him for it. Even after the noisy bedroom gymnastics in the room above mine at three in the morning, I could forgive him because of this view, this moment of beauty.

Woodrow appeared completely recovered from last night's bender with Zelda. Not I, however. But I would try to ignore my lingering headache. As I backed away from the window to wash and dress, my spirit was ready to take on the town even if my body wasn't.

Mr. Benchley knocked on the door as I was fetching my coat. He was cleanly shaved and looked refreshed after just a couple of hours' sleep. He was sporting a navy-blue wool beret.

"*Bonjour, Madame Park-aire!*"

"Oh, jeez!" I replied when I saw the dark glasses, the slanted beret, and the red-silk neckerchief. "Ya tryin' to look like a tourist, or something?"

"Don't you like it? I think it works," he said, checking his image in the little mirror above the vanity.

"The beret was a gift from Gerald last time I was here."

"What the hell is *that*? You carrying a purse, now?"

"Oh, this," he said, holding up the brown-leather bag that looked like a satchel and whose long strap was draped over one shoulder and worn across his chest like a sash. "This is my Noah bag. Gerald designed it for me, you know, and his people at Mark Cross stitched it up."

"I haven't seen you carry it before."

"Can't in New York; people would think I'm the mailman."

"Looks like a feed bag."

"Exactly! My, you are smart, *Madame Park-aire!*"

"Now you have a place to store your wild oats when not sowing them," I said. "But, why do you call it a Noah bag?"

"It's so big I can put two—"

"—of everything in it."

"*Ex-ac-te-ment!*" he said. "Woodrow and I are starving, and if we want a pail of warm goat's milk, we will have to shake a leg—or pull a teat."

"Just a second," I said, pulling on my hat.

"You have my briefcase!"

"Yes. Since the afternoon Saul died, remember? You were walking around with it and when you came to my cabin for a drink, I told you to put the damn thing down."

"That's right; you said I looked like your accountant—which I certainly *do not*. He is bald and half-a-foot shorter than I."

"You both have hair growing out of your ears."

"Yes, but I have mine Marcelled."

"What are you doing?" I asked when he removed his key ring and picked out the small key. "I thought you were starving? I know *we* are, aren't we, Woodrow, aren't we, now, sweetie pie?"

"Better not call me *sweetie pie*; Mrs. Benchley wouldn't like it."

"I call you a shit and she doesn't bat an eye."

"That's different," he said, mindlessly, because he was struggling with the key and briefcase lock. "For goodness sake, what's with this? It won't open. Don't tell me I brought the wrong key!"

"I won't, but do you have to do that now?" I asked, standing there with Woodrow on his leash, and *huff*ing my impatience as my friend examined the briefcase.

"This isn't mine. Yet, it looks exactly like mine—"

"*Ex-act-e-ment!*"

"Mark Cross, same color, the handle a bit worn, but no initials, so certainly *not* mine!"

"Now that we've got that straightened out, let's go."

"Just a moment," he said, pulling out his Swiss Army knife and finding the toothpick. "I have to return this case to whomever it belongs to; whoever the fellow is, he now has a briefcase with my initials stamped in gold on it. Perhaps there's something inside to tell us who he is."

"What would we do without that Boy Scout gadget of yours? I've grown rather fond of it. We could break into the federal mint with it if you weren't so chicken. Why else have I toted you along with me all these years?"

"Yes, a multipurpose little tool."

"My words to describe you *exactly!*"

"I'll get you one for your birthday. *Voila!*"

Mr. Benchley flipped the lock strap and pulled open the case. He began to remove a couple of books—one entitled *Succulent Plants*, the other *Winning at Chess: A Strategy for Living*.

"Why carry a briefcase for a couple of old books?" he said. "Why, there's nothing in here to tell whom this belongs to."

"All right, so you wire the steamship company and have them pick it up. Can we go? I want my goat's milk."

We walked down the narrow, curving flights of stairs and out through the courtyard, empty now of goats and milkers. Woodrow picked up their peculiar scent, and when we walked out onto the street he spotted the gang up ahead and just had to investigate. I humored him and we caught up to the goatherd, a Pied-Piper leading the way. Women who were filling their milk pails stopped what they were doing at the sight of my Boston terrier, who insisted on sniffing each goat in the flock, and nearly got kicked by one and gored by another while I tried to pull him away. He was becoming a nuisance, so Mr. Benchley scooped him up in his arms. The goatherd was a kindly soul, and asked, "*Comment s'appelle le petit chien?*"

I replied, "Woodrow Wilson."

He laughed and said the dog resembled more "*Win-stone Church-ille.*" The women were anxious to know our discussion, so the goatherd announced the presence of the great President of the United States who had negotiated the peace with the even-greater French statesman, Georges Clemenceau, for the Treaty of Versailles.

One of the ladies said, "*Il faut offrir le président à boire; c'est tout juste.*"

.

And so he took the tin cup dangling from his belt, dipped it into her pail, and offered Woodrow the milk.

Woodrow sated, we continued along the narrow street flanked by buildings adorned with the elaborate architectural embellishments of centuries past and on toward the source of fragrant baking. In the soft morning light of this false spring day I saw the Parisian streets through a painter's eyes, a canvas composed of a blending of monochromatic whites and creams with bronze finishes, where for all my life I had walked through the gray-and-lavender canyons of my beloved New York landscape.

We passed a flock of Catholic-school girls, walking two by two in their blue wool capes and wide-brimmed hats behind a pair of scrubbed-faced black-habited nuns. We skirted the splash of water from a bucket emptied by a shopkeeper about to wash and sweep clean the front pavement of his establishment. The neighborhood echoed like a bugle aimed at the sky with the voices of progress—of chores and of morning routines, of the rhythm of the goings and comings of commerce, of the clatter of wheels and horses' hooves on the increasingly trafficked cobbles—and close by a church bell struck the hour with a hearty "*Bonjour!*"

My mouth was watering when we arrived at the *patisserie* and stared at the various delights in the window. Cakes stuffed with creams and overflowing with chocolate and berries and currants and almonds and puffed and sugared and layered and floridly decorated. A little café was situated through a side door, and there we gorged ourselves on buttery, flakey *croissants* and *pain au chocolat* washed down with cups of *café au lait* until we were drunk and full and happy.

Our trunks had been delivered, but, as promised, Zelda sent a bus from the Ritz to pick them up, and as we settled our bill of fifteen francs each for the night we'd spent I felt a little sad. We were moving to more luxurious accommodations—heck, the Paris sewers would seem more luxurious—but for some reason I felt a growing nostalgia. I doubted any view from the Ritz would thrill me as much as my first glimpse of Paris at dawn from the terrace of this lodging a few streets off the Boulevard St.-Germain.

———◆———

Aleck, who was staying at the Crillon, tracked us down at the Ritz and had his itinerary ready for us to follow, with himself as our tour guide, during the afternoon. There was no arguing when it came to his plans, for he would see a suggested alteration as an inconsiderate and ungrateful challenge of his authority. He might not hold a grudge against you for long, but while he did you'd have rather been shot by a firing squad to end your misery.

So, having "wasted" his morning and our chance for a tour of the Eiffel Tower by our tardy arrival, we were duly reprimanded. It was bad enough that Harpo was "off chasing some little tart from last evening" and had yet to return to his room! He officiously instructed Mr. Benchley and me to be ready at twelve-thirty for a one o'clock luncheon at Pruniers. His nose was suitably put out of joint when we had to wait ten minutes for Scott and Zelda to come down the elevator from their suite. He was partially placated when Soledad arrived and glamorously made her entrance into the grand lobby dressed and furred in a cream-colored wool ensemble, only because she paid proper homage to the famous critic by walking directly to him with open arms and planting kisses on both his cheeks *à la française* before acknowledging the rest of us. It was when Hemingway appeared and told us he wanted to take us for a special meal at Bas Meudon, a short ride down along the river, and that he had arranged for us to later pay a call on his friend Gertrude Stein, that I was sure Aleck was about to bust a gut. Then a telegram was handed him by a bellboy. The Murphys would not be joining us this afternoon, but hoped we would stop in for cocktails before they took us all to dinner at Maxim's. I was watching to see whether *that* had pushed Aleck over the edge, but suddenly his truculence blew away with a great *huff* of resignation, and he pointedly announced, "Follow!" and led us all out into the street to fetch cabs.

"It's a place out of a Maupassant story, isn't it Aleck?" said Hem, looking out over the view from La

Pêche Miraculeuse, an open-air restaurant hung over the river at Bas Meudon. Aleck dove into his third plateful of deliciously crispy *fritures*, a delicately plump fried fish that the French called *goujon*. "And the view is like a painting by Sisley. In fact, he did many paintings of the Seine from along this stretch."

"I'm sure he did. Pour me some more of the Muscadet," directed Aleck.

He was content, now; good food always leveled his mood, and he was charmed by Hem, whom he addressed as "Ernest." He smiled as he lifted his gaze from the fish on his plate to the scene before him. "*C'est bien un poisson delicieux*, I must admit," he said, and nodded and lifted the glass of white wine to his lips.

The river shined crystalline in the vibrant sunshine of the afternoon, and the quaint village buildings were picturesquely standing guard along its banks. Occasionally, a barge would pass on its journey to or from the city. Elms leaned toward the water's edge, bearing tight buds in clusters like little yellow fists. In a few days, if the weather held, or a few weeks, if not, they would loosen their tender grasp like the fingers of newborns to canopy the gentle slopes.

Remarkably, Scott and Zelda made no improper comments, although Zelda avoided any exchange of conversation with Hem and chattered on about their plans for the summer, the renting of a house in

Juan-les-Pins where Scott could work and she and their daughter, Scottie, could sun and swim.

Mr. Benchley was unusually subdued during the meal. At one point, he passed me a slip of paper where he'd listed "words you will have little use for: *vernisser*—to varnish, *egriser*—to grind diamonds, *dromer*—to make one's neck stiff from working at a sewing machine, *ganache*—the lower jaw of a horse, and *pardon*—I beg your pardon," and then fell into a quiet funk.

As we were leaving the luncheon, he turned to me and said, "That briefcase . . . I'll bet it belonged to the deceased Charles Latham. The baggage had my ship's cabin number on it, before you changed it to yours, and my briefcase hasn't turned up. Oh, I'm not so concerned with finding mine—there was nothing of great value in it, just an address book and a notebook with a few scribbles in it. But, for Latham to carry such a briefcase containing just a couple of mundane manuals . . . it makes me think there might be a clue in the books. I think we should look things over again with a more critical eye."

"Well, you left it in my room this morning, remember? So when our luggage was sent over to the Ritz, it was probably put in my room."

"I think it's important to do it now."

We begged off the visit to Gertrude Stein's salon, but expressed our desire to do it another day. Hem looked disappointed, and when Soledad announced she had an appointment and Aleck said he was meeting Cole Porter at the Crillon bar, the party disbanded. Scott and Zelda were not invited to Gertrude's anyway—not after what Zelda had once said about the Picasso portrait of Stein hanging in the latter's parlor: "Looks like an old Roman Emperor."

Once back in my lovely, clean room—without a view—Mr. Benchley took up the briefcase, removed the books, and flipped through their pages. Nothing appeared to have been disturbed in the bindings, nor had the front or back cover papers been unglued to hide any kind of letter or document. But when he was about to return the books into the briefcase, his expression reflected the dawning of an idea. He opened his trusty Swiss Army knife and used it to pry apart the leather-lined bottom interior lining of the case.

"It seems like there is something here—see, here," he said, and I walked over to the bed on which he was sitting and watched as he pulled away the pig-skin-covered panel on the bottom of the case with a gentle tug.

"*Voila!* A secret compartment!" he said, taking out a legal-size white envelope and slitting the top fold with his knife. I sat next to him and looked over his shoulder as he unfolded the enclosed sheet of paper.

"It's a list of names," he said, staring at the dozen or so names scribbled by hand on the sheet.

"Was this what they were after?" I asked. "Was this what they hoped to get from Charles Latham? A list of names worth killing for?"

"Why else hide such a thing as this if it didn't have some value?"

"These are mostly French names."

"We need to give this to Richard Hartley," said Mr. Benchley.

"Wait," I said, as he reached for the telephone on the nightstand. "What if he's one of them?"

"*Them?*"

"Whoever *them* is . . . . What if he's on the other side?"

"Am I to gather that when you refer to *them* and *the other side* you mean the Soviets?"

"I don't know who *them* or *the other side* really is."

"Well, that clears things up. Shall we do an algebraic equation? If *them* is X and *the other side* is Y, how many miles to Cairo?"

"Well, I'm glad one of us knows what I'm talking about, even if I don't."

"I won't try to figure out what you just said. I'm having enough trouble getting along in French; I cannot allow your ubiquitous obliquity to confuse me. It's obvious to me, though, that you don't trust Richard."

"I'm not sure about Richard," I said. "I am just not sure if he is all that innocent, by the story he gave us on the train. What if he wanted to get the Duchess here to Paris and into his own clutches? What if *he* killed Latham? What if *he* set up the plan to kidnap the Duchess Sofia? What if he's one of the bad guys?"

"That's a lot of *what-if*s."

"Well, I know he didn't tell us the whole truth about what was going on."

"So, you don't want him to have this?" said Mr. Benchley. "But, what if he's not one of the bad guys? What if he's a good guy? What if—"

"Now *you're* on a roll of *what-if*s!" I laughed. And then I agonized: "Oh, I've been wrong about men so often that I don't know the difference anymore between a man I can trust and one who's a cad!"

"I'm giving this list of names to Richard," stated Mr. Benchley. "Decision made."

"Shouldn't we flip a coin, or play rock, paper, scissors, or something?"

"Or, we could shoot craps and the winner takes all," he said sarcastically, picking up the receiver.

There was no answer at the Murphys', and then I remembered that they had offered their Villa America to Richard as a safe haven for the Duchess, and the plan was to move her and Major Arbuthnot there this morning.

"We need to call him there," said my friend, and then, reconsidering: "But I doubt the telephone's hooked up; they close up the place for the winter."

"But Gerald and Sara will be back at their apartment soon for six-o'clock cocktails. They're expecting us. Maybe we can wire him at their villa."

"Claude Dubois' name is on this list, Mrs. Parker."

"I saw that."

———◆———

"They left before dawn, Dorothy," said Gerald, handing me a drink. "Richard and his friend, Dubois. Hired a car, and off they went with our blessings to the Villa America."

"Was Richard planning to return to Paris once he delivered them there safely? Did he say?" asked Mr. Benchley.

"I don't know, Bobby. But let's send a wire. They should be there by now."

The sparsely furnished apartment was decorated with an eclectic arrangement of modern fixtures in black and white and red; the walls were stark white, the floors painted with a glossy black lacquer, and on them were scattered white Mexican rugs. Upon the rugs were set black-upholstered chairs and sofa and mirror-topped tables. Sara, dressed in lovely flow-

command that had made her famous fifteen years before as a headliner. She was assisted by handsome male dancers and accompanied by a full string orchestra. Most of the audience was composed of tourists, American and British. Drunk or sober, all were in a celebratory mood. We talked about nothing of any consequence and just absorbed the festive feeling of the place.

I won't admit it to anyone, but I didn't yearn to come to Paris to see the Louvre, or the Luxembourg Gardens, or the grandeur of Versailles. What I really wanted to see and experience was the spectacle of the cancan danced to its flamboyant music that lifted the spirits as high as the ladies could kick up their skirts.

"It is a myth," said Sara, "that the cancan is, or ever was, danced sans bloomers."

"Of course, never in a public hall," added Gerald.

When the house went dark and the stage lights brightened and the orchestra played the introduction I stiffened with excitement. On the upbeat the conductor signaled his musicians and from the stage wings flew out the feathery-head-dressed, petty-coated, colorfully skirted women. In unison with each other and with the throbbing beat of the music, the line of dancers kicked their black-and-red-and-blue stockinged legs to brazenly show off their snowy-white bloomers to the crowd. It was all color and light and a whirl-wind carousel of movement—a rambunctious dance performed to the equally rambunctious and unbridled "*Galop*" from Offenbach's *Orphée aux Enfers*. It was all enough to make a grown woman squeal like a kid, and a grown man—well, Mr. Benchley grabbed my hand and led me through the labyrinth of tables, abandoning the Murphys and Aleck to get a close-up look at the stage. If I was bouncing around like a five-year-old, unable to stand still, clapping my hands and hooting and cheering and whistling with the hundreds of others watching, he stood transfixed by the fluttering of ruffled fabrics and the long, bouncing kicks. When the line of girls circled and then turned their backs to the crowd and flipped their skirts up in the air over their heads to show their ruffle-covered *derrières*, I thought his jaw would hit the floor. Of course, he was putting on his own show for me, my man-of-the-world, Fred, covering his eyes and peeking through parted fingers. And it made me laugh even more when, one after another, each lovely lady in turn leaped up and then hit the floor in a split, and my friend crossed his legs and repeated "*Ouch!*" with every landing.

I found it curious that Mr. Benchley had not checked his silk topper at the cloakroom, but carried it to the stage. There formed a line of men, in dinner wear and similarly toppered, queuing up below the footlights. Then the gentlemen in procession walked up the steps and onto the stage, as the line of dancers swished their way over to meet them. One after the other they knocked the toppers off each head with a high kick to the rhythm of the metallic crash of cymbals, affording the tramps a close-up peek at the world-famous ruffled drawers. Mr. Benchley, his hat knocked off and retrieved, bent for a flamboyantly sweeping theatrical bow before leaving the stage. What fun!

When it was all over and the audience kept on cheering, the conductor raised his baton and tapped it once again, and out returned the ladies for an encore. The crowd let out a unanimous cheer of delight, and so the foot-stomping thunder and eye-pleasing wonder of it all began again.

By the time we left the club I was giddy from excitement and, having quenched my thirst on too much champagne, was ready to perform my own cancan, an impossibility as I was attired in a simple sheath dress. As Gerald fetched a cab, I belted out my own a rat-a-tat version of the "*Gallop*," which I continued to hum until Sara and Aleck pressed Gerald to tell the cabbie to bring us to a new location in the Latin Quarter.

"There's more?" I asked, and as Aleck and Sara put their heads together in conspiracy, Gerald offered his alternative—to go back to their apartment so that he could play for us a few of his American Negro folk records. He was gently pooh-poohed for the suggestion as a too-quiet ending to this particular night on the town, and, ever gracious, he relented, directing the cab driver to take us to the Club Tango.

It was a dark little cellar, down a flight of stone steps, one of dozens of cavernous holes created through centuries of stone quarrying around the city. Paris was a city on the verge of imminent collapse; its streets and structures had been shorn-up below its cobbles and were examined by city inspectors on a regular rotation. Gerald said it was estimated that there were a hundred and seventy miles of tunnels under the city; some could be reached through grates in cellars, some via courtyards, others in the sides of hills, still others near the river, and one entrance he knew about was next to the Trocadéro. Even the police didn't know all the locations.

But here, in this windowless, smoke-fogged stone room, a little pocket of heaven and hell converged. It was a tight little space where the tables were set to accommodate a dance floor and a corner for the musicians pumping out a tango for customers who chose to dance. And the clientele were of a different class, by the looks of them—a mix of local toughs and their women and shabby artist-types huddled together at tables over their whiskeys and absinthes. Top-hatted and begowned, I suppose we appeared the high-bouncing rich Americans to the other patrons, just slumming, but we were treated respectfully, and everyone was so into their cups that I don't think they cared about or even noticed us. The exotic smoke of dope mingled with the ever-present fumes of Gitanes seems to have permeated the essence of Parisian establishments, all reminiscent of the lowliest of American speakeasies but for the openness of their service.

We had just gotten settled and had ordered drinks when the accordion music ended with a flourish and a drum-roll brought all to attention. Toward a table, where sat a man and a woman, strutted a tall, thin fellow wearing a billed cap, a red scarf, and a Breton-striped polo shirt tucked into tight-fitting sailor trousers. He lit a cigarette, took a long drag off it, and then stamped it out on the ground. The music accentuated his every dramatic gesture. He looked fierce.

He grabbed the woman at the table by her hair, and pulled her head back for a kiss, and the tango music, rife with staccato breaks, began to play.

The man sitting at the table leaped up to challenge the interloper, and there ensued a stylized fight—a right to the chin and a left to the gut—and the man-at-the-table rolled onto the dance floor and somersaulted to his feet. This choreographed acrobatic show of force was comically and gracefully repeated, until the man who'd been sitting with the woman dashed away.

The Breton-striped fellow then grabbed the elbow of the woman and lifted her to her feet, and with a swift turn of his hand brought her into a tight hold against his chest. She broke free and he caught her hand and whirled her back to him, and the dance began in earnest. They moved across the floor in long slides as if their bodies were glued together. They moved as one, with dips and twirls. Then she slapped his face, and he struck hers. The woman's head was whipped to the side at the strike of his hand. He flung her to the floor and she slid smoothly across it, only to be retrieved by her lover. He again hurled her aside until she first pawed at, and then crawled up, his trouser leg. As she rose to her feet, he gripped her by hand and by foot and flung her through the air in an arched circle until she landed on her belly to spin on the floor like a top. As if that were not enough, he pulled her up tightly against himself for another long tango stride, only to toss her away again like a ragdoll. He finally carried her offstage, upside down, over his shoulder. Now, I am a modern woman who abhors the brutish tendencies of men who might ever think it all right to strike a woman, but I had to laugh to myself at the absurd and violent drama of it all!

When it was over, and we were in the cab on the way to the Murphys' for a nightcap, Aleck told me the history of the dance, which had gained popularity with the street gangs known as The Gunmen of Paris in the *Caveau des Innocents* (the underworld clubs).

"*La Danse Apache* got its name from the Montmartre club where, outside its doors one night, two men and a woman, members of a gang, had a knock-down-drag-out fight. They fought with the ferocity

of Apaches, it was said, and so the name of the club
and the passion of the battle stuck, and the fight has
been repeatedly recreated with individual variations
ever since."

Aleck is a fount of knowledge, and this was a
story that didn't bore, so I didn't mind his pontifica-
tion on the subject.

Mr. Benchley decided that we should perfect
an *Apache* dance of our own.

"I will gladly slap your face and stomp your feet
whenever you like, Mr. Benchley."

Our taxi slowed as we approached the Murphys'
apartment. There was a crush of automobile lights
ahead on quai des Grands-Augustins, and stark light
washing up from below the street level, from under
the steps leading to the promenade walk along the
river. The gendarme walked up to the cab and told
our driver that the road was closed and to take the
detour. When Gerald asked what the matter was, the
gendarme said there had been an accident.

"Suicide?"

"*Non.*"

We got out of the taxi since it was a short walk
to the door of the apartment, only one street ahead.

Woodrow, wedged between Baoth and Patrick
like a cuddly stuffed bear, opened one wary eye when
Sara and I entered the bedroom. Honoria was asleep
at the foot of the little bed they had all piled into

for the privilege of his company. We smiled at each other and left the door slightly ajar, in case Woodrow decided to come home with me. We reentered the drawing room and Aleck poured the cognac while I walked over to Gerald and Mr. Benchley, who were at the French doors handing back and forth a pair of binoculars. Their silence was telling. I put out my hand and Mr. Benchley handed them over.

From the height of the window above the street one could see a section of the walkway along the Seine, and there, because of the illumination and the power of the binoculars, I was afforded a Nickelodeon-like view of the activities. Policemen were cordoning off the area and stretchers were being carried down the steps leading to the promenade. The prone bodies of two men were the focus of attention. A camera flash chronicling the morbid discovery brought a flash of discovery to me, when the face of one of the men lying lifeless on the stone walk struck instant recognition. I must have gasped, because Gerald asked, "What is it?" I didn't reply, but instead moved my attention toward the other victim a few paces away. The man who'd been lying face down was turned over, and when the camera flash washed over his face I saw that his features were not those I had dreaded to identify. By his size, compared to the other victim, I knew who he *couldn't* be. I handed the binoculars back to Gerald.

"Look at the man lying on the left."

"There are people in the way . . . oh! Oh, my . . . it looks like . . ."

"Yes."

"Want to let me in on it?" said Mr. Benchley as Sara and Aleck crowded into the small space.

Gerald handed Mr. Benchley the binoculars and turned toward me. We looked at each other with regret and alarm and sadness all rolled into one unspoken communication.

"Why, that fellow . . . looks like . . ." stuttered Mr. Benchley.

"Oh, for God's sake, Bob!" said Aleck pushing him aside and grabbing the binoculars. He had trouble peering through the lenses because of his own thick spectacles. When he finally focused in he said, "So, who the hell is it?"

It was Sara's turn to look through the field glasses and say, "It looks like him! I think so . . ."

"Well?" demanded Aleck.

"Someone you never saw before Aleck; you don't know him," said Mr. Benchley.

Knowledge of all that had transpired on the crossing, the accidental dangers to Mr. Benchley and Saul Gold's death, had been kept from Aleck, even the arrangement Mr. Benchley had made with the Murphys to provide a safe house for the Duchess Sofia and Major Arbuthnot. He knew nothing about the attempted kidnapping of the couple on the boat train from Cherbourg. That is to say, he knew nothing about *any* of it, not Latham or Russian spies, nothing. And because we all knew the identity of the dead man and he did not, it was now time for him to hear the gory details. I dreaded it, because Aleck not only would take the delayed report as a personal affront, a sort of betrayal, evidence of our lack of trust in him, but he would get all crazy with dread at the remote possibility of being snared in a net of fabulous conspiracy. Believe me when I say we'd been through these kinds of tangles before, Mr. Benchley and I, and we knew what to expect from Aleck. But, don't get me wrong, in our experience, after all the *sturm und drang*, Aleck would always pull himself together to help save the day. So, we all sat down to give him the scoop, about the Duchess, that is. As Mr. Benchley and I had promised Richard that we would not discuss the Latham spy-ring incidents, we left that information out.

"So, you're saying," he began after the telling, with his "back up" as predicted, "that we're dealing with Soviet kidnapping and now murder and intrigue and you didn't say a word to me? Did you ever stop to think that I might be in danger?"

"Come off it, Aleck; nobody here is in any danger," said Mr. Benchley. "As it stands now, the spies are doing a very good job of killing each other off. By the time it gets to be your turn to die, there'll be nobody left to do the job."

"All right, all right!" barked Aleck. "So, now what'll we do?"

I knew the switch was coming—the man of action winning over the sissy—but this was a little too fast. I figured we'd have to wait a week or so before he settled down.

"There is nothing *to* do," I said. "The way it stands, the way Richard Hartley arranged things, we are not, nor do we appear to be, in anyway involved in this affair. So forget *doing* anything."

"But, one of the men involved in protecting the Duchess Sofia has just now been discovered dead a few yards from the Murphys' front door!"

"But no one could have known the Duchess was here, or that Richard Hartley has taken them to the Villa America," said Sara with the steady voice of reason.

"They were probably followed here, and you have innocent children asleep in their beds—"

Gerald raised a hand to stop Aleck's tirade. "I'm sure that the Duchess and the Major have enjoyed, over the years, innumerable weekend parties on country estates. I doubt, through mere association, their hosts have all been done in, Aleck. Not to worry, old sport."

Sara added, "Richard arranged for a bit of *mis*information: Anyone would think the couple was on their way to Venice."

"But the dead man out on the quai!"

I looked at Aleck. "His name is—*was*—Claude Dubois."

Hemingway's bull

Zelda and Scott

The Fitzgeralds and their daughter, Scottie

Gerald and Sara bookend Linda and Cole Porter

Sara and the children

Mistinguett

Passionate Apache dancers

A couple of fun lovin' kids

Artists at a good cafe

Chapter Eleven

I woke up the next morning to a knock on the door and practically leaped out of bed, expecting a telegram from Richard, or Mr. Benchley with news from him, although I knew it unlikely that we would ever hear from him again. Woodrow jumped off the foot of the bed and beat me to the door.

When I opened it I was greeted by a bellboy delivering a huge package tied up with pink ribbons. The size of the box was ungainly, so I asked the young man to place it on my bed as I fetched a five-franc note from my purse as a tip.

I looked at Woodrow; he looked at me. "What are you waiting for?" he was saying in dog language.

I tore off the ribbon, expecting to find some magical treasure inside, perhaps a gift from Seward Collins, the man I'd been seeing a lot of back in New York, and who was to join me in Paris in April. The card must be inside. But before I could lift the lid off the gift box, there was another knock at the door.

I opened the door into the eighteenth century, for there he stood, a sad, defeated Mr. Benchley, dressed in the garb of King Louis XVI, all ruffled lace, with royal-blue velvet waistcoat, white hose and buckled shoes, and a black curly wig with tresses flowing down below his shoulders. He indeed looked like one of the Gish sisters. The homely one.

"You look like an idiot," I said, turning away and back to the task of opening my present. "And you can't hide behind those dark glasses, you know."

"It was worth a try," he said taking them off. "And, no," he said, anticipating my question. "No news from Richard, yet. I just got off the telephone with Gerald. He's heard nothing, either. And we agreed, for everyone's safety, it was best if we didn't. I see that your costume has arrived."

My expectations were dashed when I realized that within the box was the promised Little Bo Peep costume sent over by Aleck for tonight's Festival of Fools.

"Oh, yes," said Mr. Benchley retrieving the be-ribboned shepherd's crook he'd left in the hallway. "This is for you, to complete your look."

"Don't make me tell you where to stick it."

"Now, now, my dear, let's not shoot the messenger!"

"This is all so . . . oh, how can we pretend to be merry and enjoy ourselves with all that's happening? I'm worried sick about Richard and the Duchess and Major Arbuthnot."

Inside the box was the costume of a fantasy shepherdess, for no real live herder of sheep would wear such a thing. They'd freeze to death up on the bonny highlands of Scotland, or Switzerland, or wherever the hell one walked around with sheep.

"I ain't goin'!" I said, knocking the box and all the silly frou-frou onto the floor, upon which Woodrow decided to nest until my temper cooled.

"No use arguing with Aleck, my dear."

"I wouldn't dream of it."

Mr. Benchley admired his luxurious black curls in the mirror. "It should be powdered . . . . So, you don't want to go to the Festival of Fools?" he said, and then frowned at his image. "It really should be powdered."

"Yes, I want to go, but I don't want to look like a fool."

"But that's the point, Mrs. Parker. Look at me! I look the biggest fool of all, and I'm not complaining—mainly because I'm afraid of Aleck and I don't want him sitting on my head like the last time I said *no* to him; I still have problems focusing. Anyway, in this getup I have a real chance of being named King of Fools, and as I'm representing the last Louis of the royal line, who actually *was* a fool, I may have a shot. This outfit could use a crown. After all, if I can't win a Pulitzer, well it's something, anyway . . . ." He then turned back to the mirror and with a look of disdain said, "It really should be powdered, you know. Think I need a beauty-mark on my cheek?"

"Don't get carried away; I won't be able to explain it to your wife."

"What are you doing?"

"Telephoning Harpo," I said.

At noon, with still no word in reply to Mr. Benchley's wire to Richard, Mr. Benchley and I accepted Hem's invitation to have lunch at his favorite café, Closerie des Lilas.

It was a pleasant little café in a nice neighborhood a few streets from the Luxembourg Gardens, just around the corner from Hem's apartment over the sawmill at 113 rue Notre-Dame-des-Champs. Hem said he liked to spend a few hours each day writing over a café crème, or visiting with the usual "suspects" who frequented the café on a regular basis. He was not so happy with the new management, however, who had made all the waiters shave off their moustaches and were trying to cater to a higher class of clientele. But, it was still a "good" café, said Hem, and we had an enjoyable hour.

Harpo telephoned from the lobby to say he was coming up to my room with a solution to my costume problem for this evening. And as Mr. Benchley had expressed concern about his wig, he had acquired a more suitable costume for him as well. Mr. Benchley arrived at my door with Harpo, who was carrying a burlap sack over his shoulder and dressed in the wild wig and old brown coat that he wore when on stage with his brothers.

He opened the sack and pulled out my costume in sections, tossing them on the bed. Woodrow became very curious and began leaping about Harpo. The Marx Brother said, "I know what you're after, Woodie, old dog. I've been carrying this around all day," and then from his spacious coat pocket he pulled out a greasy paper bag and from it pulled a Delmonico steak, which he then presented to my pup. "Nothing but the best for my friend," he said. "Direct from the kitchens of the Crillon!"

Harpo's attention returned to the task at hand, and he began pulling items of clothing from the sack. "Now, Dottie, here's the blouse of a virgin, the vest of an *Apache*, the skirt of a taxi dancer, and some jewels I snatched from a dowager princess."

I wanted to ask how he'd gotten a virgin's shirt, but was afraid to. And at this late hour, when we were to meet with Soledad, Aleck, Hem, and Mathew at the Murphys' for drinks before walking on to join the crowds at the festival, I had little choice: Put on the items he'd brought, or freeze my ass as Little Bo Peep.

"Whattcha got for me?" asked Mr. Benchley. "This wig is itchy and it really should be powdered."

From the sack Harpo pulled out what looked like a cotton nightshift and a tent of purple-and-white fabric embroidered with gold thread. "Not so bad, hum?"

"It's a vestment!" said Mr. Benchley. "Where on earth did you get a vestment?"

"Well, there's this little church, see, just a couple blocks down from—"

"You stole a Catholic priest's vestments?"

"*Borrowed*, *procured*, *snatched*, what's the difference?" said Harpo. "At least no one has to look at those bowed legs of yours."

"I'll have you know that Mrs. Benchley thinks I have very shapely calves."

"So," said Harpo scrutinizing my friend's legs, "when she asks you if her outfit makes her ass look big, do you tell her the truth?"

I came out from the bathroom where I had changed into my new attire. I looked at Mr. Benchley, robed in swaths of purple and gold. He looked at me with reproach.

"Well," he said, "do *you* have something to say about my legs, too?"

"No, I think they're darling, and best unseen, but I could sure use that wig you're wearing," When he pulled it off his head and handed it to me I said, "Well, now that you're all covered up you look better."

I appraised myself in the mirror. "Who am I supposed to be, Harpo?" I asked, straightening the wig on my head and arranging the long curls over my shoulders.

He pulled out a tambourine from the big coat pocket and rattled it. "Esmeralda!" He handed it to me.

I liked banging and shaking it. "Esmeralda who?"

"The gypsy girl from *The Hunchback of Notre-Dame*."

I needed more baubles, so I opened my jewelry case and took out a number of beaded necklaces and a couple of bangle bracelets. I began to add more rouge to my cheeks and darkened my eyes with pencil and mascara. I looked like a floozy.

"Who are you going as, Harpo?" asked Mr. Benchley. "Yourself? You're famous enough."

"No. There'll be too many Harpo Marxes at this party. Can I borrow that pillow, Dottie?"

He didn't wait for me to answer. He loosened his collar and jammed the chair pillow between his shoulder blades, tightened the rope he had tied around his waist so the pillow wouldn't slip down, and pulled a face.

"Oh, I get it," I said. "You're going as Quasimodo!"

"Harpo," said Monsignor Benchley, "didn't your mother warn you about making faces like that?"

"She told me not to cross my eyes, too, 'cause they might stay like that." He crossed his eyes.

"Oh, one more thing to complete the look, Bob," he said, reaching back into his burlap bag of tricks and pulling out a tall, white miter bordered with an embroidered leaf motif. He ceremoniously placed it atop Mr. Benchley's head.

"Oh, I *like* it," said Mr. Benchley. "I'll probably go to Hell for wearing this."

"You're scheduled for Hell, anyway," said Harpo.

"Very clever, Harpo, to do the *Hunchback* theme, especially since in the book Quasimodo is crowned King of Fools at the Festival of Fools," said Mr. Benchley.

"And you, Bobby, are the crazed Archdeacon Frollo! What a trio we'll make!"

"May the Lord bless you, my son," replied Mr. Benchley, making the sign of the cross.

When we arrived at the Murphys for cocktails Hemingway and Mathew were already there, neither costumed. Gerald offered to find them something from out of a trunk. He had the makings of an *Apache* outfit he'd worn for a party he'd hosted a couple years back and Sara had an old Indian chief's headdress hanging on the wall in the children's bedroom. With a bit of war paint and a linen caftan hanging in her closet, it would serve well as a costume, but when Hemingway declined, Mathew followed his lead and, I have to say, regretfully refused to dress up with the excuse that he would go as a foreign correspondent for the *Detroit Register* and file a report on the Parisian Mardi Gras as his first, if only, human-interest story for the paper's readers.

We had a couple of drinks and then Sara and Gerald emerged from their bedroom dressed in the most peculiar and humorous costumes made of sheets of tin and silver-painted leather and wire and nuts-and-bolts fittings. While we waited for Aleck and Soledad to arrive, we tried to guess which automobile parts each represented. Rack and Pinion? Spark Plug and Cylinder?

When Gerald answered the bell, Soledad entered as a world-weary, green-velvet-suited Oscar Wilde. She wore her trousers magnificently and walked about with the most casual of masculine strides, dropping Wilde quotes with the sanguine ease of the great man himself. I cannot understand why it is considered outlandish for women to wear pants!

Aleck, of course, intended to arrive last—I suspected he was sitting out in a taxi waiting for all of us
to arrive at the Murphys before he made his entrance.
And a grand entrance it certainly was, as befitted the
royal personage of Catherine the Great!

To say he looked spectacular, in the sense of
appearing as a spectacle, is precisely what he accom-
plished. He was all trussed up in a golden gown of
silk taffeta with an off-the-shoulder bodice embel-
lished with jewels and a wide skirt supported by wire
panniers in which he had to turn sideways in order to
make it through the apartment door. Of course, he
never could have gotten into a taxi in that outfit, and
I wondered for a second how he'd made it all the way
from the Crillon to the Murphys'.

The flamboyant Mr. Woollcott was dripping
pearls—a choker to cover any razor cuts along his
stubby neck, and great drapes of them to fill in where
cleavage ought to have been. Above all, he was properly coiffed, noted Monsignor Benchley, with a fashionable *powdered* wig, atop which teetered a birdcage
among plumes of ostrich feathers. He had tweezed
his brows, which had the effect of giving him a startled
look, and powdered his clean-shaven face ghostly
white. His cheeks were rouged like a fuzzy ripe peach.
A beauty-patch slapped on next to his reddened lips
looked like a squashed fly. He was a spectacular spectacle, all right.

Hemingway's face froze and he laughed nervously, but when Aleck raised his fan and peeked over it coquettishly, he announced that he and Mathew had to be on their way. They were meeting Daphne and Ronnie for dinner and would catch up with us at midnight at the square at Notre Dame Cathedral, where the procession would end.

"Where's your Bo Peep dress, Dorothy?" asked Aleck.

"I lost the flock."

"And your costume. Robert, what's the meaning of this? What happened to Louis the Sixteenth?"

"I lost my head."

"Enough with the puns! You two look like you're going to a tarts-and-vicars party."

Sara laughed and handed Aleck a glass of his favorite Madeira.

"And you! Court Jester! Why are you dressed—like yourself—and what's that lump—Oh! Think you're very clever, don't you, boy?"

"Trying to live up to what you always say about me, Acky."

"How did you get into a taxi wearing those running boards?" Sara asked as she circled Aleck, giving him wide berth.

"You're as wide as our dining room table, extensions and all!" said Gerald, dropping umlauts all over the place.

"Coach-and-four."

"Shit! You hired a hack?" I said.

"We will ride to the Champs de Mars in style, and then we will be met at the square at Notre Dame at midnight for the journey home."

"All the makings of a Cinderella story, if you ask me," said Mr. Benchley, taking a chair and arranging his skirts.

"I'm not asking you," replied Aleck.

"I think you look grand, Aleck, dear," said Sara. "I'd offer you a chair, but I don't know how you can possibly sit down."

"I'd kiss your lovely cheek, Aleck," said Gerald with tongue in cheek, "but there's a fortress at every approach."

Aleck raised a tweezed brow and took from his purse a Sherman's cigarette, which Gerald lit for him.

"I didn't know Catherine the Great smoked," I said, trying not to burst out laughing when he took out his black-rimmed eyeglasses and put them on.

"There are a lot of things you don't know about her."

"She was quite the vamp," said Soledad.

"You know what I always tell the girls, don't you, Aleck, darling? *Men seldom make passes at—*"

"I wouldn't finish that sentence, if I were you! Are we bringing *that* dog?" said Aleck with peremptory disdain.

"*That* dog versus *this* dog? There is only *this* dog," I said pointing at Woodrow.

"It's not *comme il faut*. He'll need a costume."

From his purse Aleck pulled out a pink tutu. "He must be properly attired. He'll go as Pavlova."

I was not about to argue with the haughty Queen, so I fastened the little tutu around Woodrow's waist. Gerald buttered a cracker with pâté and held it over Woodrow's head, and, after much encouragement, Pavlova rose up on her hind legs and begged the treat, just as the Murphy kids came in to see our costumes and bid us all goodnight. Once again the children were enthralled by my Boston terrier's charm, and paid little attention to ours. And so for the next ten minutes they were preoccupied with feeding treats to my shameless prima donna, much to the relief of Aleck, who had braced himself against a wall in fear that his gown might be thought a tent for them to make camp under.

I don't know why I was surprised, but when we left the apartment there was a coach-and-four awaiting us on the street, its liveried driver dressed in the costume of an eighteenth-century royal coachman. Aleck did nothing small.

After Aleck had been helped onto the open landau, his skirt's guardrails positioned so that he could sit alone on the rear bench of the coach, we squeezed into the carriage, Woodrow on my lap. Off we headed for the Champs de Mars for the start of l'Académie des Cinq Arts Festival of Fools.

It was a big party with thousands of people: artists, dancers, and actors mixing with Parisians from all walks of life and droves of tourists. What had centuries ago been banned as sacrilege, when the lowly dregs of Parisian society behaved with depravity and were allowed to don bishops' robes and conduct mock masses on the first of January, the Feast of Circumcision, was now an organized artistic event with a parade route and food stands and little bands of dancers and music at every turn. That's not to say there wouldn't be the usual number of pickpockets and unruly drunks along the way. It was a carnival like New Orleans' Mardi Gras.

As Aleck might say, many of the costumes were *splendiferous* and ranged from sad attempts to the *fantastical*. Where costumes had failed, faces were painted or masked, and more important than the display of creative attire was the revelry of the gathering. It was to be an evening of robust fun before tomorrow's somber Ash Wednesday, marking the beginning of Lent. It was the last chance before Lenten sacrifice to dance in the streets, to abandon the commonplace drudgery of day-to-day routine. Tonight, the old could relive the lightness of youthful antics and the young could indulge in uncensored fun. Tourists would create a memory of this night of festivities in Paris to conjure up for years to come as they rocked on their Boise porches or sat snug by the hearths of staid Philadelphian drawing rooms. As in any parade or circus, there was the high celebratory energy that stirred the crowds. The night was mild and clear and windless, and the city shimmered with light as bright as diamonds tossed on a black velvet tray.

The carriage let us off at a street corner leading into the great square on which stood La Tour Eiffel, glimmering and shedding its blessed light over the crowd. As we blended into the assemblage of revelers, we made a plan that in case we were separated we would meet on the rue du Cloître, the street running alongside the cathedral, at midnight.

The Parade of Fools began its march heading east on rue de l'Université, and as we proceeded the police made their presence known to the participants as well as the onlookers crowding the sidewalks. I took Mr. Benchley's arm and as tart and vicar we followed Soledad and Aleck out onto the street. It would be difficult to lose sight of Aleck. In his wide-angled green dress he looked like a moving Ping-Pong table.

Mr. Benchley said, "No, more like the fairway to the ninth hole at St. Andrews." Gerald and Sara were up ahead, Gerald's sheet-metal headgear like a castle turret landmark. I had no idea what had become of Harpo. One rarely did. He is an aberration, and there is no point in trying to apply logic to his behavior.

As we continued onto the beautiful Boulevard Saint-Germain, I had the oddest feeling that we were being followed, and I turned to look at the masked faces: a man dressed as a cowboy, a woman in a black-and-red flamenco dance dress and lace mantilla, a Musketeer sporting a white-plumed hat on his head, a brown-cowled monk. Mr. Benchley asked what was the matter, and when I told him, he said, "Followed? Why, by about ten thousand, I would say." Still I couldn't shake the feeling that a pair of eyes was watching me in particular.

We had paused for a moment to watch a group of jugglers near the side of the road, performing to the peppy music of a brass trio, while keeping sight of Gerald's "turret" ahead. I turned to look at the passing crowd, and there, behind us, was the wave of a white plume behind a trio of East Indians dressed in tunics and brightly colored turbans, their faces and eyes darkened. Mr. Benchley put Woodrow down and he pulled my friend in closer to the circle of performers. I started to follow, but my path was blocked by other bodies filling in the space between us. Being short of stature and unable to see above the heads in front of me, I felt a rush of claustrophobia as if walls of people were pressing in. And then I felt a hand at my shoulder. I figured it must be one of our friends. But when I turned it was the ruffled cuff of a white shirt and the sleeve of a velvet tunic that met my eye. I froze.

And then a voice whispered in my ear, a familiar voice with an edge of warning in it. When he was gone, I stood rooted where I was for a long moment, until I saw through a gap in the crowd the flash of white-and-purple brocade that was Mr. Benchley. I stepped into the space to see Woodrow, my little Pavlova, upstaging the jugglers, prancing up and down on his hind legs, tutu bobbing up and down, and begging crackers from Mr. Benchley to the tune of "*Alouette*"!

I let the little dance go on another minute while I composed myself and until Woodrow had had his fill of crackers and sufficient approval from the audience that had assembled around him. Mr. Benchley scooped him up in his arms, answered the applause with a bow, and stepped to my side.

"Don't trip on your dress," I said, as we turned to move on along the parade route, "but Richard is here and is waiting for us in a courtyard half a street down on the rue Saint-Jacques."

I was nervous about meeting him there. His whispered plea had been full of urgency. With Claude Dubois dead, I was worried about trusting Richard.

There appeared to be intrigue at every turn. *Why couldn't Richard talk to us openly in the relative obscurity of the crowd*, I wondered? Unless there was someone else sneaking around behind us whom he didn't want to hear what he had to say. That thought made me more uncomfortable about the whole affair. And now we'd lost sight of the others since Woodrow's sideshow exhibition; there had been safety in numbers, and the number had dwindled down to just the two of us and a dog in a pink tutu. Not very promising in light of a possible ambush.

The procession turned left onto rue Saint-Jacques and, as Richard had intimated, the first building that led into a courtyard on our right came into view. We dodged the onwardly moving stream and passed through the line of police and spectators to slip around the archway leading to the cobblestone court, which was set back from the street. I spied a flash of reflected light and recognized the long blade of a sword and the white plume that betrayed Richard's presence in a darkened doorway off the court. I grabbed at Mr. Benchley's elbow at the sight of the weapon.

"Here!" Richard called *sotto voce*, and Mr. Benchley moved under cover of the stone entryway. I followed anxiously, like Bo Peep's lamb.

"We don't have much time," said Richard. "I may need your help, as a distraction, that is. I don't want to put you in any danger."

"It's a little late for that now," I said.

"They've taken Duchess Sofia."

"And they've killed your friend, Claude Dubois," said Mr. Benchley.

"I know he's dead. *I* killed him."

Richard killed Claude. He murdered the man who had been protecting the Duchess. His sword was still drawn, and he kept a steady eye on the arched entrance into the courtyard. Was this a maneuver to get us away from the crowd and kill us as well, out of sight of any help?

Did he need to kill us because we knew too much, because we were too involved and could name him as an associate of Claude's, thereby linking him to the murder on the quai? But, why confess the deed to us? He must have seen my skeptical expression, or sensed my shrinking from him, for he grabbed my arm with his free hand to pull me in closer, out of any light that would give us away.

"It was me or him," he said. "But I couldn't fight them off alone. They took her."

Mr. Benchley had no qualms about the man's integrity, because he pulled out the sheet of paper that he had carried around in his pocket for the past two days and handed it over to Richard, saying, "It's a long story, Richard, but I think this is what your Mr. Latham wanted you to have."

As he unfolded the paper he told me to keep an eye on anyone entering through the archway. Mr. Benchley struck a match and in the weak illumination Richard read the names on the list. "Claude Dubois," he said quietly, and I turned to look at his face before the match burned out.

Above the noise of the procession came footfalls on cobbles and a gruff, masculine voice. A man and a woman had entered the courtyard, singing loudly. They stopped to kiss, and the girl did a little spinning dance, and then they kissed once more. From my place, now pressed against the wall of the wide stone opening, Woodrow panting in my arms, I could hear the French banter escalating into a definite drunken argument. I peeked into the yard and as the fight continued I glimpsed the sudden arrival of a dark figure in the shadowy archway. A lamp went on somewhere in a window above us, casting enough light for me to see the interloper was cloaked and hooded in a monk's cowl. Arms crossed and hands hidden within the wide bell sleeves of the robe, he stealthily approached the man and woman in the throes of their argument, said something I could not hear that got their attention, and, when they turned to face him, he turned away and quickly made for the street.

"That man was following us—and you," I stated.

"Yes, and now he thinks we got away from him, so we're safe for a short time."

"Good," I said. "He thought that couple out there were a tart and a vicar."

"Pardon me?"

"Never mind. Want to tell us what's really been going on?"

"Well, this list explains a lot to me, but we've no time for explanations right now. I've got to get the Duchess away from the people who are holding her hostage."

"Answer just one thing, Rich," insisted my friend. "When anyone is held hostage, it's because they are worth something to the kidnappers—or they know something they shouldn't know."

"We don't buy the story you gave about their wanting to take her back to Russia because she has gained sympathy and money and they want her silenced, or any of that stuff. What is really going on?"

He seemed to weigh the value of disclosing some of the truth that we sought against the ramifications of our possessing that truth. It took a few moments for him to reply and, when he did, we were no better enlightened than before.

"She knows too much."

Automobile parts

Catherine the Great Woollcott

Chapter Twelve

Richard turned in the shadowed entryway and opened the door. We followed him into a hall lit by a single gas jet, and then into a small, windowless sitting room. He lit a lamp and told us to sit. And then he spoke: "We are fighting a war. A different kind of world war. A covert, subversive war. You don't see the victims, not yet, anyway, but the fighting is going on, underground.

"What I'm about to tell you is a tale of espionage: Charles Latham, U.S. Intelligence, was murdered in Manhattan, as you know. There is a communist network in England, and there is what's been going on here in France.

"Back in 'nineteen, the Soviet Union created Communism International, or *Comintern*, as they call it. One of its functions outside of the Soviet Union is to expand their government worldwide by financially supporting efforts by communist groups around the world in the systematic destruction of democratic governments.

"Now, the Communist Party of Great Britain has been causing tremendous concern in the country, and MI5 believes CPGB members are actively engaging in military espionage. As a matter of fact, evidence ties CPGB members to the Soviet Embassy in London, and there are current investigations into the suspected involvement of collaborators in Scotland Yard. These investigations are partially the result of an accidental discovery made by the Duchess Sofia. I'll get to that later.

"About this list, now. On the other side of the pond, in the United States, Charles Latham, working for U.S. Intelligence, infiltrated secret communist networks of spies based in New York and Washington, D.C. While he was busy undermining the flow of information acquired by this network, he stumbled upon information about a communist spy ring active in France. All he was able to find out was that these people were based in Paris, and that there was an *Inspecteur Principal* involved in it. This list you gave me contains the names of the leaders of several spy rings here in France. This is a real coup. Latham must have obtained these names very shortly before we were to meet on the *Roosevelt*. It's what he wanted to pass on to me. With this list of names and through U.S. contacts here, along with French military intelligence, the exposure and disbanding of these Soviet spy rings would result in many arrests.

"Where before I had one, I see now that I have two missions: Secure Duchess Sofia in a safe home and get this list to French Intelligence. But first I must find her."

"What about Dubois?" I asked. "Did he give Latham away?"

"Unlikely, but that is of no importance at the moment."

"His name is on that list."

"Yes, he is—was—working on the Paris front for the Soviets, that's for certain, now; I discovered that too late. But, the way things happened, I don't think he ever knew who Latham was. You see, Dubois and I were aboard ship when Latham failed to show up before departure. Dubois was never privy to information concerning Latham's activities. I, too, knew nothing about Latham or any New York spy ring until my superior contacted me and set up the assignation. My only mission had to do with the Duchess Sofia. And I suspect that's all that Dubois was involved with. His plan was to see to her capture. He probably would have retained his cover had the clock tower bell not struck five, moments before one of his cohorts asked the time."

"The clock tower bell?" I asked. "What about a bell?"

Mr. Benchley interrupted. "So, what you are saying is that none of the Soviet spies here in France have any idea that they've been exposed?"

"There are two dead men on the quai. Soviet agents know their men are dead, even if the police don't know who they were and why they were killed. They have the Duchess, and unless I can stop them it won't be long before they dismantle their headquarters and scatter like roaches to set up at another location."

"Oh, my God!" I said, and clutched Woodrow tightly against my chest.

"All right, so they have the Duchess. But there is more, isn't there? She knows something, doesn't she?"

"No. Although they think she's a spy—that's why they want her. But all she ever was privy to were details she accidently overheard about Soviet spy activity in England.

"You see, Duchess Sofia had acquired information by chance, in a country home outside London, by accidently overhearing a clandestine midnight conversation between two men who were unaware of her presence in the library. She'd fallen asleep in a fireside chair, out of sight of these men, who had come in there to talk. Their voices woke her; she stayed hidden and she listened. They didn't discover her while they made their plans and named names. But, it is possible that she may have been seen leaving the library, or that something else tipped them off. She sought the advice of Major Arbuthnot, an old friend who'd been in love with her for many years and had been supporting her since the Russian Revolution. He plays a good game of cards, as you know, and, other than his small army pension, that has been their source of income. He insisted they go to MI5 with the information she'd overheard. Not long after that, things started to move against the British communist spy network. She came to the States to get away from possible retaliation, but she was not safe there, either. There were orders to capture her. They think that she has always been a spy and that her brilliant cover of 'harmless little old lady' is false. They want to send her back to the Soviet Union, to tell them what they *think* she knows about the European networks and find out about our government's espionage activities. She is, after all, a Tsarist, an escaped member of the royal family. So, these suspicions about her involvement in espionage appear to them to be confirmed."

"Wait a minute," I said. "Go back to the ship. It they killed Latham in Manhattan, why did the spy ring there try to kill him aboard ship with the poisoned fruit and the poisoned orange juice?"

"You forgot my *swimming with the fishes*, my dear Mrs. Parker."

"All right—that, too."

"I surmise that Latham's cover was blown a short time ago. The poison may have been a backup plan in case they were unsuccessful in grabbing him before he sailed. Of course, as I told you, he had no intention of remaining on board that ship. Trunk-loads of rocks, remember? It was all a ruse.

"They must have sent an agent on board who'd never seen Latham and was going by the room number and general description of the man. Six feet tall, dark hair, middle-aged, and rather nondescript—"

"Mr. Benchley!"

"I don't know if I appreciate the *nondescript* part."

"—and possibly travelling under an assumed name."

"Benchley?"

"What about Dubois?"

"I killed him. I killed him when he tried to kill me and the Major and take the Duchess hostage. I had arranged a car, through our contact here in Paris, to take us to the Murphys' villa on the coast. But I never intended to take the Duchess there. Instead, we would drive to a little village where I had arranged for her safe residence at a convent. Dubois knew nothing of that alteration in my plan. I had always told him *only* what I thought he needed to know. I'd begun to suspect his real affiliations on the boat train. He was slow to foil the kidnappers' getaway, and when he fired his gun I thought he deliberately missed his mark.

"So, before dawn yesterday, when the car drove up in front of the Murphys' and we got the Duchess settled into the backseat, a man appeared from the steps of the river's walkway and approached us, asking Claude the time. But the clock tower bell had just moments before struck five o'clock. I knew for certain, from the way the man approached us from out of nowhere, that these were not my people; a bloody smear on the door handle of the car confirmed the switch had been violent. It was all very fast, and the Major's cane proved useful in preventing the driver from shooting me. With it he knocked the gun out of his hand, and that gave me enough time to save myself from Claude's switchblade. But that didn't save Claude from my bullets. The Major picked up the gun and shot the driver dead, and then the man who had approached us to ask the time wrenched the gun away from the Major and, knocking him down, got behind the wheel and took off before I could stop him. I wasn't able to get the Duchess out in time."

"So they have her."

"They have her."

"I stripped the bodies of identification, pulled them down to the walkway and put them in a motorboat docked alongside and covered it with a tarp. I suspect that's how the man who had asked the time had arrived on the quai, by the motorboat."

"Where would they have taken her?"

"I found a telephone number in Claude's pockets, which I was able to trace to an address off quai de Montebello—just a few streets from here."

"What's happened to the Major?"

"I have him tucked safely away. He was very heroic trying to save the Duchess, but he can't be part of this rescue. They know what he looks like."

"The people in this spy ring don't know us, do they?" I asked. "Oh, I'm not scared or anything; I just wondered if we could be useful."

Richard smiled, but Mr. Benchley had my safety in mind, and, I'm sure, his own, when he said, "Have you called the police?"

"I couldn't chance it. Remember what I said about the French *Inspecteur Principal*? Good thing I didn't call; his name's on this list. I can rely on only one other trusted agent. There is some risk to you as bystanders, but I was hoping that you could help as well."

"Tell us what you want us to do," said Mr. Benchley.

———◆———

"You're going to knock on the door?" I said in disbelief.

"What would you have me do, storm the place?" said Richard with a smile. "Actually, I need *you* to knock on the door. I'll be coming in through the window."

I looked over his swashbuckling costume—the wide-brimmed hat with the luscious white plume, the sheathed sword hanging from his belt, the britches tucked in the high boots—and said, "What? You gonna do a Cyrano act?"

"I suspect it'll be more like Douglas Fairbanks," said Mr. Benchley. "But will a sword serve you well against a gun?"

"I have my trusty musket," said Richard, showing us his holstered forty-five under the mantel. "Don't worry about me; I probably won't need the gun. Not all of these people are murderers."

"We're worried about *us*," said Mr. Benchley. "But it's a good plan, and I suppose there isn't any other way."

"We can't wait to get the Duchess when they decide to move her. That would be too risky. This way we have them contained."

Richard told us that during the afternoon, after he was able to find the hiding place, he had sent his one trusted agent to check out the place, and after hours of surveillance it appeared there were only two people guarding the Duchess.

Mr. Benchley and I were among the stragglers bringing up the rear of the procession, and we continued along the rue Saint-Jacques and then veered off onto the rue des Grands Degrès and into the courtyard of the building where the Duchess was being held hostage. We had started our staged argument while still with the procession, and carried it into the courtyard with us.

Soledad suddenly appeared and joined the staged fray, brandishing a gun. I begged for my life, and she threatened loudly to kill me if I did not come home with her. I screamed with blood-curdling effect, and Mr. Benchley shielded me from the mad Oscar Wilde. Soledad shot the gun twice, and Monsignor Benchley performed a death scene worthy of any Puccini opera. Just as two gendarmes out along the parade route came running into the courtyard, a number of costumed paraders on their heels, he fell down dead.

I ran into the building, up one flight of stairs, with Soledad in pursuit, screaming like a banshee for my life to be spared, that "the priest meant nothing to me!," and banging on the doors leading to the apartment we needed to enter.

Coming up the stairs behind us were the gendarmes, just as we reached the door. I banged and begged to be let in, and when the door was opened, in flew Richard from the balcony, brandishing his sword.

Soledad stormed in waving her gun and a man who was hiding behind the door knocked it out of her hand. Woodrow ran in like a surprise and leaped up to bite the man on his ass, and when I yelled, "Fetch a cab, Woodrow!" he performed his little figure-eight maneuver around the man's feet, just the way Mr.

Benchley and Aleck had taught him years ago on the streets of Manhattan. Just as the man regained his balance and aimed his gun at Woodrow, Richard unsheathed his sword, knocked the weapon out of his hand, and, with a flourish of the blade, stuck the man to the wall by his coat tails. A gendarme entered and took in the scene, Mr. Benchley bringing up the rear as the other hostage-taker made his escape over the balcony.

The Duchess was nowhere in sight.

Richard followed the escape route, while Soledad remained behind to explain as best she could to the police that a woman was being held hostage. She was showing her identification to the police when I said, "Take care of Woodrow!" Mr. Benchley and I ran back down the flight of stairs and out into the courtyard where a crowd had gathered. A gendarme called out after us to stop. We didn't.

On the street we blended in with the stragglers continuing along the parade route and I saw the familiar white plume that showed Richard's location on the rue Saint-Jacques. We followed in pursuit, keeping sight of the plume, which rose at the incline to the Petit Pont leading over the Seine to Île de la Cité.

Here, on the bridge, the crowd had thickened as the procession culminated and filed into the great square before which rose the foreboding Cathédrale Notre-Dame de Paris.

I lost sight of the white plume. Being small in stature, I couldn't see more than the backs of the people in front of me. Mr. Benchley grabbed my hand and pulled me in tow.

It would be easy for a criminal to get lost in this crowd, I thought. What chance was there of catching him? But, if we didn't catch him, how would we ever find where they had taken the Duchess?

I felt like I was caught in the boxwood maze of an English garden for all I could see to get my bearings. Bodies were pressed tight at first, and then Mr. Benchley led us into a small clearing in the forest of brightly colored costumes. Vendors were hawking their goods, drunks were behaving lewdly, and it was a pickpocket's paradise.

Towering above us stood the eight-hundred-year-old Roman-Gothic cathedral; its statuary of Judean Kings, luridly lit for ominous effect, glowered over the crowd that was packing the square. Gargoyles bared fangs; grotesques leered. The festive music of an orchestra set up on a stage on one side of the square sharply contrasted with the imposing architecture of the church. The crowd was cheering at something that was happening beyond my field of vision. Mr. Bench-ley pulled me in close to him and we moved with the pressing masses toward the sound of amplified voices when the music came to an abrupt halt.

"But, where is Richard?" I asked my friend as we searched around us. A couple of times I thought

I had spotted him, only to find the white plume was attached, once to the hat of a brigadier general, and another time to the headdress of a cancan dancer. And when Mr. Benchley laughed, and I asked what was so funny, he pointed to the stage. All I could see was the top of a familiar head of wild strawberry-blond curls. Mr. Benchley lifted me from my waist so that I could better see what was going on. Harpo was up there, on the makeshift stage, and a pair of hands was placing a big, gaudy crown on his head while the crowd broke out in thunderous cheers and applause. *King of Fools,* I thought; *how appropriate.* And from my higher vantage point I saw Richard Hartley giving chase to the escaped kidnapper before his bobbing plume disappeared around the south façade of the cathedral.

"Oh, brother," said Mr. Benchley with a chuckle, referring to Harpo.

"There!" I yelled, and he put me down on my feet. "There's Richard!"

He followed my pointing hand but saw nothing.

"They just went around the church, that-a-way."

He bolted away from me, pushing through in pursuit, almost losing his miter along the way, and in a moment the crush of bodies had cut off sight of him. I tried to move in the direction he had gone, but I was grabbed by a rambunctious young man dressed as a Roman senator, who twirled me in circles for an impromptu dance. Several other couples dressed like nymphs and fairies joined in as a costumed Pied Piper began playing his flute for a medieval dance, which turned into a quadrille. Every time my hand was released and I tried to get away I was handed from one to another in a frolicking tug-of-war.

And then rough wool fabric rubbed against my cheek and I felt smothered. When my eyes refocused I was staring into a field of brown. That was the last thing I remembered until I awoke to the terrifying sight of long black curls dangling before my eyes and the dizzying impression of a deep abyss between wooden slats in a dark and perilous place.

I must have gasped for fear of tumbling down into a dark oblivion I could not understand, and my hands shot out to break my fall. But all I could find for a stronghold was the scratchy wool. I was dangling head-over-heels, being carried up a dark stairway over a man's shoulder. The sounds of ten thousand collective voices rose up from below at a distance. I stiffened with vertigo; I wanted to fight for my freedom, but reason told me if I broke free from the man's grip, I would only fall to my death down the long and perilous spiral stairs. When I was thrown to the floor in a heap at the top of the landing, my head hit hard on the old and petrified wooden boards and I passed out again.

I came to; I didn't know for how long I had lain there unconscious. The man, the hooded "monk," was gone, and I looked around to get my bearings. Arched and wood-slatted windows allowed in the illumination of the cathedral's exterior lighting. I couldn't miss the bell: It was frighteningly huge and hung above me like a thirteen-ton threat. I scurried along the floor of the loft toward one of the arched openings and, when the sharp pain in my head subsided, peered out through the bottommost louver.

I yelled, "Help!" But the force of my breath shot painfully through my head and I fell back in agony. Waiting until the pain subsided so I might try again, I attempted to reason my way out of panic.

The monk had left me there. Why? I realized that he wasn't coming back for me. Why bring me up to this bell tower, just to leave me here, concussed? The blow to my head must have knocked some insight into me. *That's when I figured it out.*

I was the decoy, the distraction. I knew that my friends, coming to my rescue, would allow the culprits get away, to take the Duchess to another location, safe from police capture. I heard a sudden rustling and my heart leaped in my chest. Could there be bats in the belfry?

No, I realized, there were *rats in the belfry!*

A flash of light through the louvered arches revealed the dark specter of a huge rat scurrying across the floor. When the light wavered and then dimmed, I saw the critter was much smaller than its inflated shadow, and I waited in frozen anxiety for it to scamper down the suspended stairs.

I began to rise to my feet, but didn't make it all the way up for the wave of nausea that pulled me back down and the ache throbbing in my head. I would have to wait until I regained some stability before I tried to descend the circular stairs.

The loft was flooded with light—suddenly—before the shadows returned once again. The phenomenon of intense light repeated; I managed to get to my feet and peer out through the louvers, shielding my eyes from the direct glare until the searchlight moved on to throw me into darkness once more.

Down below, in the square, faces were looking up at the tower. I needed to signal for help, somehow. I took off the red scarf from around my neck and waved it out between the louvers, hoping it would be seen when the searchlight passed. I heard calls from below and saw raised arms pointing. There was movement just outside the opening, and when my double vision cleared I thought I was hallucinating because Harpo Marx was only a little way below me, scaling the Grand Gallery between the towers.

"I'll be there in a minute, Dottie," he called to me.

"Oh, crap!" I replied, relieved and yet scared to death he would fall. And then I couldn't see him anymore, and was wondering whether my fears had become reality when I heard the collective hush cut through the noise of the crowd.

Footsteps pounded on the stairs, louder with every successive tread, and there appeared Harpo on the landing, followed by Monsignor Benchley, miter still secure on his head. He was out of breath and wheezing.

"Four-hundred . . . and . . . twenty-two . . . steps," Mr. Benchley huffed.

"Forty-seven crawls, my way," said Harpo.

"You could have come in through the front door, Harpo," said Mr. Benchley, "like I did."

"You take the low road and I'll take the high road."

"Help me out of here," I ordered. "I don't think I can take the stairs alone."

"I'll carry you down," said Harpo.

"Not on your life, you crazy fool!" I said, as Mr. Benchley gave me a swig from his flask and then took me in his arms to guide me down the stairs. We had made it to the first landing when the clapper of the ancient bell, *Emmanuel,* struck its mark. I thought my head would explode. Startled, we looked up to see Harpo, dangling in recoil from the bell cord, lifted into the air. We braced ourselves and covered our ears when the clapper struck alarm once again.

Down into the sanctuary we went, without any interest in the magnificent vaulted ceilings, the rose windows, the impressive altar, and exited through a side door.

"Did Richard catch the man?" I asked, leaning into Mr. Benchley as he led me away from the cathedral and toward the street.

"I don't know."

"Just as I feared."

"All I knew was when the crowd started pointing up to the South Tower, and I saw your kerchief—well, my priority was fetching you back safely. I got you across the Atlantic, warding off icebergs in our path, and I wasn't going to let you die in France."

"Yeah, thanks. If Oscar Wilde wanted to come here to die, fine with me. I'll take Manhattan. Speaking of Oscar Wilde, Soledad has been working with Richard all along."

"So it appears."

"She has Woodrow."

"Yes, I know. Let's hope the police didn't arrest them. After all, Woodrow did take a chunk out of that fellow's behind."

"He does me proud!" I said, and when I laughed the pain in my head struck hard like the bell clapper hitting its mark. Another thought made me ask, "How could they know? How could they know I was there, unless someone—"

"There was this fellow dressed like a monk who went up on the stage and said you were up there." Mr. Benchley repeated, "*Monk!* He was the man we saw earlier, wasn't he?"

"He clobbered me and carried me up there."

"Oh, my dear!"

"No thanks to you! Where were you when he knocked the daylights out of me?"

"Are you hurt?"

"Just stop patting me on the head, you damn fool." I said truculently. "I was used for diversionary tactics so that those kidnappers could get away, and nobody would be any wiser 'cause while they were sneaking off, everybody's heads were in the air."

"Harpo climbed the walls, you know—"

"He's always climbing the walls."

"—and I pushed past the guards outside the church to save you. They only let me in when I threatened Papal action if they didn't. This outfit does get one into the best places."

"*Phooey!*" I said.

"Well, that's a nice thank-you-sir!"

"Now what'll we do?"

"Go back to the hotel, I suppose. Aleck is probably waiting for us. It's almost midnight, so the coach should be coming to meet us down that-a-way."

"Fred," I said. "Why go to the bother of setting up a diversion for a getaway, when it was so easy to get lost in the crowd and just disappear? Do you think the kidnappers have the Duchess close by and they were about to move her while I was being rescued?"

"I see your point."

"Well, it appears that they've arrested Harpo. Look. He's got an escort of five gendarmes."

"It's tradition in these European countries to send their royals to a dungeon or a tower now and again, so King Harpo is just one in a long line of fools."

"And this crowd has gotten out of hand," I said. "There's an ambulance, and they're taking someone away on a stretcher. Looks like the poor soul is dead. He's all covered up."

We spotted Aleck—but then, how could we not? His Renault-tank of a skirt forced people to give him a wide berth to avoid being knocked over. He stood alone on the street across from the North Door of the cathedral. Sara and Gerald stood partially obscured behind him. Aleck spotted us and waved. We began to cross to meet our friends when seemingly from nowhere appeared Richard, hatless, staggering and clutching his arm. Mr. Benchley went to his aid, holding him up to keep him from falling.

"I'm fine," he said. "They had her here, down in one of the underground vaults. But they've taken her elsewhere—"

"The doctor needs a doctor!" I shouted, and my head throbbed mercilessly.

I ran toward the ambulance in search of a medic. But as I approached the driver glared at me and yelled something in French, and the two medics who'd loaded in the stretcher looked over at me and then quickly slammed the back doors in my face.

Why a knock on the head should lend me such clarity, I don't know. But I just *knew* that these were not ordinary ambulance men. I ran back to where Mr. Benchley was holding up a wounded Richard Hartley; Gerald, seeing the distress, had come over to them.

"I'm really all right now," insisted Richard. "It's just a surface gash, but they knocked me cold and took my gun."

"They have her in that ambulance," I said, "and they're getting away!"

The street had been cleared of automobile traffic for the festival, and except for police on horseback and one or two police vehicles, only pedestrians took to the streets. The cathedral clock struck the hour of twelve. Aleck's hired coach-and-four had arrived and the coachman was awkwardly trying to assist Aleck up onto the back bench, before resuming his place at the reins.

Richard's attention returned to his mission as he watched the ambulance pull out from the curb. When he saw the coach pulling to the opposite side of the street, he yelled, "Let's go!"

Adrenalin renewing his spent energy, he hobbled over and instructed the coachman to get down from his perch. To everyone's surprise, the coachman did as he was told.

Aleck was outraged, and yelled, "What the hell do you think you are doing!"

"Commandeering this vehicle!" replied Richard. "In the name of the United States of America!"

Flummoxed, jaw dropped, Aleck got his back up, quite literally, and the movement nearly sent him tumbling backward off his precarious perch. Mr. Benchley, Gerald, Sara, and I got into the carriage. Richard cracked the whip and reins and we were on our way after the siren-blasting ambulance.

Because of the siren, pedestrians cleared the way for the ambulance, and we were so close on its trail that the crowd cheered us drunkenly as our coach-and-four barreled after it. Very quickly we bore to the left. Before us was the Pont au Double, leading off the island and onto quai de Montebello. The streets were now open for automobile traffic to our left, if not to the right, which had been the parade route, so the ambulance turned sharply left, knocking down a wooden traffic barrier that had yet to be removed. We followed closely, and I saw policemen's startled expressions as they made haste to their vehicle to bring up the rear of the chase.

Onward, then, along the quai, past other bridges linking the Île de la Cité and the Île Saint-Louis to the Left Bank, while skirting motorcars and buses. The police car added its singsong siren to the whining warning. We moved at a fast clip, but the ambulance was maneuvering on four tires, not sixteen legs and wooden-spoked wheels. When the truck ahead turned right on quai Saint-Bernard, it slammed on its breaks to avoid a horse-drawn farm truck entering from the rue Culvier. Our front horses reared in startled fear at the near collision, as the ambulance scooted around the wagon and down a side street, cutting its siren to stealthily escape its pursuers. The wagon driver cursed at Richard in French words we were not taught in school, as half-a-dozen crates of live chickens on the flatbed tumbled out onto the cobbles, blocking our way. Mr. Benchley leaped from the carriage and moved a couple of the squawking caged birds in an effort to clear our path.

There were words shouted back and forth between Aleck and the wagon driver in guttural, angry French. The driver called Aleck "Madame de Pompadour" and Aleck tossed back a few obscenities, but was silenced when Mr. Benchley hopped back into the carriage and Richard took off down the street.

I turned to see the fist-shaking poultry farmer cursing future generations of our offspring as Richard reined the horses to turn onto a narrow cobbled residential street, quiet now at that late hour except for a gang of young men and women loitering outside a rough-looking bar. Sirens signaled the imminent arrival of the police cars that were closing in. Slowing down, Richard asked if an ambulance had passed, and when one of the young men pointed ahead we proceeded slowly down the street. When we came to an intersection where we had to go right or left, I saw a glimpse of the red cross against the white field just as the ambulance disappeared into another side street. I shouted for Richard to bear left, and when we arrived where we thought would be another cross-street, we found ourselves dead-ended and facing the iron gates of a garage that had once been a horse stable. There was only a courtyard to our right, but we didn't see the ambulance.

"Where did they go?" asked Gerald, standing in the open carriage and peering about for a clue. There was no way for Richard to turn the horses easily in the narrow road—that maneuver would cost us valuable time—so he came down from the seat, and we all got out, helped Aleck down from his lofty post, and walked back from whence we had come, with a hobbling and rather disagreeable-looking Alexander Woollcott bringing up the rear. And there, in a narrow alley between two buildings, was the abandoned ambulance, its doors ajar, the stretcher bare.

Hearing the hollow clunking of heavy metal on stone, and then the scrape of a shifting weight, Gerald said, "*Aha!*" and scanned the area for its source. He walked down to the end of the dark alley, which led into a small, square yard, overgrown with weeds and scraggly, knotted fruit trees. "We need light," Richard said, and told us he would go back to the coach to fetch one of the oil lanterns that were sometimes used to illuminate its interior. Mr. Benchley told him to stay with me and Sara, as Richard's shoulder was bleeding and he looked awfully pale. Mr. Benchley soon returned with the lantern.

Gerald took command now.

"Aleck, Sara, you stay here and direct the police in through the yard when they finally arrive."

"But, where are you going?" demanded Aleck.

"Down into the underground tunnels, if my suspicions are correct."

"Why can't I come?"

Sara shook her head and stifled a laugh; Gerald gave him a withering look. "Really, Aleck! Need I say it? Your skirt's too wide."

This time Gerald led the way, and when Mr. Benchley asked what he was looking for he said, "The entrance. I'm looking for a covering in the ground, under the overgrowth."

But the ground was firm like packed earth under the bramble and interwoven grasses of a summer past. The little plot of weeds ended in a five-foot hillock covered in brittle and twisted vines. "It's here," said Gerald, and he and Mr. Benchley found and tore away the flap of burlap disguising an iron grate in the wall. The grate lifted away, Gerald whispered, "Let's go!"

"Go the hell where?" I screeched. "Down in that dark hole?"

"There are hundreds of these around the city."

"Sewers?"

"No, an underground passage, one of the caves, the tunnels I told you about. Some are offshoots of catacombs. Come on." And then as he started to descend and found his footing, he smiled at me and said, "That's all right, darling. Stay put. Someone has to let the police know where we're going."

"I'm coming," I whined, my head aching and my future looking dim. What would I have said to the police? "*Ici est où nous used to come quand j'étais ici pendant la guerre?*" Perhaps they would take me out for breakfast if I said, "*N'avez-vous pas des griddle-cakes?*" I spoke almost no usable French. Of course, after they took me away and locked me up, they would understand and shake their heads if I yelled, "American Embassy!" Anyway, they'd find us soon enough. It's hard to miss a coach-and-four. And Alexander Woollcott. I heard their siren warbling close by. It was only a matter of time before they found the ambulance in the alley.

I ducked down and entered into the dark cave. The three men stared at me ghoulishly in the flickering light of the lantern. "We don't know how far we are going, and we don't want to get lost in the maze, so let's start by dropping markers for our return," Gerald said. "I'll leave my vest," he said, shrugging out of it and dropping it to the damp stone ground when we came to a turn in the carved-out tunnel.

I tried to shake off the heebie-jeebies, but the tinkling drips of water echoed loudly along the stone walls. I expected rats and snakes and spiders to crawl up my legs at every turn, and the musty, stagnant air lent a tomb-like atmosphere to the narrow space. I shivered from the damp and the feeling of doom.

Mr. Benchley laid his miter cap on a shelf-like protrusion of rock as we moved along, guided by the light of Gerald's lantern. From the distance came echoing voices, but it was impossible to know how far away or from where they emanated. Two paths now presented themselves as the tunnel split into a Y. We stopped and Mr. Benchley and Richard conferred with Gerald, who lowered the wick and concealed the lamp behind Mr. Benchley's robes. This way we could see if any light was burning around the next corner a couple of hundred feet ahead in each direction. Our eyes adjusted to the darkness, and to our left there shone a faint glow in the distance.

"What do we do now? I asked, dropping my red neckerchief to the ground like a child dropping crumbs in the forest.

"We sneak up on them," said Richard.

"But, you don't have a gun. They took it," said Mr. Benchley.

"But, I have my sword."

"Not a good match for a gun," I insisted. "Shouldn't we go back and let the police handle this?"

"Dorothy's right," whispered Richard. "I want you to go back and get the police here. They're probably at the ambulance by now."

"Great!" I said, "And how are we to do that without a lantern to see us through?"

"Yes, I see your point . . . . All right, then," said Richard with a grimace. "Grab a rock from the ground over there."

"Sticks and stones?"

"Take off your socks, gentlemen, and put a rock inside each one."

The men were armed with improvised bludgeons—clever, but not the best weaponry. I wore no socks, so I was told to keep out of the way.

Richard took the lead, sword drawn in his hand.

If I were the betting kind (and I am), it wouldn't be on us four against God-only-knew-how-many killers lurking around the next bend.

Mr. Benchley dashed the light, and slowly we walked along the pitch-black passage, hugging the nasty damp wall for guidance. I kept one hand on Mr. Benchley's shoulder, the other along the wall. The ground was uneven, and a couple of times I felt my heel slip out from under me on the slimy surface.

This is the stuff of nightmares, I thought.

And then, finally, I could see the faint figures of my friends in the weak light coming from the next turn. I froze, as did Mr. Benchley and Gerald, against the wall as Richard peered around the rocky edge. I was rigid with terror; my pulse throbbed in my throat. With the blow to my head earlier and the tension I was now feeling, I thought my brains would explode out the top of my skull!

And then Richard was gone, and I panicked as next I lost touch with Mr. Benchley. I cringed at my fate, but took a deep breath and started to make the turn toward the raised voices, looking back toward the pitch black from which we'd come, and seeing a reassuringly bright and welcome light instead.

"In here!" I yelled, and the footsteps and calls of men thundered on with more urgency. I let the half-dozen men in armor rush past me into a cavernous room where the frail and courageous Duchess Sofia Louise of Russia was held captive.

Notre Dame de Paris — Where's Woollcott?

The Final Chapter

The Duchess Sofia is resting comfortably and safely in a secret location in Provence. Major Arbuthnot resides in the same village below the convent where the sisters reside in their life of Christian devotion. He visits the Duchess daily, and is teaching the Sisters of Divine Patience how to win at whist and how to bluff in poker.

Harpo Marx was at first charged with attempting to deface a historic and sacred structure, but he hired a lawyer after the Murphys paid his fine. (Aleck refused to pay it because Harpo had refused to wear the court jester costume he'd rented at great expense.) Anyway, Harpo is famous in France. And as he had not despoiled any of the ornamental carvings, or caused any damage to the noses of the statues along the Gallery of Kings, or broken the ears or chipped the teeth of the gargoyles along the Galerie des Chimères on his climb to the South Tower, and he was nowhere near the West Rose Window (installed in 1220 A.D.), and it was never his fault if there appeared a ding in the glass, he was released with a warning not to try to scale the Eiffel Tower. (The authorities must have had Harpo figured pretty well by now, for he *did* intend to do just that.)

Soledad returned Woodrow into my arms when she arrived at the entrance to the tunnel, after having telephoned the *Préfet de Police* and waking him from his mistress's bed. As a personal friend and a great fan of her books, he had been a constant resource of information for her mystery stories. It was upon his orders that the police force had launched a dragnet of officers to find the kidnapped Duchess. She admitted having from time to time assisted Richard in U.S. Intelligence affairs, and asked that that fact remain confidential.

The spy ring in Paris and England disbanded and arrests were made for some members' involvement in espionage, murder, and bombings that were previously attributed to anarchists.

Saul Gold's body was sent back to New York for burial. He is remembered by those who love literature and poetry.

The Lady Daphne Twinton and the Marquis Ronald Everett Hampton-Crispin-Jones accepted Hemingway's offer to show them around Spain in July, and the plan included taking me and Mathew and Mr. Benchley, if he could make it, along for the trip. Hem talked about the thrill of the Running of the Bulls and the life-and-death drama of the matadors in the ring at the bullfights during the Festival of San Fermin in Pamplona. I wanted to go, but the thought of spending nearly two weeks with Lady Daffy and her Marquis didn't seem like a good time. And I remembered what Zelda had said about all "the bull."

Hemingway left his wife, Hadley, a few weeks later after joining her at Schruns, for another woman he'd been having an affair with since before I'd ever met him in New York. Surprise! Pauline Pfeiffer, working for *Vogue* in Paris, was to become his second wife.

His new assignment as foreign correspondent for the *Detroit Register* has built self-assurance into Mathew Hettinger, something that his wealthy parents could never buy for him. His job is one most coveted by young reporters, and he is building a name for himself with his weekly syndicated column, *Across the Pond*, in which he has been reporting on Germany's admission into the League of Nations, the growing fascism in Italy, and speculation about Trotsky's expulsion from Moscow. At first, I wondered if Mathew was the secret agent working alongside Richard Hartley. I asked Richard about that.

"The man you said reminded you of Jimmy Durante?"

"Yes! I suspected he was a Bolshevik. He was following us!"

"He was *my* agent. He's U.S. Military Intelligence."

As for Dr. Richard Hartley, he delivered his paper on treatments for infantile paralysis at the Académie Impériale de Médecine and was duly lauded for his work. We had a lovely dinner together before he sailed back to America and to his research institute in Washington, D.C. His life is a busy and complicated one. And whenever he comes to mind, so does that corny expression: that we were like two ships in the night, passing each other on our separate journeys.

Gerald and Sara invited me to spend the summer with them at their home, the Villa America, in August. They will give me a little cottage on the property so that I can work in peaceful comfort and enjoy the lovely, warm, blue waters of the Mediterranean. They are truly a remarkable couple, and I hope to see them often. Mr. Benchley will come for the summer with his wife, Gertrude, and their boys.

I gave back the Cartier watch—in truth, I threw it out the window of my hotel room during an argument with Sewie Collins. He went home, I'm happy to say, and I stayed in Paris.

Before Mr. Benchley returned to New York we had lunch with Hemingway at Lipp's, a wonderful brasserie where we ordered the pommes à l'huile, as recommended by Hem, a lovely marinated potato salad, and *portugaises* (oysters), and enjoyed the wonderful icy-cold beer for which they are famous.

I asked Hem, "What is a *fine?*"

"Brandy. Do you want one?"

"I'm disappointed. I thought it was something exotic!"

After lunch, we relented at Hem's suggestion that we meet his friend and mentor, Gertrude Stein.

"You are really going to like her," he said with youthful enthusiasm.

The door of 27 rue de Fleurus was opened by a housemaid, who took our coats. Then we were greeted by a little mousey-brown lady, who gaily ushered us in through the foyer. When Hem inquired if Miss Stein was at home, she replied, "Of course, Ernest, always for you. Miss Stein is outside in the garden. There are early tulips. You'll find her there." Off he went to fetch his mentor.

The little brown mouse, a Miss Toklas, asked how I was enjoying my stay in Paris, as she touched my arm and then led me by the elbow into a little parlor.

"Sweet little dog," she said, patting Woodrow's head when I had removed his leash. She offered me a chair while she went to prepare the tea. I turned to see that Mr. Benchley had not followed me into the room.

"Hello? Miss Toklas?" I called, but she was apparently off watching water boil.

Woodrow followed me as I retraced my steps and found myself returned to the foyer. Ahead was the front door, and to my left, closed pocket doors. Behind me was the staircase to the upper section of the house. Did Miss Stein have her salon upstairs? Could Mr. Benchley have gone upstairs to wait while Hem went to fetch Miss Stein from the garden?

I heard voices coming from behind the pocket doors, so I slid back an opening through which to peek. Across the room French doors opened onto a garden; Hemingway was standing just over the threshold beside a stocky, wiry-haired woman with a superior air. Although their backs were toward me, I could see affection between them; they looked like a father and son reviewing the day's work. I spied Mr. Benchley hidden from their view in an alcove of the large parlor, looking at one of the many paintings that crowded every inch of the wall.

"What have you been reading that's good?" asked Miss Stein as they remained rooted to the spot, looking toward the little garden.

"Poe and H.G. Welles," replied Hemingway.

Miss Stein shook her head: "One unleashes his nightmares on the world; the other his perverted fantasies. Now, answer the question: What have you read recently that is good and true?"

"I read *Sons and Lovers*."

"Yes?"

"By D.H. Lawrence—"

"I know who wrote it."

"I liked it very much."

"It's a terrible book! The man is preposterous! A very sick man—"

"I couldn't read *Women in Love*, though . . . ." faltered Hem, almost as an apology, a sort of placating concession to an unintentional insult.

"—a sick man—no! A *dead* man! Why do you read a dead man?"

"And Aldous Huxley; I like Huxley."

"Why do you read trash?" she asked, and then: "Never mind, sip your *eau de vie* and tell me all about your time in New York and your new publisher— they've taken your book?"

"Yes. But the editor, Max Perkins, he wants me to remove certain words."

"Is that bad for the book?"

"I don't know if it will be good and true."

"And the company you kept? Those senseless dilettantes your friend, Don Stewart, told you might help you along?"

"No! I mean, *yes!* They are nice. As a matter of fact—"

"They do nothing of value, I'm told. They make foolish jokes. *Une Génération Perdue.*"

Hurriedly, Hem tried to stop her as Mr. Benchley had walked out from the alcove and was within
earshot. "Please, Miss Stein, I want you to meet Mr.
Robert Benchley, *who is a friend of Don's.*"

Miss Stein and Hemingway turned from their
discussion of dead and trashy authors and the malign-
ing of my friends, as Mr. Benchley said, "Oh, it's all
right, Hem. There's a little bit of truth in that. *The
Lost Generation* . . . yes, I suppose. Why, a couple of
years back, we misplaced Warren G. Harding only to
have discovered he had died and failed to tell anyone.
And now I hear Miss Stein say Lawrence is dead?"

"Madame," sounded a voice from behind me. It
was the little brown mouse. Gertrude Stein opened
the pocket doors and Woodrow ran into the salon.
She stared at me as if I were an interloper.

"You should come with me," said Miss Toklas.

"Sorry, I'm lost."

Woodrow lifted his leg on a potted palm.

"The wives have tea with *me* while Miss Stein
discusses—"

Hem's face darkened with a blush as he bounded over toward me. "I was hoping for something a
bit stronger," I said, circumventing him and, as the
bounder that I am, walking full into the room. "Got
any scotch in here? I see you do. I'll have what he's
having," I said, pointing at the tumbler Mr. Benchley
was holding.

Miss Stein looked at me with curiosity in her eyes, as Hem made the introductions: "This is Mrs. Dorothy Parker, Miss Stein." And he added, to shore up my credentials, "A good writer and poet."

"I thought you were Mrs. Benchley!" said a horrified Alice B. Toklas.

"So it's been said," I replied, and caught Mr. Benchley's quiet chuckle as I took stock of the artwork. "Nice pictures," I said, looking around at the collection on the walls before leaning in to scrutinize Picasso's portrait of Stein. "Admiral Hornblower?"

Fin

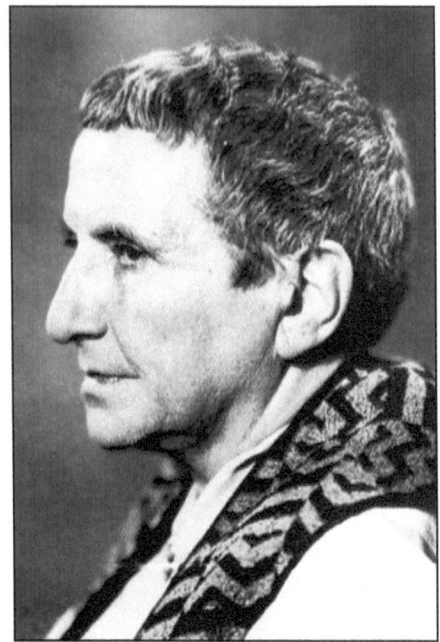

Miss Stein

Admiral Hornblower

27 rue de Fleurus

A view of the garden at Gertrude Stein's

Afterword

Robert Benchley accompanied Dorothy Parker on the *S.S. Roosevelt* crossing in February 1926 for Hemingway's return to France. As his decision to sail was made at the last minute, he was put on the cancellation waiting list, so for a while he had no accommodations until he was assigned a cabin. From this bit of information and my imagination I have built my story.

Captain George Fried became an international hero after the crew of the *S.S. Roosevelt* daringly rescued the crew of the British ship, *Antinoe*. The tickertape parade in New York was held for him and his crew days before Parker, Benchley, and Hemingway sailed to France. As captain of *America*, he was to be honored with another parade in 1929, after he commanded the sea rescue of survivors of the Italian freighter, *Florida*. He has been largely forgotten, and I just chanced upon his name during my research of the *S.S. Roosevelt*. Through newspaper articles of the 1920s I identified Fried as the captain with whom Parker, Benchley, and Hemingway actually dined on the crossing to France.

Dorothy Parker came to love the Murphys. She admired their courage and stoicism in the face of tragedy, after the death of their son, Baoth, from meningitis, and several years later, following a long struggle with tuberculosis, the death of their youngest child, Patrick, each passing at the age of sixteen. Because of her high regard for them, Dorothy accompanied the Murphys to Switzerland to help where she could during the time of Patrick's treatment, and made numerous crossings from New York to be with them.

Picasso spent the summer of 1923 as a guest of the Murphys at the Villa America. He sketched and painted numerous portraits of Sara. The paintings of Gerald Murphy are in the collections of the Whitney Museum of Art and the Museum of Modern Art in New York, and the Dallas Museum of Art in Texas. His modern style prefigured the Pop Art movement. *Boatdeck,* which caused a sensation at the Paris exhibition of the Salon des Indépendents in 1924, has been lost for decades.

Both Robert Benchley and Alexander Woollcott became lifelong friends of the couple. Harpo Marx was Aleck Woollcott's guest for the summer at a rented villa in Antibes and saw the Murphys often.

Sara and Gerald were parental figures to both Fitzgerald and Hemingway. F. Scott Fitzgerald dedicated his novel, *Tender is the Night*, to Gerald and Sara, and modeled the two main characters of that novel, Dick and Nicole Diver, after them. By the second half of the book, though, Dick and Nicole more closely resembled Scott and Zelda. The obvious portrayals were upsetting to the Murphys, because they were far from flattering; aside from the physical similarities and character traits, the actions of the characters were untrue to their natures. Still, Scott and Zelda always remained in their hearts, as did Ernest Hemingway, for whom they served as constant benefactors early in his career, reading his first drafts, encouraging his work, providing financial assistance and a home for his wife, Hadley, and son, Jack (Bumby), during the child's illness, and paying their medical bills. As he eventually did with most people who championed his work, including his longtime mentor, Gertrude Stein, and Sherwood Anderson, Hemingway finally turned against the Murphys, quite publicly, in his memoir, *A Moveable Feast*, proving true the old adage that no good deed goes unpunished.

Dorothy Parker, who, as a critic, was known to cut to the bone the work of so many artists, reviewed all of Hemingway's novels with effusive raves. Fortunately, she was never told by her friends how Hemingway had viciously disparaged her in a verse he wrote in the fashion for which she had become famous, and which he read aloud to their mutual friends at parties. What Hemingway thought humorous was seen by her friends as a cruel attack. Among those friends was playwright Donald Ogden Stewart, who had spent much time with Hemingway in France, as well as on the trip to the Pamplona bullfights, during which Hemingway recorded the conversations of the people involved to use for dialogue, using their real names in his first drafts of *The Sun Also Rises*. Don Stewart never talked to Hemingway again after he ridiculed Dorothy behind her back. After Ernest Hemingway's death, Dorothy Parker naively asked a friend, "Do you think Hemingway liked me?"

Robert Benchley wrote the humorous *French for Americans*, parts of which, along with my dialogue, he recites aloud in my story.

Praise for *Dorothy Parker Mysteries*

Those of us who since childhood had wished there was a time machine that could let us experience and enjoy life in other periods, should read Agata Stanford's "Dorothy Parker Mysteries" series. They wonderfully recreate the atmosphere and spirit of the literary and artistic crowd at the Algonquin Round Table in the 1920s, and bring back to life the wit, habits, foibles, and escapades of Dorothy Parker, Robert Benchley, and Alexander Woollcott, as well as of the multitude of their friends and even their pets, both human and animal.

—*Anatole Konstantin*
Author of *A Red Boyhood: Growing Up Under Stalin*

Agata Stanford's "Dorothy Parker Mysteries" is destined to become a classic series. It's an addictive cocktail for the avid mystery reader. It has it all: murder, mystery, and Marx Brothers' mayhem. You'll see, once you've taken Manhattan with the Parker/Benchley crowd. Dorothy Parker wins! Move over, Nick and Nora.

—*Elizabeth Fuller*
Author of *Me and Jezebel*